ALIVE

ALPHA'S LITTLE PSYCHO
BOOK 1

K.A. BAUER

Alive (Alpha's Little Psycho 1) by K.A. Bauer

Cover Artwork by K.A. Bauer

Copyright © 2023

All Rights Reserved

Paperback ISBN 979-8-9892840-1-6

CIP data for the individual books are available from the Library of Congress

TRIGGER WARNING

PLEASE DO NOT PROCEED IF YOU ARE NOT
COMFORTABLE WITH THESE ELEMENTS.
YOUR MENTAL HEALTH IS MORE IMPORTANT
THAN MY BOOK SALES.

Please be advised that this book contains mention or depiction of the following elements which may be upsetting or triggering to some readers.

BDSM

AGE PLAY

CHILD ABUSE AND NEGLECT

SEXUAL ASSAULT

TRAFFICKING

PTSD FLASHBACKS

BULLYING

SUICIDAL IDEATIONS

EXTREME VIOLENCE

EXPLICIT LANGUAGE

ALIVE

ALPHA'S LITTLE PSYCHO BOOK 1

PROLOGUE

<u>Ethan</u>

8 years ago

"You promise you're going to be back in time to make it to my party?" I don't like being whiny with Connor. He's eighteen now and going off to college in the fall. In fact, he's visiting the university in Pittsburgh with Ric today. I really wish he didn't go almost five hours away with his best friend on my birthday, but it's not like your little brother turning thirteen is important in college admissions. Mom told him to go, and I agreed. Connor is the one with a bright future ahead of him right now, and he has to pick the best school for the best big brother ever.

"I'm sorry I wasn't there to wake you with birthday pancakes, Little Blue. Tomorrow will be epic though. We are gonna rock out to the fact that you got your wolf now. And Ric is gonna show you all the best places to go running while me and Dad get a surprise set up for you. Every wolf in our family gets it."

Supposedly, being in the Beta's family means something special that Dad is going to explain to me tomorrow. Something about my wolf being blessed or some witchy woo stuff like that. I don't care. My party is gonna be all about me having fun and running around getting used to my furry side. I can't wait to show Connor and Max and Ric and Shaun how cool I am now that I have my wolf. I just need to make sure they all see after the party tomorrow.

"See you tomorrow then, Connie," I yawn into the phone. "Tell Ric-Roll we're racing and I'm gonna leave his butt in the dust!"

Before Connor disconnects, I can hear Ric's deep chuckle coming through the speaker. That laugh started doing things to me a few months ago. Hearing it right before bed is really going to ensure a changing of the sheets in the morning... but oh, the dreams will be worth it.

I thought it would feel different having my wolf. Everyone is always going on and on about having this other side of yourself and the clash of personalities that can happen inside your head. Either my wolf is chill as all hell or I'm defective because dude ain't talking to me at all. I'm just me, but with a built-in winter coat and claws. He was supposed to talk to me a while ago, but only Max knows about the radio silence from my furry side. I kinda wondered if I would even shift at all today.

Mom freaked out a bit when I shifted this morning before breakfast. I'm not sure why, but Dad said it's all part of our talk tomorrow before the party when my brother gets back. I'm not going to worry about it. I think Mom is only worried about Connor being away. I mean a silver wolf might be rare, but it's not unheard of. She just doesn't like when Connor isn't in her line of sight.

Taking a deep breath to help me relax for bed, I notice a strong chemical smell coming from the hallway. Funny, I didn't know

Mom decided to change the air fresheners tonight; although, it makes sense with the party. She's always complaining about the teenage wolf musk coming from our floor.

I hate these chemical smells so much. I'll ask her in the morning to switch back to natural stuff. She should be in a better mood with Connor being back and more likely to listen to reason. As I lay back on pillow, I can't tell if the noise I'm hearing is coming from downstairs or just a part of the dream I'm trying to enjoy. Must be my imagination. Dad will wake me up if there's something wrong. I reach for Mr. Whiskers to help keep the nightmares away so the good dreams can come through, only to remember he's not here. Frowning, I try to open my eyes, only to realize I am trapped in dreamland. The last thing I remember is the smell of peppermints, before oblivion takes over. At least that chemical smell is gone.

Ric

That little boy really knows how to get me to laugh. I've known Ethan almost as long as I've known Connor. The kid was born when we were in kindergarten together and I've gotten to watch him grow up. The two of us try our best to make Ethan's birthdays special, but we're eighteen now and deserve to have some fun. I just hope my little boy Blue doesn't feel too abandoned. Ever since the day I gave him the nickname, I hate seeing him upset. I'll do just about anything to put a smile on that kid's face.

As Connor finishes putting away his phone, we pull up to the curb at the frat party we got invited to. The original plan was to head home tonight and surprise the little shit for breakfast. For once, I just wanted us to be able to be regular guys. One night of fun isn't going to hurt anyone, so I convinced my best friend we should at least swing by.

"Why are we here again?" Connor asked with an exaggerated sigh.

"Dude. For the first time we got invited somewhere truly because we are regular guys. Damn fine-looking guys, but just us. For once, I want to have fun being Ric, not future Alpha of the Jameson Pack."

Connor sighed again and we got out of the car to walk up the street to the party.

"One hour and we have to get on the road," he tells me with a glare.

I nod in agreement since it's not likely that a human party is going to have anything on hand to make it worthwhile to stick around. Regular alcohol stops getting our kind drunk by about sixteen.

I get where he is coming from. I really do. Family is everything to him and his little brother totally idolizes the dude. The man doesn't want to do anything to disappoint the pipsqueak. To be honest, neither do I. Ever since my eighteenth birthday last week, I find myself worrying more and more about Ethan.

I talked to our dads about it, and they said it's likely just my alpha genes manifesting themselves. I'm not so sure. When I asked why I worry over Ethan more than any other member of the pack, I got some line about his age and his wolf is technically not pack until he shifts but that he's of the age where his wolf is present. It makes as much sense as anything else right now.

I get the feeling he's going to be crushed when I scent my fated mate, though. I already know she isn't a part of our pack, since I've scented every wolf there. Being the future Alpha, I know I'll be needing an heir, so it's looking like I'm going to be stuck with a she-wolf. Goddess help me, but I'm not looking forward to that process. Maybe, I'll get lucky and fate will send me an omega, but I'm pretty sure there isn't an unmated omega wolf anywhere east of the Mississippi.

Walking through the door, I shut down my thoughts regarding my future mate. Right now, it's time to drink some humans under the table and try to forget being a wolf for a while.

"Remind me again not to mix tequila with grain alcohol ever again." I say reaching for the ibuprofen we bought before leaving the city. My head is feeling like it is being split in two by a lumberjack with a rusty dull hatchet.

"Or rather, remind me to make sure the grain isn't mixed with aconite before I start drinking" I add. Wolfsbane liquor is expensive and pretty much the only thing that will get us drunk. I wasn't expecting to find it in the moonshine that was being passed around. It wouldn't affect the humans that much, but to us werewolves, even a small amount puts us at a human tolerance level.

"We should have been on the road hours ago," Connor scolds me as we cross the border into Ohio. "Ethan is going to be so mad at me for missing pancakes, again. He never lets me live it down when I break a promise."

Connor seems more amped up than usual, but then again, his little brother has always been kind of a master of vengeance if you cross him. My last girlfriend insulted him and treated him like a toddler, even going so far as kicking him out of his own living room when we were all hanging out at the Beta's house. I still don't know how he got into Jessica's bedroom without leaving a scent trail, but he definitely made sure the point was made to not talk down to him. She still hasn't managed to get rid of the smell of dead rodent. Every single thing in the room has since been changed out, but it still reeks of decaying rat if the room temperature goes above sixty degrees. The kid is a master of his craft.

The traffic in front of us is finally starting to clear again after a bad accident around Columbus and we are once again on the way home. When we take our exit near Dayton, my phone starts going nuts in my pocket. I know the plan was to be in at like 2am according to the itinerary I gave my parents, but it is only 7am. Even if we came back last night, I'd still be dead to the world this early in the morning.

Rolling my eyes, I swiped up to only hear my mother's frantic voice and the sound of sirens... a lot of sirens. There isn't even a chance to say hello before the questions are being shouted at us.

"Alaric?! Please say that you're all ok and... and... *RIC* talk to me and say you're alright! You all have to be alright!"

I've never heard my mom like this. What the hell is going on? Connor has already pulled off to the shoulder so we can focus on the call. I put the phone on speaker and try to answer her before she goes off and starts again.

"We are still on the road back from Pittsburgh, Mom. Connor and I are just fine. A bit hungover on my part, but we're almost home. What is going on?" I tried to exude the calmest energy I could. Mom just found out she's expecting again, and she seems to be really freaking out over whatever is going on back at home.

Before I could even wrap my mind around why she could possibly be freaking out, Connor grabs my phone.

"Why are there sirens? Why did you worry about us? Why did you say *all* of us. It's just us two. Who else is supposed to be with us?"

My best friend is in full business mode, and it just registered in my brain... she doesn't know that we were delayed in coming home, so where did she assume we were?

"Did Mr. and Mrs. Sinclair ask about us not coming home last night? That's all on me," I say to try and make sure they knew Connor isn't to blame for this delay. "I wanted to check some things out in the city before we headed home."

My father's voice cut in behind my mother's sobs, "Boys, come straight to my office. Something has happened. Ric, take over driving," My father commands.

My hungover ass really did not want to be driving anywhere, but you don't disobey your Alpha. As I walk around the front of the car, Connor slides across to the passenger seat, warily eyeing the phone sitting on the dash.

After I am in the driver's seat and shut the door, the Alpha continues, "Connor, my boy, I'm so sorry," he begins again with a weary sounding sigh. "They're gone, son. They're all gone."

My mother's sobs increase in the background, so my father hastily ends the call with no type of goodbye. There is no hesitation in me as I peel out back onto the highway to get us home. *He's mistaken. They're just mistaken.*

It takes me a record thirty minutes to get back home. I purposely don't drive past the Beta's house. Something is telling me not to even look that way until I see my father first. Connor was ready to jump and run as soon as we hit pack lands, so I had to order him to stay in the car. I've never had to use my authority on anyone before this. I hate having to use it on my best friend. I know all he wants is to make sure his family is alright, but the way my parents were on the phone... I'm pretty sure Connor is going to need all of us.

As I pull up to the building that holds the offices, I notice a lot of crying faces. I also notice about a dozen of our warriors waiting for us. This is wrong. Something is really wrong in our pack.

My father speaks before we can even take a seat in his office.

"There was an accident. They're gone, son. I'm so sorry. They're all gone," he tells us again. It's the same tone of voice, like it's just a recording going over and over again.

"What happened?" I choke out.

"Gas leak," Dad says. "It was right below Ethan's room."

My head starts shaking back and forth. No, he can't mean what I think he does.

"All three are gone. They think Ethan's alarm triggered the explosion and that's why he..." he pauses as if it's too difficult to say. This is the Alpha who recovered his father's body after it was desecrated by filthy bloodsuckers. How bad is it? "Connor, there's no chance of identifying him. There wasn't enough left to even take to the hospital. Your parents were taken there but didn't make it."

Connor explodes in rage, and the cracks in my heart shatter. *Ethan is gone. My little boy blue has been taken from me.*

From US, my wolf reminds me. *He was ours, too. Our pup to protect.*

While my wolf howls in my head, I'm left staring at my best friend sobbing in a ball on the floor of my father's office. He lost everything because of my selfishness. There's no coming back from this, not ever.

It's been three months since the funeral. Connor is getting worse by the day. He wakes up in the night screaming. I wake up to him trying to leave to find Ethan. He swears he hears him calling out for help. The guilt and grief are killing him. I know he blames himself for not being there. He should be blaming me. He didn't want to go to that party. I kept us away.

Because we weren't there, no one noticed the gas leak. The report said by the time Mr. Sinclair smelled the gas and went to investigate, Ethan's alarm was already set to go off. The bodies of the Beta and his wife had catastrophic burns but were mostly identifiable. Ethan's body was little more than charred bones.

Because dear old Uncle Carl was too busy, Connor had to see it all. Connor had to identify his parents' and little brother's remains. I couldn't let him go through that alone, so now that image haunts me as well.

Connor shouldn't feel the guilt. It's my fault we weren't there. Had we been back when we said, we would have been downstairs to smell the gas long before the smell could reach the third floor where Mr. and Mrs. Sinclair had their suite. We could have gotten everyone out. *I could have gotten Ethan out.*

Connor's guilt is eating him alive. It's almost like the less he has the hallucinations of hearing Ethan, the more he lashes out. We're all trying to tell him he needs to let go of his grief. Mom and

Dad are both worried. They are thinking about moving the pack, relocating further south.

I say it's running away, but I can see the appeal. I see Ethan everywhere. My wolf smells him everywhere. I hear him sometimes. It's not the cries for help that Connor is hearing. No, my guilt manifests itself into my Little Boy Blue telling me stories. I should really stop falling asleep with the television on. Too much late night drama manifesting in my subconscious.

But Mom and Dad are right. Our pack needs to leave the site of the tragedy. Connor needs to heal.

As I start to drift off on the eve of the big move, I swear I hear Ethan. Maybe it's just that his loss is weighing so heavy on me with leaving our memories behind.

I wanted you to be my first. I'm sorry... I'm so sorry...

I hear his whisper. I'm sure it's just my guilt manifesting itself, so I turn up my music and continue packing up the last of my room. I hope I can let it go in time.

ONE

<u>*Ethan*</u>

I have no clue how long I've been in this decrepit place. I know it's at least changed seasons a few times because Needle Dick Noah over there had snow on his boots a while back. I was brought here in May, on my birthday. Was it this year or last year? Maybe the year before? It doesn't matter anymore. Noah and Petey are arguing over some kind of draft for sports. I'm pretty sure those happen in the summer sometime. That was always Dad's thing with the Alpha, Ric, and Connor. I never really could get into the sports stuff.

I'm being led from my cot room for my daily dose of fun, and I wonder which activity they have planned for me today. Since Needle Dick is here, it could be anything. He gets off on being told what to do by the docs. I think it's a kink thing. Putrefaction Pete only appears to do as he's told. If no one's watching, he's the kind of guy who will take an extra fiver to get himself off using us. Most days, I wish he was told to take a shower and pop some breath mints. He could peel some paint with the smells coming off of him.

Hey, that's a good name update. Paint Peeler Pete, sounds off in my head.

Yeah, my wolf found his voice pretty much right after I woke up in this place. He insisted that we could reach anyone we could picture in our heads. Took us a while to adjust to the fact that no one could hear us calling out. Mom and Dad didn't answer. Connor didn't answer. Ric didn't answer. No one is coming for me, and I accepted that long ago. Yeah, the hope of rescue kinda left me the same time my virginity did.

Nothing like being a thirteen-year-old kid discovering consensual non-consent, minus the consensual part, to really drive it home that I must have been the only one to survive that night. There's no way Connor would ever give up finding me, unless he is already dead. I figured Mom and Dad must be dead. No one could've taken me from Dad. He might not have been the most loving man out there, but he was the strongest wolf I ever met. He and Mom wouldn't ever let a kid of theirs be taken. It would look really bad if they did.

Kinda wish these guys killed Uncle Carl though... considering the second he realized I was an omega, he sold me to the highest bidder. And man, they didn't waste any time. Less than twenty-four hours after my first shift and I ended up holed up in this lab. Good old Uncle Carl. He's the only reason I'm looking forward to getting out of this place. I want to handle that bastard myself. He deserves some of the "special treatment" I've received during my stay here.

"Prepare the subject for the procedure," comes cutting through my thoughts. This dude's voice cracks more than mine does. At least I have the excuse of puberty.

Per the usual, Needle Dick and Petey boy strap me to the table and put in the gag so that my wolf doesn't bite them... again.

It's an automatic response to fight when they hurt us, my wolf whines at me.

Yeah yeah. I know. But we get it worse when we fight back so I have to let them do this or else we won't get to heal right. I don't want to try to deal with half a lung again. That shit was a bitch, I reply to my beast. It sucks that we have to put up with this, but it's just not worth the extra pain to fight back anymore.

I'm guessing this time is going to be something a bit different when they start taping my hands into fists and securing them to my sides. Looking down at my body, I'm giving them both a very quizzical look. They know my looks by now. This is my "What the hell is going to be happening that this is necessary?" look. While I'm pondering all possible reasons there could be to completely immobilize my hands, the squeakster says something I miss. I just hate his voice and try to tune It out as much as possible.

Next thing I know, my head is getting slammed back on to the table and a strap is placed across my forehead. Oh, so it looks like we're doing full restraints today. This means my wolf is REALLY not going to be happy about today's activities. I just take a deep breath and prepare for the pain. They don't even put me under anymore. They want to see my honest reactions or something. I think they're just sadists who are too chickenshit to admit they aren't up to snuff to find willing participants for their kink.

Mentally, I'm preparing for the first slice. That's always the worst. The anticipation is so much worse than the actual cutting. I mean, yeah, it really sucks having to regrow a liver and it was definitely not fun feeling my intestines filling back in. The amputated toes coming were really bad for my balance for a while there too. Point is, I know what comes after sucks, so I wish they'd just get on with it already.

While I'm waiting for the prick of the scalpel, I feel a pressure on my neck. Could they actually be planning on decapitation? That will be nice. I've been wondering if it's my body that regenerates or if it comes from my brain. I think I snuck too many comics from the library. And bright side is, if I don't regenerate my head or body and I die, at least I'll be free of this place.

Ah, nope. It's just a collar. I can't hold back the laugh that bubbles up around the gag. Thinking I might be choking, Noah goes to adjust the gag and I can't help myself.

"What's the tag say, Needle Dick? Fido? Lassie? Old Yeller? Spot?"

I'm cackling like a loon as he shoves the gag back in hard enough to break a couple teeth. Hell, guess I'm gonna have to pull those out later. But the look on their faces? So worth it. I even had a few more to throw in there... Spike, Scooby, Tank....

The scalpel finally starts slicing through my abdomen, so I let my mind drift. This is when I tell my stories in my head. I come up with my daily soap opera of who is fucking who in this hellhole. Who got the clap and is spreading it around the building? It's something I started doing back at the beginning. I used to tell these stories to Ric in my head. He was never really there. He would've sent a rescue party for me by now if he ever cared... if he's even still alive. Still, it feels better to tell a story to someone else. Otherwise, I'd have to admit I'm all alone. Nah, that's not a good idea. I don't like that thought.

Hey, Uncle Carl is still out there. Sometimes I send him the ways I'm going to handle him when I'm free of this place. Dunno if I imagine it, but I'd like to think I can feel his fear. That old piece of crap needs to feel some fear. I think he's always reeking of it but constantly eats those damn peppermints to cover it up.

"Subject is sexually mature and able to self-lubricate. Next phase is to induce pregnancy to observe..."

HOLD THE FUCK UP! Did this weaselly little piece of shit just say they want to knock me up?! Hell to the no! This ain't gonna fly. It's bad enough that the guys use me to get their jollies off, but at least they pull out. Now, this little rat bastard is saying they're gonna TRY to make me a baby daddy/mama/papa... whatever... against my will? OK now I understand the extra restraints cuz I'm pissed. The growl that escapes my throat echoes in the chamber before I black out, having control wrested away from me by my wolf.

I'm not sure what happened next because suddenly waking up on my cot with a bandage on my throat and wrists and a hastily glued incision down my torso.

Sorry. My wolf tries to apologize to me. *I tried to shift when you lost it. I didn't think the collar wouldn't give or that our claws would slice up our wrists before we got free of the restraints.*

Can't really blame my wolf. I forgot about all that shit too. But now I have to figure out a way to get out of this place without carrying the spawn of the unwashed out with me out the door. Or worse, not getting out and raising a kid in here, if they'd even let me keep it.

"Perhaps I can help you, my child," said a woman's voice from nowhere. I'm pretty sure my mind has officially broken at this point and I need a permanent padded room, but I reply anyways. Can't hurt to double check, right?

"Uh, lady. You ain't my mom, number one," I say into the darkness that is my cot room. "And number two, if you can get me out of here, don't waste my time with talking. Hop to it. I got an uncle to take care of."

"If I grant you my assistance, you cannot kill." Her voice warned. "No one in a sworn deal with me is allowed to take a life without my blessing."

"Well how in the hell can you help me, then?" I ask, "Killing the bastard or not, I still gotta get out of here." She slowly appears in front of me. She kind of looks like the princess rebel chick at the beginning of that one science fiction space movie. Max would remember the name. He's a geek like that.

Holy shit. I'm pretty sure I'm talking to the freaking Goddess. This will be good... or bad. Either way, I'm in. You don't turn down a Goddess.

"You will survive these ordeals physically intact. You will not die in this place. You will conceive no child other than that of your true mate."

"Wait up... my true mate? I'm fourteen. How in the hell am I supposed to find my true mate and get knocked up being trapped in here?" I ask in confusion. I can't even smell him out for another four years. This sucks. She's telling me I have another four years of this shit ahead of me?

"My child... You are seventeen years of age as of ten minutes ago," she gently corrects. "You will not know your true mate's scent and he will not recognize yours on you as a cost of my interference in these events."

Seventeen??! I've been in this hellhole for four years. I guess time really flies when there's no calendar or entertainment.

"OK Sweetheart Goddess Lady, how do we cut this deal so I can get on out of here and get with the mate situation?" I ask and she smiles at me. This is either the best idea I've ever run with or the worst. Either way, I'm not dying in here.

TWO

Ethan

Since the Goddess visited me that night, each day I'm stuck here gets a little bit harder. I started sucking up to the boys a while back to get "favors" for when I have to undergo procedures. The docs are still cutting out organs and cutting things off every day, week, whatever, but I get to watch now. They hung a mirror on the ceiling for me. They don't even gag me anymore and I get to ask questions about what they're doing to me now. The docs look at me like I'm a pet that learned a cute trick. That's fine. This is all going to be used in some very creative ways once I'm out of here.

See, the nice Goddess Lady gave me a goal. Sure, I can't kill because of our deal. But she never said I can't maim, disable, or disfigure. And I'm learning an awful lot about the body and what incapacitates the human body. They keep doing things to me and then based on their level of amazement on my survival, I can gauge just how lethal what they did to me should be. I probably should be more worried about the fact that they're trying to permanently disfigure and disable me, but the G Lady gave me her word. I'm safe enough with her deal in effect.

"Why won't it take?" like nails on a chalk board…

Oh, why won't his balls drop already? It's been years apparently and even my voice finally stopped cracking. Still isn't as deep as Ric's but no voice will ever hit like that dark chocolate ganache with whipped cream and…. Ok don't want to pop a boner on the operating table… again. I think Needle Dick Noah has some package envy going on after the last time.

"If it doesn't get pregnant, we can't continue the study." Squeaky is complaining again.

Best I can figure out, these numbnuts are trying to use science to understand magical creatures. They've had a few fae, multiple beta wolves, a couple human hybrids (poor bastards), even a vampire or two… and they're still not understanding that magic isn't just science that we don't understand yet. Magic is magic. There is no science that can explain a 150 pound skinny little ginger twink like me turning into a 225 pound moonlight silver wolf. Conservation of matter and all means it will never make scientifical sense, and yet they keep killing us to try and make it work.

The next voice on the other end of the phone is one I would recognize forever. This is the asshole in charge. This is the guy who paid Uncle Carl twenty thousand dollars for his nephew, and then proceeded to up it to fifty when Carl revealed I was an omega upon drop-off.

"Remove the womb and see if it will re-grow it like the other organs," he says. "If it does, we continue once it's regenerated. If it doesn't regenerate, we will terminate and find another specimen."

OK, I know I'm able to regrow pretty much anything and the G-Lady promised me I'd survive this place, but this is cutting it pretty close, right? The womb is not something that will always come back though. I'm pretty sure Mom had to have hers removed after me and it didn't grow back. I mean they said I was the baby they didn't plan for and didn't want any more.

And if it doesn't grow back, how do I find my mate? I can't smell him. The only clue I have is that he'll knock me up. If I don't have my baby bits, how can that happen? I'm an omega. The only way to stop having my heat is to be fully claimed by my true mate. I don't want to go through that every six months for the rest of my life. But would that be irreparable harm? Would that be enough to void the deal? Would that mean I can finally die? I need out of here now or I'm not going to care.

Goddess? Sweetie? Hello? I'm yelling in my head as loud as I possibly can. Panic is taking hold for the first time in years. *I think it's time you step up the timeframe and get with the escape plan cuz if I lose my baby bits, our little bargain is null and void and I'm going apocalyptic on everyone's ass.*

As I feel the smooth glide of the scalpel, I hear her sigh.

Then I'm confused when I hear what sounds a lot like my Uncle Carl making a very unique grunt. Why the hell am I hearing that ass rubbing one out? I never should have trusted anyone ever. I guess even the G Lady has given up on me.

Ric

Connor should be home soon, I hope. It's been almost two months since he left to deal with the legal crap regarding the death of his uncle. What should have been a quick in and out trip back to our old hometown has apparently turned into a major shit show. Dear old Carl was apparently into some rather shady stuff and it's left my Beta with the task of determining what needs turned over to the authorities and what we will have to handle ourselves.

That heart attack couldn't have happened to a better guy. The jerk deserved it after he abandoned his nephew, his only living relative, over seven years ago. I mean, I get the guy wasn't close to his sister, but to leave an eighteen-year-old kid to grieve his entire family and arrange a funeral by himself... the Goddess did right by taking him. Although I do feel kind of bad for the human authorities who discovered his body months later.

The sounds of Green Day's Basket Case starts blaring from the desk drawer pulling me from my musings. Seeing the face of my best friend and Beta on the screen, I quickly swipe across to answer.

"Con, man. What is taking so long?" I ask before he can say anything. "Just bring it all back here and we'll sort it together already. I need someone of the adult persuasion with a brain around me. I need you back here. *We* need to have you back."

The silence greeting me kind of starts worrying me. Connor may have turned a bit stoic and quiet over the last seven years, but this silence feels weighted. I am not going to like what comes next. I just know it.

"Ric..." he stops.

Is he crying? My Beta hasn't had a breakdown in years. I knew I should have gone back with him. He always would backslide when we went back before visiting the graves. The hallucinations almost always come back as soon as we get outside of Dayton and don't leave him alone until he's back on a plane.

"Alpha, it's Ethan," he chokes out.

I freeze. That name hasn't been spoken in over five years to my knowledge. The last time either of us heard the name was at my parents' funeral. Some well-meaning pack member mentioned that our pack is due for good times after all the losses and they named him along with Mr. and Mrs. Sinclair. Connor lost it. I lost it. The only reason no one ended up in the hospital was the fact that I was holding a toddler at the time. His name is never spoken. It's an unspoken agreement between us and everyone else.

"Connor, don't go there," I beg him. "We both saw the body. You can't go through this again. Hell, *I* can't go through it again. "

The pain of losing Ethan hasn't dulled at all over the last seven, almost eight years. I just got better at hiding it. I know Connor is the same way. If he starts hoping again, I will lose him too. I can't lose them both. I can't be alone in my grief. I need him as an anchor or the entire pack will be swallowed by my guilt and grief.

"Ric, that body wasn't him! I have proof now," he's shouting. "The bastard stole him and sold him. The idiot kept the record of the sale."

My wolf is perking up at this information. Even he never got over losing Ethan. Every time my parents pushed me to find a mate, he growled. The elders in the pack won't even push it after the last outburst. My wolf has refused to even consider another for a mate since we failed our little boy blue so badly.

Can't protect mate. Don't deserve mate, chimes my wolf for the millionth time since the accident.

"It's dated the day of the party, the day we came home," Connor continues, "The *item,*" he growls, "is listed as male, thirteen, omega."

Omega? Ethan was an omega? How didn't we know this?

It's been almost eight years. Could he even still be alive? And if so, what condition would he be in?

I'm falling apart here while hope is blooming inside my Beta. I don't think he's thinking about what would happen to a young omega not under the protection of an honest Alpha. He's still caught up on the fact that Ethan apparently didn't die in the fire.

"Ric, he is still out there. I'm sure of it! I just need to dig a bit deeper and find this lab."

The excitement in Connor's voice makes the guilt weigh even heavier on me. Was he really hearing Ethan for those first few months? Maybe it really was his little brother begging for help the only way he could, and we just abandoned him. *I abandoned him.*

A crash sounding from the other side of the phone breaks through my guilt spiral. It sounds like Connor found something he doesn't like and the leaden ball of fear grows in my gut. I hate that he is getting his hopes dashed, but I would rather he be crushed now than having months or years of searching turn up nothing... or worse...we could find out he's already dead and we missed him. That would crush us both irreparably.

"Alpha," The rage in his tone takes me by surprise.

"I found the address for the lab," he growls. "I found what they were doing... are doing. There are multiple reports. He's listed as subject 17."

More crashing comes over the line. This is bad. Connor is the most levelheaded of all of us. "He was getting updates like a freaking magazine subscription!"

"Send me the documents before you destroy something by accident," I tell him. "We might need a record just in case we need to bring in the human authorities"

I have to repeat myself a couple times to get through and almost had to force him with my authority to calm down. Can't have an out of control werewolf in an area that is no longer home to a pack.

"I doubt we'll need the human authorities once we finish," my Beta replies. "And if there is anything left, we'll give it over to the vampires."

I tense when I hear that word. My grandfather was killed by vampires. We were all raised on tales of how cold and cruel and vicious they are.

"Why the vampires?" I ask, not sure if it's worth knowing the answer if it makes us have to deal with those filthy animals.

"It looks like subject twenty-three was a vampire prince," he replies flatly.

"Was?"

"The report says subject twenty-three was lost," Connor says coldly as he hangs up on me.

After Connor disconnects, I'm waiting on the email with the documentation. I boot up my computer and wait for the ancient thing to load. Sometimes I wish I could justify spending money on a new one, but seeing as I only use it for email and storing my excess of photos, I don't see a point. My phone does everything else I need to take care of anyways.

Jack is the one who gets the fancy computer. He gets pretty much anything he wants. I shouldn't spoil him as much as I do, but it's difficult trying to be a single parent and big brother all at the same time. I don't always see the line.

As if thinking of him was a summoning, the door to my office flies open with a bang and in rushes the most adorable little tornado of sass and spite. He is almost immediately followed by the most annoying person on the planet. I know I haven't met everyone on the planet yet, but I'm sure Jessica beats them all.

"Brotato! You need to check your woman!" he giggles through

his attempt to speak like an adult. Seven-year-olds should not be this endearingly exasperating.

"Alpha, you really need to consider sending this one to a boarding school or something," Jessica shrieks in my direction. "He's completely out of control and has damaged my personal property... again!"

Wow, her voice sounds even worse than I remember.

"Jessica, like I've told you before, don't antagonize him and don't leave your things accessible to children in the pack. We all know you have some rather adult things that I don't need our pups finding." Yeah, she's into some crazy stuff and has been for a while.

I recall the memory of the first time Ethan admitted to messing up her room and his eleven-year-old self regaling us with the tale of the things he found. For the first time since that hellish day, I'm remembering Ethan with a smile. It feels foreign on my face as I reach up to touch the raised corners of my lips.

Apparently, my non-reaction is too much for Jessica who storms out of the room leaving me with a giggling Jack to handle.

"You know you can't keep messing with the grown-up wolves," I try to explain to him for the millionth time. "Not all of them will let it go just because you're a pup and my little brother."

He cocks his head to the side, reminding me of a puppy, and after pondering it for a minute he fills me in on what he did. I'm really trying not to laugh at the sheer genius of this kid. He didn't just hide food in her closet to make it all smell. This little gremlin smeared anchovy oil on the bar in her closet and let it drip on all of the clothes and furniture so it would soak into the wood and fibers and be impossible to get out without a remodel. Then he removed part of the buckles from every pair of those stupid strappy shoes she wears.

Just then, my computer dings to let me know the email has come through. And then it dings again. And again. There are about fifteen in total once I'm sure that the computer is done receiving them. It's time to send Jack out because this is a way more complicated and adult situation to have a six-year-old in the room.

"Jackie, I gotta take care of some Alpha business. You gonna be ok heading home on your own?" I ask.

I don't wait for him to respond before I shoot a text to one of my warriors to come escort him home. Finding out Ethan had been taken from us means that Jack is never going to be left alone again. I failed one boy. I'm not failing the only other one to ever touch my heart.

As soon as the door to my office closes behind Max and Jack, I open the first email. My wolf is bursting to escape. These sick fucks took a thirteen-year-old boy to *research the regenerative abilities of an omega wolf compared to beta wolves.*

Obviously, they couldn't seem to capture an alpha wolf because one of us would have torn them apart. Hell, an adult omega could rip apart a human if needed. I guess that's why they took a child. I guess we're lucky that omega doesn't manifest until puberty starts or Carl might have sold him off earlier. I wish I could bring him back so I can kill him again... slowly and painfully.

I am still growling as I open the second email. The date on the document indicates it was six months later. It says that

---

"the omega subject seems to have better regenerative abilities than those of its beta counterparts, but still inferior to those of the undead subject number twenty three."

What the hell? They were comparing how a thirteen-year-old

wolf compares to a vampire when it comes to regeneration? He's lucky he was healing at all at that age. We don't get our full healing abilities until around sixteen usually. They could have easily killed him!

My wolf is becoming more and more restless as I'm reading on through each of the emails. Over and over, they document what seems to affect "regeneration" and the subtle changing of his anatomy as he matured into a full omega.

My wolf goes silent and I swear my heart has stopped beating upon reading the ninth report.

Subject shows sexual maturity. Its body appears to self-lubricate like that of a female during heightened stimulation. Verified through most recent vivisection that subject has grown a vestigial womb. Unclear if womb is mature enough to conceive and carry young. Seeking permission to proceed with phase two to impregnate the subject.

Omega wolves don't start to have slick until they are seventeen at the earliest. This means Ethan was alive three, almost four, years ago. He was there, being cut open over and over again for at least four years.

Then it hits me: *impregnate the subject.* I don't want to keep reading. I'm sure that human scientists would have initially tried some form of artificial insemination, right? Has to be the case I'm sure. Although the thought of a seventeen-year-old Ethan being forcibly pregnant in a lab somewhere is a bad enough thought, I can't allow myself to entertain the other possibility. Call me an ostrich, but I want my head so far buried in the sand on this one.

After some deep breathing and psychological gymnastics to calm myself and my wolf a bit, I continue to the next report.

Artificial insemination does not appear to be a viable method to induce pregnancy in the subject. Introduction of donor semen has not yielded any results. Lack of ovaries eliminates in vitro fertilization as a possibility. Upon further inspection in last procedure, we can conclude without proper force, the womb does not appear to allow entrance to any fluids. Commencing direct stimulation with living donor to induce pregnancy.

My desk goes flying across the room. I don't even remember touching it. The door opens and three warriors rush in only to see my face and back out again slowly. No one wants to face me like this. Even I don't want to face what I've just read, but it's in there now. It won't leave my head.

They raped him. My wolf growls in my head. The anger. The rage. The guilt. It's all too much for me.

Connor's face shows up on the screen of my phone again as the sound of music draws my eyes to the floor where my desk used to be. I almost don't answer. I have four or five more of the emails to read through. I don't want to know what's next in the nightmare that we abandoned Ethan to.

The phone doesn't stop ringing. It's battling my heartbeat for the loudest sound in my head. Without realizing I've even picked up the phone from the floor, I answer it to Connor's growl in my ear.

"I'm going to get him out, Ric. You aren't going to stop me. I'm bringing my brother home," he says before I can even react.

"I haven't finished reading everything yet." I growl back. "I can't risk losing you on the off chance of him being alive. At least wait for me to send some guys to back you up."

"Read the last report and then tell me this can wait even another six hours for backup to arrive," he tells me, "I swear if you make me wait and I lose him all over again, you'll wish for death before I'm done." My Beta snarls at me.

Connor has never threatened me like this. That means I have to read the rest, or at least skip to the end. I pull up the last email on my phone screen and my blood freezes in my veins.

"Bring him home," I whisper to Connor and end the call.

Womb removal successful. Regeneration does not appear to be initiated even after three months. If subject does not show signs of regeneration by next scheduled exam, seeking permission to terminate and find a replacement subject.

Based on the time that I can figure out, these reports were done every six months starting right when he was taken. If that's the case, the next "exam" will be any day now.

THREE

Ethan

"What's up, Doc?" I ask as I'm being strapped in for yet another fun day at the office.

Needle Dick ain't here today. That's a first. Usually, he's first in line to tie me down. Gets his jollies off, I guess. Petey boy has the honor of getting me tied down all on his lonesome today, and I gotta say he is enjoying himself a little too much. Wish he would enjoy a toothbrush a bit more, though. Ugh, I'm really hoping this ain't the last thing I smell because I'm pretty sure the rat intestines I put in the insulation in Jessica's room smelled better than Paint Peeler's breath here.

Per the usual routine, the weasel ignores my greeting and squeaks into the recording app on his phone, "Commencing exploratory to determine regeneration. Permission has been granted to terminate if no evidence of reemergence of removed organs."

What did that jock-stain say?! Terminate? Ah, hell, G-Lady, your time is up! You gotta get me out now!

Apparently, my reaction is not unexpected because next thing I know, there goes that chemical smell again. Is it weird that I find it comforting that something else is replacing Petey's god-awful putrefaction breath from my nostrils before I die? Whatever. Doesn't really matter at this point. This time is different. I don't really know if I'm going to actually wake back up after this one.

I'm struggling to stay alert as I feel the scalpel slide across my lower abdomen. I need to know the outcome before I go. I need to know how screwed I am before I let the darkness take hold.

The nails on a chalkboard squeal again, "No sign of regeneration to be seen upon initial incision."

"Terminate the subject." That is most definitely not the voice I want to hear right now.

The weasel wasn't recording. He was on a phone call with his boss. Oh, damn. Well, that sucks for me. There's no reprieve. I'm not waking back up this time. If I do, the last thing I'm going to have to worry about is a baby.

Goodbye world. As the chemicals start to pull me under, I get a sense of déjà vu. There's a loud noise and I think I can smell some smoke. Figures, I'm going to hell. Not that I haven't lived there most of my life, but why should my afterlife be any different?

"Ethan! Hold on, baby brother! I'm bringing you home." That sounds a bit like Connie.

Huh...

My own personal hell is apparently going to be my worst nightmare on repeat. Time to check out of this life. G-Lady, you lied to me. We're gonna be squaring this up soon.

So...

Apparently, I wasn't dreaming there at the end, or what I thought was the end. Connor really did finally find me and bring me out of that place. According to what he's told me so far, I'm the only one who got out of that place alive. I'm still not willing to say anything to him yet. This is way too much like my dreams slash nightmares from the beginning.

I used to dream that my big brother and his best friend would barge in and beat everyone up who was hurting me, both on the table and in the other room. They'd save me and bring me out into the sunshine or moonlight. I'd get a big hug from my brother and my first kiss from Ric and they'd drive me away and never look back.

Then I'd wake up to being in there and it hurt even worse. That's why they had to be dead in the beginning. The dreams hurt less if they're dead and can't come save me.

Yeah, that dream died pretty much the second that they tied me to the bench... to get me used to it "for when the omega is ready to breed." Even then, I held out hope that someone would save me. Then Petey forced my first kiss and I puked in his mouth. Honestly, I think it improved the smell. But that little upchuck resulted in my first open mouth gag and my first trip on the bench for its intended purpose.

I cried that night. That was the last time I cried. It was the realization that I had no more firsts to give that broke me. Hell, Ric was the one in all of my fantasies, but the guy didn't even know I had been in love with him forever. I spoke my wish and my apology to him that night before I cried myself to sleep. That was when I knew no one was coming to save me. I just hoped he and Connor had gone quickly when they died.

Finding out they were both alive and well and not even

looking for the last however many years kinda hurt. I mean I already knew that fairy tales are bullshit bedtime stories and prince charming is a self-centered prick just looking for a piece of arm candy. But to realize the prince in my dreams is that guy, it really cuts deep.

The beeping of the heart monitor is really starting to get annoying. Doctor Weasel never used them, so the sound is just pounding away at my sanity, what's left of it anyways. It's like the beeping is competing with the incessant ticking noise coming from the other side of the room. I'm feeling like I'm about to jump out of my skin this is so uncomfortable.

The only thing stopping me from stripping down, shifting, and bolting out of this place is the fact that my brother is asleep in the chair right next to the bed. I know I can get away from him easily. But I need answers first. I need to know why it took him so long to find me, to save me. I need to hear from him that he never gave up. Connie never lies to me. He will tell me he was looking all this time even behind Ric's back. I'm sure of it.

That's another thing. Ric is Alpha now. I never thought his Dad would give up the title and the power that goes with it, but at least I won't have to deal with the old bastard looking the other way next time something happens. Something always happens in that pack. At least Max should still be there. He's at least good people.

While Connie is snoring loud enough to wake the dead, I start taking in my surroundings. I haven't seen actual moonlight in years, so I'm a bit disappointed that it's not some magical sight thanks to my connection with the G-Lady and all. Maybe it's because of her that I don't care about the moonlight? I mean she did pretty much force me into a lifelong deal by allowing them to remove my baby bits.

We'll never be a papa. My wolf whines at me, coming fully awake after our ordeal.

This just means we never have to worry about losing anyone again. No womb means no mate or child to be taken away from us. I reply to him neutrally. I can't think about it without going under and I need to be alone for that. I won't do it around someone I don't know if I can trust.

Looking around the small room, I start feeling really out of place. The clock on the wall is making that god-awful tick tick tick noise. I stare at it hoping to have some sort of superpower to shut it up. After about fifteen minutes, I've admitted defeat to the clock. Finally looking at it to read the time, I see it's after midnight. I know it's been at least a couple of days here, but I really wish I could find something to give me the date. Connie hasn't said it yet.

Looking at the table next to the bed, I see Connor's phone. I pick it up and the screen lights up for me. The screen is dominated by a picture of him, Ric, and a little kid. Looks like they're all pretty happy, too. Guess if you lose your little brother, it's easy enough to replace him, right? The date showing on the phone finally registers to me. Huh, I'm about three days away from twenty-one.

Fuck answers.

I spent almost eight years of my life getting cut open. I've been gutted like a fish. I've been hacked to pieces. I barely got to eat real food for eight fucking years. Oh, and let's not forget the fucking. Yeah, I had no say in that either.

Eight years and you move on to be the perfect big brothers to some other kid while I was forced to die over and over and over.

Next thing I know my wolf is crashing through the window and we're racing for the closest woods. I can faintly hear the sound of the heart monitor alarm blaring and Connor yelling in the distance.

Connor can go back to his perfect little family. Him and Ric both can go to hell. Maybe they'll actually experience a fraction of what I went through the last eight years....

Eight years.

Fuck.

Ric

He's alive.

Ethan is alive. My Little Boy Blue didn't leave this world behind.

We left him. We left him in a place like that...

Connor slams open the door to my office, interrupting my perusal of the bottom of the fifth bottle of tequila for the night... or is it the sixth?

"He's gone!" he gasps, having obviously run here straight from the hospital.

The sight of him covered in blood with his insides trying to be on the outside... I can't ever get that picture out of my head. Hence the tequila. Connor made a six-hour trip take under four to get Ethan to a shifter hospital we could trust. That was two days ago, maybe three. They're all blurring together.

"Ric, sober your ass the fuck up! We have to find him!" Connor starts trying to get me standing. The movement and the tequila don't mix well and the floor is rapidly rising to meet my face.

My Beta saves me from the faceplant only to slap me hard enough to have my ass meet the floor instead. The pain manages to pull me to at least a little bit of clarity. Enough to respond anyways.

"How did anyone get past you to get him out the door?" I slur in his general direction. It was a logical question. Connor is the lightest sleeper on the planet.

"He didn't go out the door!" Connor growls back at me. "Either he jumped out the window or someone threw him out and went after him."

"I'm mostly sure no one came into the room," he seems to be talking to himself now, "Why would he run from me?"

My Beta collapses as if his strings were cut. The pain we have both been fighting to keep inside is trying to break free. This guilt will kill us all if we let it. Of course, he ran. We never even looked for him and something tells me Ethan at least suspects it, even if he doesn't know the reasons.

"We'll find him," I tell him. "He can't get far with the injuries he has and the other packs in the area will put out an alert on any new wolf trespassing on their territories." I try to reassure him and myself at the same time. "Ethan doesn't know the area and his working knowledge of the world is that of a kid. We'll get him back. We won't lose him again."

Connor panics and tries to rush out the door to search for himself. I hate having to restrain him, but it's the only way to stop him from making things worse.

"He's keyed up, Con," I explain while holding my Beta in a choke hold. "He just woke up in a strange place with strange smells and last thing he knew was being cut open by docs over and over.

"Of course, he ran from a hospital." I'm trying to logic my way through this for both our sakes. "He'll settle once he's alone and we can always follow his scent and track him."

"Tracking, right," Connor replies as I release him. He starts to pull himself together and stands up. "You're the best nose. You need to help me here, Ric. I can't lose him again. I just can't..."

His sobs are pulling my own to the surface. This damn metabolism refuses to let me stay drunk enough to not feel this shit. It looks like I'm going to have to face a conscious Ethan sooner than expected. Maybe I'll get lucky and only have to meet his wolf and Connor can take over? That would be better. I don't think I can handle seeing the betrayal in his baby blues. At least our wolves' eyes aren't our own.

I find myself nodding in agreement as I am pulled up from the floor. Connor's right, though. I am the best tracker in the area, even in comparison with the other packs in our region. The hospital is located at the junction of our territories, so it, the shopping district, and the surrounding woods are considered neutral. Hopefully, Ethan doesn't go beyond there into another pack's land. I really don't need the headache on top of the hangover I'm already starting to form.

Leaving my office behind, Connor and I start the drive towards the hospital just as it starts raining. Wonderful...

"What do you mean you can't identify his scent?!" Connor screams at me in the hospital room.

It's the damnedest thing. I can smell that a wolf was here. I can vaguely identify the wolf is related to Connor since siblings always smell similar. For some reason, that's all the identifying aspects I can get from Ethan's bed. I can scent each of the doctors and nurses and even Connor on the bed, but there's only enough from Ethan to know that someone else had been there.

"His scent has no unique identifiers. I've never come across this before," I tell my Beta. "They don't make scent blockers that still leave something behind." I'm just as confused as he is. I can't track this. I can't find Ethan.

"I don't know what you're talking about, Ric. I can scent him just fine. We need to go before the scent trail is washed away by the rain." Connor spits out as he jumps from the broken window without bothering to shift.

I follow only to discover him kneeling in tears at the edge of the parking lot. "It just ends as it hits the back of the parking lot." Connor is spinning out again. My mind and my wolf are thinking the same thing *Did they find him and take him away again?*

Suddenly Connor jumps to his feet and starts pacing in the downpour.

"Why didn't I think of this sooner? I mean, I haven't done it in years. I only ever did it with Dad since he said it was dangerous, but this is a last resort, right?" he looks up at me, but before I can respond he continues, "Right. I gotta do it..."

I'm listening to my Beta ramble and spin out and I have no clue what he's talking about. I grab him by the shoulders and shake him hard enough to get his attention. It takes a few tries to snap him out of his internal debate on the ramifications of whatever he's thinking about doing.

"What are you going to do? Explain it to me." I order him, using my authority as his Alpha. I hate using it, but I can't afford to have him lie to me now. There's a secret here that I don't know about and apparently it can help us find Ethan. My wolf refuses let go unless Ethan himself tells us to leave him alone.

Connor takes a while to clear his thoughts and focus back on me. He's fighting my authority, trying to figure out a way to keep this secret. After about five minutes of resistance, his shoulders slump and he starts to explain.

"My father's family line was blessed by the Goddess long ago. Every male wolf in the line gets gifted a psychic ability of some sort when their wolf emerges," he explains. "All of the alphas in the line have the same basic ability, although it differs slightly based on the individual. We can basically take over the senses of another. For my dad, that meant he could listen in on anyone as long as he was thinking about them. For my grandfather, he could see through another's eyes. I can do both; however, there are risks involved."

My mind is reeling. My Beta has had this ability for over twelve years now and this is the first time I'm hearing of this? The risks had damn well be big or else I'm going to be pissed that this was kept from me.

After pausing to let me digest what he's said so far, Connor continues," For me to see through someone else's eyes, I'm temporarily blinding them and myself. Although there is no lasting harm to use this outside of a killer headache according to my dad, if I were to look through your eyes while you're driving for example, it could cause you to crash. I will incapacitate the person I'm seeing through.

"For me to hear through their ears, I'm creating sensory overload and overstimulation to my own auditory processing system. I can go deaf if I listen too long... or go mad."

As I take the time to process what he's telling me, Connor resumes pacing and muttering under his breath. I know he's thinking of the pros and cons of using these gifts to find Ethan. Another thought occurs to me as I'm watching him pace.

"Why haven't you ever used this gift to help the pack? You could just pop in a listen to our rivals to get ahead on deals and such." I must ask. I know he's too honorable to do that kind of stuff, but even I would have used it in school to get test answers or something.

He sighs like he expects the question, "I asked my dad about using it for that kind of stuff too. I mean I was a kid. Turns out, I can only use it on those I have a blood tie with," he explains. "So, I can use it on you or any of the pack through my blood tie with you. And I can use it on Ethan. And before you ask, no I couldn't use it eight years ago when we lost him."

He continues even before I could ask, "I can't use either ability on anyone under the age of maturity without causing irreparable harm to either their hearing or their sight. To use it before I'm sure their healing ability is fully developed could be disastrous."

The silence hung in the air between us. We both knew what

he wasn't saying. He didn't even attempt to look through his brother's eyes or hear through his brother's ears before now. He couldn't risk it in the beginning. Then, we believed the lie that Ethan was dead all this time. And now, what if he distracts Ethan and he gets hit by a car or falls off a cliff or worse? It's not worth the risk.

Before I can voice my objections on the subject, I see Connor's eyes glaze over. He isn't kidding about the being blind thing. It's like there's a golden film over his eyes as he's looking out of Ethan's eyes. This is freaking me out, so I grab him by the shoulders to stop him from trying to walk anywhere while he's like this.

"He must be in the neutral area somewhere in the woods. He's found a cave for the night. I can't see any real markers to identify where he is though. I wish I could share smells..." his voice cuts out as he gasps in shock.

"What happened? Is he ok? Did he get hurt because you're using his eyes?"

Connor blinks and his eyes are back to normal and starts laughing. I don't see what's so funny.

"Well Ethan got a gift too apparently. Turns out I wasn't crazy back then." Connor suddenly falls on his rear end right in the middle of the parking lot as he continues in between the sobs, "my baby brother was calling out for help and we all left him. I knew it in my gut that it was him and we left."

My blood freezes in my veins. He really was calling out for help. He was speaking into Connor's mind. Why didn't he ever reach out to me? Is it a blood thing for him too? It must be. The kid has to know I'd have done anything for him. I'd have burned the world to find him.

And since you're there with him, Fuck you too, Mister Alpha Asshole Alaric. You both seemed to move on just fine without me so why don't you both just fuck off and leave me alone. You're good at that.

I crash to my knees in the middle of the parking lot next to my sobbing Beta. The sound of a wolf howling echoes through my head. When my warriors come running up to us seconds later, I realize it was me.

***

Coming back to the house that belonged to me and Jack, I realize just how empty I've left my life become. My wolf never moved on from that morning eight years ago. Honestly, neither did I. Ethan's rejection from tonight is still slicing through me as I shower and prepare for bed. Before I drift off completely, I send a message to Max, the head of my warriors:

> Jack is to have guards 24/7 unless he is in my direct sight. Send over two men to guard the house tonight and we'll set up a rotation and schedule in the morning.

I'm not losing another person from my life. Goddess help me, I'll destroy the world if I lose him, too.

FOUR

<u>Ethan</u>

It's been roughly two weeks since I ran from the hospital. The doozy of a headache I was rocking after that mind trip in the rain that night managed to stick around for a few days afterward. I've been wandering around the woods and the immediate area since just to get an idea where we are.

I know we aren't in Ohio anymore. Ohio doesn't turn everything yellow in the spring. It's also warmer than I know it should be, or maybe it's global warming? I hear that's a thing now.

This section of woods and the little shopping district on the other side of the hospital all seem to be a kind of no man's land for shifters. I'm able to smell a mix of pack scents in the shopping areas but the woods have a distinct lack of pack scents. Looks like I found my place to be then. I'll just hunker down in my little cave and live out the rest of my life alone and in peace.

Yeah, that lasted a whole two days. Once I *relieved* a man of his wallet in the hospital, I was able to get some decent stuff for my cave. I never thought a sleeping bag and fuzzy slippers would be the height of luxury, but damn these are close. I also got some friends for Mr. Whiskers.

Damn.

I gotta go back for Mr. Whiskers.

Does Mr. Whiskers still exist?

Did Connor give him to the new little brother?

He's my teddy! No one else can have him!

Where is Mr. Whiskers?! I demand in my brother's head.

Let's give him a headache this time. His stupid double vision trick hurt me for days.

Little Brother, you have no clue how happy I am to hear from you.

Oh, shove it! I interrupt his bumbling attempt at an apology. *I loaned you Mr. Whiskers for your college trip and I'm calling it due. I want him back. TODAY!*

Tell me where, Little Brother and I'll bring him to you, he says in my head. *Just don't shut me out. Please, Ethan.*

Oh man, he actually sounds like he misses me.

If he missed me.

If he loved me, why was I there for over a third of my life? Why didn't he come to get me? Why didn't anyone save me?

Shaking myself out of these thoughts is a lot easier when it's the same four walls and handful of dickwads staring at you every second of every day. This freedom shit is messing with my head.

Meet you at the hospital. Dunno what time. I don't have a watch, I tell him. *Sundown-ish I guess. By the blue car that never seems to leave. I like that car. It smells nice.*

I cut him off before I got a response. I just want Mr. Whiskers. I don't need anyone or anything else. I'll be just fine. He's the only one who never let me down. I know at least *he* never forgot about me.

Ric

It's been a couple weeks and we can't seem to get any news on Ethan except that he apparently stole a wallet from a guy who was in for a colonoscopy and then used his credit cards to buy clothes and stuffed animals. For a guy who is running on an eighth grade education, the kid is good at covering his tracks. He crosses so many scent trails in town, none of my warriors can track him down. Even when he goes into the woods, he's able to cover his tracks to the point his scent just dissipates about a dozen yards in. It would be impressive if it wasn't so infuriating.

Connor looks up at me with a huge smile on his face. I think he's totally lost it.

"He wants Mr. Whiskers" he says in awe.

"He broke two weeks of silence to demand a teddy bear?" I'm totally skeptical of this reasoning. Ethan had already grown out of the teddy by the time he hit middle school. "How are you gonna manage that considering the thing is long gone. Nothing survived the fire, let alone a stuffed animal."

The look he's giving me is making me really wonder what all my Beta has kept hidden from me over the years. I could almost describe the look as bashful. Yeah, this is really creepy. "Spit it out, dude. You're creeping me out." I tell him.

"Well," he starts hesitantly, "the thing is, Ethan used to worry about sleeping alone, like if Mom and Dad were out late by the time it was bedtime or whatnot," He explains to me. I nod for him to continue because I can't see where this is going.

"It became a routine for him to have Mr. Whiskers in his bed under his pillow just in case. For years, I forgot about it. It wasn't until the night before we left to go to Pittsburgh that he reminded me. I ducked into his room to say goodnight since we were leaving before he would be up in the morning. I thought he was asleep," he chuckles at the memory.

"But before I was able to leave the room, he threw the ratty ass bear at my head. He said, and I quote, *This is only a loan. He comes back to me the second you see me...*"

"And you've had it ever since." I finish for him.

His nod and his glassy eyes are all the confirmation I need. This is a promise between the brothers that Connor thought he'd never get to fulfill. This is their second chance. I can't stand in the way of this. I would do anything for Jack, even holding onto a ratty old teddy bear that probably looks more like a chew toy than a teddy bear at this point.

My mind is made up for what needs to happen next, so I let Connor know I want to go with him to do this teddy bear exchange. I need to see him for myself, alive and well, to be able to even attempt to move forward. And I'll give him some things I've been putting together for him as well. He's going to need these things whether he stays with us or not.

FIVE

<u>Ethan</u>

I'm getting Mr. Whiskers back! It's a good day. Mr. Whiskers always protected me from the bad dreams. I can really use his protection now. The nightmares have started. It's been a while since I've had one bad enough to remember in the morning. Last night's was the worst. The other stuffies try their best, but Mr. Whiskers is a professional nightmare fighter. That's why I need him back.

Making my way back to the hospital using the upper limbs of the trees is a fun game I thought up. My parents and Connor never understood how I got around everywhere without leaving my scent. It's because I have always loved to climb. My scent trail is there. It's just about ten feet or higher above the ground. Most shifters don't think to sniff up, so they think they've lost the trail. Bonus perk for this game right now is that no one can track me from the town to get me in trouble for the things I've swiped.

Speaking of town, I should really avoid that side of the hospital just in case the dickheads decide to plan an ambush to bring me back with them. I see anyone but my brother, I can just keep to the trees and head on back to my cozy cave.

A sound like a deer crashing to the ground gets my attention. I can't kill one, but if it breaks its own neck, my wolf can at least get a good meal. *Sounds like a plan to me* my wolf responds, so I turn back into the woods towards the direction I believe is Alpha Asswipe's pack lands. After about a quarter mile, I see that it is indeed NOT a deer.

It's a kid. Wait, that's not just any kid. That's the kid from Connor's phone... and he's terrified. Maybe he's trying to catch up to Connor to get Mr. Whiskers. Maybe the kid needs the professional nightmare fighter, too.

Nope. That's not it. Coming out from the trees behind the kid is none other than Needle Dick Noah, and I know the look on his face.

Shit.

I'm gonna have to play hero here aren't I? No time to think. I just need to act.

Hey kid! When you see the signal you need to run straight to Connor and give him the message I'm gonna give you. Word for word. You understand? Don't speak out loud. Just think it and I'll hear you. I throw out there into his head.

His tiny voice tugs at my heart and I understand why Connie took him in.

I understand, Mister. Straight to Big Brother Connor. I'm really scared, Mister. The bad man is trying to take me away from Big Brother Ric.

And right here is the moment I wish I could kill Noah. I would kill for this kid if I could. Right now, there's only one thing I can do.

My name is Ethan. You run straight to Connor. He should be at the hospital parking lot by now. Tell him they wanted you but Ethan went in your place. Tell him it's one of the same guys as before. Oh, and tell him not to take eight years this time, eh?

Before the kid can respond, I jump down behind Noah so the kid can run.

"Hey Needle Dick!" Yep, that got his attention. "Looking for someone? Sorry your lousy skills in the sack translate to the rest of the world, too."

Oh snap. He's pissed. Too much? Possibly, but I cackle with glee as he takes off after me instead of the kid. I just need to put enough distance between us and the kid so he can reach Connie and then I'll take to the trees and slip away from Needle Dick Noah.

Good Luck, Kid

That's the last thing I am able to get out before the sting of the tranquilizer dart registers. I wish I had enough time to tell Ric to protect that ray of sunshine but looks like it's back to the cot room for me.

Ric

I'm going to kill him. Not really. But I really want to sometimes.

Jack has slipped his protection detail and I can't go with Connor to meet up with Ethan because of it. I know it's not right to be angry at a seven, almost eight, year old kid for what is essentially just being a kid. Kids hide and want to play. I know that's all it is with Jack, but my gut won't let go of the fact that it's after dark and my warriors still don't have eyes on my kid brother.

That's it. I'm going out looking myself.

The phone ringing stops me from opening the door. Connor is calling, probably to gush over his brother and he reconciling. Or else he's calling to wallow in the fact that Ethan told him where to shove it after getting his bear back. Or maybe he's calling because his car broke down?

Swiping across the screen, I also grab my keys so I can get out to search for my little brother.

"He didn't show," Connor says before I can even say hello.

"What do you mean he didn't show? I thought he wanted his bear?" I ask while trying to locate something on my desk. I don't even remember what I wanted to grab. Phone? Check, I'm on it. Keys? In my hand. What else do I need to grab to go looking for Jack?

"He did... does... Something feels wrong. I tried listening instead of looking and I can hear him running and breathing hard. I can't tell if he's running from something or running to something. And he's shut me out so I can't ask him"

The sudden screech of tires has me holding my breath. Oh Goddess, please don't let Connor have to watch his little brother get hit by a car, not after all they've been through.

But the voice I hear through the phone next surprises me. It is not my Beta... it's my little brother.

"Ethan said to say" Jack gasps out between haggard breaths, "they wanted me but he's gonna take care of it. He said this time don't take eight years." I flinch, as I know Connor is doing the same at that little dig from our little brothers.

"Connor, who is Ethan?" Both of us gasp at the realization that Ethan is in trouble and managed to save Jack from the same fate.

My wolf sits up in anticipation. It's time to go hunting and this time nothing will stop us from finding Ethan.

SIX

RIC

Yet again we can't find a scent trail for Ethan. Connor insists he's alive, but he can't see anything and every time he tries to hear, it's like static. We don't know if it's because he's unconscious or if something is interfering or if they're using some sort of sensory deprivation to torture him.

I don't want to speculate. My wolf is restless with the need to find him. It's been a few hours and the only clue we have is that we know he was put into the trunk of a car thanks to a doorbell camera. We don't even have the plate number, just the make, model, and color of the car. We couldn't even get a good shot of the guy who stuffed him in there.

From what Jack has told us about the guy who was chasing him, he's just a human, maybe a bit faster than usual, but still a human. Humans don't usually get involved in were business. Maybe he has a werewolf parent but never manifested a wolf. That isn't all that common, but it's been known to happen.

However, those humans are generally part of the pack as well as their offspring, so why doesn't this guy have a pack scent on him? Considering what we've since discovered about the lab where Ethan had been, I'm not too happy about this turn of events.

Following the dick's scent is easier than trying to pick out Ethan's so I trace it back through the woods... to my own pack lands. This *human* encountered Jack inside the safety of our pack. He chased my little brother away from the safety of our pack. My wolf is hungry for blood.

First pup, now mate. Human needs death, my wolf growls to me.

Mate?

I'll have to unpack that later because the scent trail is crossed by someone who shouldn't have been here. It's familiar as it's pack, but the volume of perfume attached to it makes it indistinguishable. It's so strong it muddles the scent of the dick I'm pursuing to the point I've lost the trail.

So now, there's a traitor in my pack. It's the only way a human who isn't part of my pack could come onto my land and get anywhere near my brother.

Connor catches up to me to ask why I stopped. He clearly has done the same mental gymnastics I have. There's no way we are ever letting Ethan stay in human hands ever again.

As he takes a whiff of the area, his nose wrinkles in distaste.

"Why the hell do our she-wolves think we would ever like perfume?! All it smells like is chemicals and all it does is fuck up our noses for hours," one of my warriors complains loudly while the surrounding warriors hum an agreement. I can't say I disagree with him.

At the thought of she-wolves, I remember Jessica is supposed to come over for some special dessert thing tonight. I really need to call her to cancel. I didn't want to do the thing in the first place, but especially now, we need to find Ethan. He is more important than some chocolate thing our parents started doing when we were in high school. My dad was the one who said it should be a tradition, not me.

As I pull out my phone, I notice Connor has managed to get that distracted look on his face. He's got a bit of a smirk going, so I'm guessing Ethan is not in immediate danger and is instead being a bit of a smartass. Safe to say, we are going after him now that we've made contact, so I hit Jessica's contact to call her.

As the phone is ringing, Connor cocks his head to the side. The line connects and I hear her overly sweet voice trill out, "Alpha, I'm so sorry I'm running late. I will be *right* there."

Ugh I hate her voice.

Looking up, I see the face of my Beta contort with rage as a growl is building in his throat. I'm looking into the eyes of his wolf as the realization hits me. He's hearing my phone conversation in stereo.

Ethan

Waking up from the tranq feels kinda like getting thrown overboard but landing on a piece of driftwood. You're not drowning, but you aren't fully on deck and in control of everything. "What the hell? He died eight years ago! Why the hell is he here and not the twerp?!"

Oh she could give weasel a run for his money on the screeching. Although she does sound kind of familiar, so maybe they're related? I don't really care. I need some water. Cotton mouth is a bitch to deal with when you first wake up.

Speaking of mouths, yay for gags. I knew good old Pencil Dick over here had some kinky shit outside of the lab. Based on the size of this one though, it won't actually keep me quiet if I wanted to make noise. Maybe he made it based on his... It's about the right size for that. As for me making noise, I'm just too stoned to really care at this point. My wolf will burn off the rest of the drugs eventually and then I'll just rip out the gag.

Or maybe not. Trying to move even a little bit results in pain, so either Noah darling has gotten better at the knots or the she-bitch knows how to tie someone up. Kinky little minx. She even got the good blindfold going on. I can't see a thing.

The she-bitch just keeps whining and complaining that Noah is a waste of space who can't do anything right. His mother should have drowned him as a baby... ouch that's harsh. Accurate? Absolutely. Still harsh though.

"I don't know why Dad insisted I keep you around. You can't even grab a little kid!" she's practically screaming and I barely hear Noah breathing. Come to think of it, they smell similar. Your mom, Dad... holy shit! They're siblings.

"How in the hell am I supposed to be his mate if that little shit is in the picture, huh? Answer me that! The kid tortures me worse than this one ever did!"

Why do I feel like that was directed at me? I haven't tortured anyone in over eight years, unless you count verbally with Noah and Pete and the gang. But I have the feeling I'm supposed to know who this she-bitch is. She-bitch is kind of redundant, of course but just saying bitch is less satisfying somehow.

Man, these were the good drugs.

I'm just trying to float away on these unexpectedly fantastic sensations and her voice keeps bringing me back. Are there cosmetic surgeries for voices? If so, she-bitch over here really needs to save up and get one. Judging by the smell of this place, though, she needs to invest in a cleaning service or a good air freshener first. Why am I smelling anchovies?

For a bit I zone out of the incessant screeching of why the she-bitch is mad that she can't get her dick wet by the guy she wants. Wait, reverse that. She can't wet the dick of the guy she wants. Right? I think that's the way it goes. I don't really know. I never saw much point in the va-jay-jay with me being omega and all.

Ok drifting away again seems like a good idea. I'm sure Noah wants to get away from here too. I kinda understand him a bit better now. I get why he's such a dick. I would be too if I had to share DNA with someone like the she-bitch here.

And why in the hell does she keep acting like she knows me? This is really going to bother me until I can figure it out.

Right then, my head feels like it's going to split in two. That is NOT the way I want to come down from this high. Based on the last time this happened, I assume the cause is that jerk-face Connie. I guess the kid found him after all. Good for him.

Took you long enough you old jackass. So I'm a little snippy. These headaches are almost as big of a bitch as the dentist drill still going over there.

Why can't I see where you are? Just open your eyes an let me look around. He says to me.

Huh, so that's his trick for the migraine inducing. That's kind of cool actually. Not exactly safe, but cool. Prank ideas start to form in my head. I am struggling to hold in my giggles as I'm imagining me calling on him to look while I'm in the middle of one of my epic rub sessions.

What's so funny, Little Blue? I thought you got nabbed again. Are we all out here on a manhunt for you just playing hide and seek? Connie asks me. He's not mad. I can tell. He's got that confused lilt to his voice. I'm pretty sure he's starting to catch on to just how long it's been since I've been what one could call sane.

Hide and seek is so last season, man. Don't you know you gotta step it up? It's all about the kidnap and rescue games now. And let me say this, the she-bitch here is really fucking good at her ropes, but gags? Not so much. I give it an eight out of ten.

Connor's chuckle seems to come through just fine. I'm enjoying this little break and it almost feels like I've got my big brother back. I really do miss him.

The screeching is increasing in the background. Oh? Was that a slap? Things are getting good. I just wish I could see it. The most drama I've seen in the last eight years is people fighting over a parking spot in the shopping district last week.

Man, blindfolds suck. Things are heating up over here between the she-bitch and Needle Dick and I don't get to watch. Although some ear plugs would definitely be nice if she's gonna keep squealing like that.

I didn't mean to send that to Connor, but the next thing I know, it almost feels like there's cotton shoved in my ears. I can still hear, but it's muffled. Feels kinda nice after the axe to the brain his eye trick hit me with earlier.

I'm not really paying attention and the floatiness of the high is starting to circle back to me when a phone rings. If it wasn't for the gag in my mouth, I would probably puke. Who puts a ringtone like that on their phone when it could ring in public? Ugh, can I dislike the she-bitch any more?

Wait, why am I hearing growling? That isn't my wolf's growl in my head. Is that Connie's wolf?

Then it hits me. I know who the she-bitch is now!

I feel another pinch from a needle as the giggle fit takes over. Jessica really should have taken the loss eight years ago. She-bitch is gonna die for this one and I don't have to lift a finger. G Lady I think I found another loophole.

Ethan?! Answer me buddy!

Oops. I guess I tuned out Connie with my revelation.

We're on our way to you. Just stay with me...

Connie's voice is getting softer. Usually when someone starts losing the volume in the mind speak, it means they're getting farther away. Something tells me this has more to do with whatever was in the needle than the direction Connie is moving.

Sorry, Bro. Looks like I'm checking out for a bit. Hey, do you know how Jessica got the good drugs? I might need to know... for future... reasons...

I don't know if Connie even got that. I don't know if I even thought it in words. I just know that the darkness is soft and quiet and the ride is smooth, so I drift away.

SEVEN

RIC

As I hang up the phone, Connor looks murderous. I can't say I blame him. At just a glance, we both take off towards Jessica's cabin. She's been living at the guest house since Jack's little prank with the anchovy oil, but she'll never give up the old cabin towards the back edge of the territory. We used to go there for parties in high school and she never lets anyone forget it.

Connor stops like he needs to concentrate. He looks scared. "He's unconscious... at least I hope that's all it is." He tells me. "She drugged him."

At this, he starts a bit of a panic giggle. Never thought I'd see my stoic and dignified Beta giggling like a school girl.

"Ethan said she got the good drugs." He explains between gasping breaths, trying to calm down. "he's high as a kite and I think she just gave him more to make sure he's out. Pretty sure she's taking precautions to make sure he won't be found while we're searching tonight."

I hate to admit it, but she is the last person I would have thought of going after Jack. I mean our parents were good friends, especially after the deaths of the Sinclairs. Jessica has been there for every one of Jack's milestones. I didn't really invite her around, but she was always showing up. I thought it was because she cared about him, so why is she hiring some thug to take him away?

"What's this about a problem with the closet that she had to move?" Connor breaks through my thoughts.

The anchovy oil. As I'm describing how Jack pulled off the prank that caused her extended stay at the guest house, Connor is trying to fight the smile breaking onto his face.

"Sounds like something Ethan would've pulled on her." He sighs with a smile.

We're a little under a quarter mile to the cabin. Connor explains to me that the closet with the anchovy smell is where we will likely find Ethan. She apparently was telling her brother... didn't know she had one of those... to put him in there so that he wouldn't be scented while we are running our searches. If we didn't know better, we absolutely would miss him.

As the cabin comes into sight, I see the car from the video footage pulling away from the back of the building.

"Shit. What if he's in the car, Ric?" Connie whispers to me in terror as we pick up the pace.

I signal my warriors to follow the car. They know what it would mean to lose it, so they won't. It's not the best solution, but it's the only one I have. Jessica is still in the cabin at least and she's the one I need answers from.

Connor and I stop before the trees end to take everything in. My mind is bouncing around like a ping pong ball at all the different things fighting for my attention right now. Ethan, the guy in the car, Jack, Jessica's betrayal, Connor's sanity, clothes, shoes...

Wait? Shoes? Oh yeah, the other part of Jack's prank. Sleep. I need sleep.

But first, I have to take down a bitch. Before we can even knock, she's opened the door to usher us inside.

"Oh Alpha, you didn't have to come see me to apologize. I understand things come up for someone as important as you." Her voice is so overly sweet it's making me nauseous as she continues, "Although you are always welcome to come in to relax, I'm afraid I still can't get the smell out from little Jackie's last escapade."

Connor growls at the mention of the smell. It's not like we can't tell. The smell of anchovies is overpowering. How in the hell did Jack get the smell to be this strong in such a short amount of time?

It's to the point that I can't even smell her except her perfume. I understand now why she's been using so much of it. She needs it. But it also spells her doom as the scent puts her at the scene of meeting a stranger inside pack lands and not informing anyone.

"Where is my brother?" Connor demands as he grabs her by the throat and slams her into the door as she closes it behind us.

"Your brother? He died in a fire, didn't he?" she says in apparent confusion.

She's good. If I didn't already know Ethan had been here, I might have believed her.

"I know he was here, "Connor growled out. His wolf is starting to break through. Although I don't mind my Beta taking out a traitor to the pack, we both need answers first.

"Con, go check the rooms. I'll get the answers we need," I tell him as I sit down in the old recliner that I'm pretty sure has been here longer than we've been alive. It smells like the dick, who I guess is her brother. Still going to have to work through that one.

Connor throws her on the sofa and storms out of the room. He's heading straight for the master bedroom, her room, to check the closet. That's the place that makes the most sense based on what he overheard while Ethan was still conscious.

Jessica looks pissed. No, she looks jealous. She seriously looks like she's mad that I'm putting someone else's welfare above her comfort. Wow. And the bitch wonders why I never want to be around her outside of mandatory social obligations. Between the narcissism and the voice, the guy who the Goddess pairs with her has to either be a saint or the worst scum of the earth to deserve a punishment like being with her.

Connor calls out that he needs some help looking, so I call in a warrior to watch Jessica. As she starts to get up, my wolf growls in a way that even I didn't know was possible. The bitch actually pees herself in fear. My wolf is happy about that, watching her sit back down soaked in her own urine. The authority in my voice rings clear as I order, "Bind her and take her to the cells. She is a traitor to the pack and will face judgment at the next gathering, once we're done questioning her brother."

My warrior does a double take, but complies. I'll have to unpack that later as well. Just how many people are unaware that she has siblings. How many secrets am I going to uncover? Just how out of touch am I now?

Running to the bedroom, I see the open closet and the contents everywhere in the room. Connor is at the edge of the bed with his head in his hands weeping silently.

"He's not here, Ric," he gasps out between sobs. "He can't be gone, again.

"Tell me I'm missing something! Tell me I'm blind and he's lying right here asleep." Connor is breaking. I won't be able to put him back together this time. I have to find Ethan.

One of my warriors comes through the door, pointedly ignoring my Beta sobbing on the bed, to hand me his phone.

Looking down at the screen, I see the number belongs to Max, the head of my warriors.

"Did something happen to Jack?" I panic. Max is supposed to be with Jack personally until I get back. I didn't know who to trust right now aside from him and Connor. But now that I know it was Jessica behind the incident with Jack, I can start to increase the people I trust with my little brother.

"Little man is fine. We went out for ice cream and on the way back saw a bunch of my guys wrestling a human from a sedan," he states with a bit of a question in his voice. Yeah, I forgot to give him a heads up that I gave the warriors that specific task.

"So then, little man here tells me that this is the guy who chased him," Max continues, "and took Ethan... is this Ethan the same as the little shit who thought it was funny to cut all of our jocks during junior year? The same Ethan we all were told died in a fire eight years ago?"

I forgot to inform my head warrior about Ethan being alive at all. I'm dropping the ball everywhere. I should have remembered that Max would need to know about this. Come to think of it, Max was around a lot when Ethan was when we were kids. We were like the Musketeers and Ethan was our D'Artagnan. I'm pretty sure it was Max who got him started on that fries with ice cream thing. Even Jack has picked that one up.

Connor is staring at the phone in hope. If Ethan isn't here, he should be in the car, so I ask, "Did the guys find anyone else in the car? Even in the trunk?"

I hear Max ordering the guys to search every inch of the car that could possibly conceal a person. I can hear the straining of metal and the breaking of glass, but ten minutes later our hopes are dashed.

"Sorry, Boss-man. No one else in the car."

He sounds curious more than disappointed. "You gonna

answer my question?," he pushes me. "Little man here doesn't know Ethan. Said he just met the guy when he *spoke in his head* and told him to run to your Beta." Max is pushing me to talk. He's making me ask for help. I'm bad at that.

"Max... yes," I say into the phone. "Ethan is alive and it's a long ass story that I don't have time for. Right now, we have to find him again." While I watch, Connor shrinks in on himself at the news his brother is still missing.

"All we know is he's tied up, blindfolded, gagged, and drugged..." I add, "by Jessica."

I let that one sink in for a minute as silence steals through the night. Max hums in a very noncommittal way and I hear Jack commanding in the background that they need to get more sundae fixings for when we bring Ethan back to the house. I can hear the hero worship in his tone already. I can't let my little brother down. I can't let any of them down. I will find Ethan and bring him home. There is no other choice. I am the Alpha and it is my duty and responsibility to keep my pack whole and sane. We need Ethan to be alright for that to happen.

EIGHT

<u>Ethan</u>

Ok those were definitely not the good drugs.

The headache I'm rocking is telling me that either the stuff in that needle was meant to kill me or my brother somehow thought I'd magically lost the blindfold. Either way, I'd kill for some ibuprofen.

Not kill. Maim?

Yes. I would maim for some ibuprofen. The G Lady's deal really makes me think about learning some new colloquialisms.

Ha. Big words.

Ok so maybe these drugs aren't too bad. I think they interacted with the others and that's the problem. Maybe. I don't know. I'm too stoned to think.

Speaking of stoned, I have got the worst case of the munchies I think I've ever had. I don't even know what the munchies are supposed to feel like. I know what hunger feels like. I know what starving feels like. Multiple organ failure due to malnutrition... been there, done that. Zero stars. Would not recommend.

I could really use a double cheeseburger with barbecue sauce and pickles... oh and fries with a chocolate shake to dip them in. That used to gross the hell out of Ric and Connor. Their buddy Max thought it was good tho. Kinda wish I had that lug in my corner right now. Dude gave me Stabby, my first switchblade. Can't buy one without an ID, so I kind of need that one back. Or maybe they're illegal now? I don't know. Hopefully Connie didn't take it out of Mr. Whiskers. Mr. Whiskers does a lot of jobs for me.

Waking up from induced sleep is extra confusing with the mind vortex thing I got going on upstairs. The filter that people are supposed to have up there to keep thoughts in line and organized? Yeah, it barely functions when I'm completely cognizant. And times like this? It's flat out broken. So, my thoughts just come and go, with nothing holding them in line.

Speaking of going, I have to pee really badly. Thinking about it is making it worse. I need to think of something else.

How long has it been since I was supposed to meet with Connie? I really should get a watch, not that it would help me right now. They got me trussed up like a pig at the county fair. And with the blindfold, I can't see squat.

But the point remains, I can't keep being time blind. I used to have a really cool superhero watch that Connie gave me for my ninth birthday. I took it off to go to sleep so I'm sure it was thrown out when they cleaned out my room.

Maybe there are voice activated watches now. I mean that would be so cool. I could feel like I'm in an episode of Star Trek or the really old cheesy Power Rangers show. *Beam me up.* That would be really helpful right about now.

I start to giggle at the thought, but the tickle in my throat makes me remember, I'm still gagged. They didn't even spring for a good one for sound. This one is the kind that is meant to replicate a particular appendage. It's too long and not thick enough to muffle any sound. Uncomfortable as all hell once you think about it, but as long as I stay calm, it won't be anything to worry over.

So let me take stock of my situation here. Blindfolded? Check. Gagged? Check. Unable to move? Check. Hearing? Huh... I can still hear things. Didn't even think about hearing things outside my brain. I usually don't anymore. I rarely hear anything worth listening to.

I can kind of hear voices, but I can't make out who it is, let alone what they're saying. At least the she-bitch isn't one of the ones talking. That much I can tell. But the voices sound kind of familiar, I think. My wolf is almost purring at the sound of one of them. That's new. I didn't know wolves could make that noise.

I can do a lot of things that we just haven't figured out yet, my wolf tells me.

Good to have you back, I tell him. If I can talk to my wolf now, hopefully I can reach out to someone who can actually help me get untied so I can find a bathroom.

I guess I should try to reach out to Connie first, since I went unconscious in the middle of our conversation earlier. You'd think he would have found me tute-suite considering he knows it was Jessica who has me. It's not like the she-bitch is rolling in dough judging by the smell of her place.

Or is it had me? Was that even her place or was it a drop off point?

Did she manage to get me away so there's no new clues now? Yeah, I need to reach out before I panic and the gag causes me issues.

Connie? You almost here, man? I really need to pee and don't want to piss myself.

There's a crash from somewhere nearby followed by some shouting. Someone's keyed up over something around here, but my bladder is screaming at me. Forget the bladder. I need to get out before I hyperventilate and die choking on a penis gag.

Ethan? Where are you, bud? Connor sounds almost as frantic as I'm starting to feel. *We're looking but can't find you. Can you identify anything? I can't hear anything but mumbling from you and I'm guessing you're still wearing a blindfold.*

Well, damn. I guess the bitch moved me after all.

Why am I still smelling anchovies? I ponder. *This is really going to mess with me. The munchies god is demanding a cheeseburger but all I can smell are those damn little fishies that Mom liked on her pizza. She should have never been in charge of pizza procurement. Olives and anchovies do NOT belong on something as magnificent as pizza.*

At Connor's startled squeak, I realize I apparently sent that thought to him and not just to myself.

See? No filter after drugs.

Little Blue, it's super important to answer this question. Ric pushes his way into the communication. I guess he's here, too. I didn't know I can do two at once. *Is the anchovy smell on you or around you?*

Connor is really fucking excited about the damn fishy smell, and Ric is getting insistent. I really can't understand why this is so important, but I try to settle my brain enough for my sniffer to figure out the difference.

After a few minutes, I answer. *It's not coming from me or my clothes. Maybe a little from the ropes, but it's mostly all around me, like it's soaked into the wood and padding around me.*

Padding? I didn't realize it at first but I'm surrounded by some sort of padding or clothing or packing materials. That could explain the sound issue.

Oh hell, did the she-bitch pack me in a crate to ship off to some overseas oil tycoon who wants a harem of exotic little twinks to feed him grapes and make pretty mixed babies?

I don't want to be in a harem! I yell into my brother's mind. *You better find me now, asshole. I'm not popping out little ginger sheik babies!*

Ric

Connor has gone from weeping to pacing. He told me Ethan is talking to him so I let him pace.

As his head snaps up, he locks his gaze onto me and says, "He's still here somewhere."

How is that possible? We have torn apart this house. We've gone through every floor and room and closet. We've looked under the beds, behind dressers, opened chests and trunks. There's nowhere else he could be...

"How do you know he's still here?" I ask because I'm at a loss. There's nowhere left to look.

"He is still smelling anchovy, like an overpowering odor of anchovy." He tells me.

The closet. It's the only place that absolutely reeks of it and the only place that would completely overpower our noses. But there is nothing in there. We tore everything out of the closet. We ripped all the drawers out of the built in. We even tore up the floor of the closet and pulled down the ceiling. There's nowhere in there he could be.

I reach out to Ethan, hoping he will hear me. I don't know how this mind speaking ability of his works, but I've picked up a few bits and pieces from his mind since he's been back. I thought I was imagining it before, but I'm pretty sure I can reach him as well.

It worked!

We both race back to the master bedroom and try again to look at what we could be missing in the closet. Connor is looking a bit green, like whatever thought is going through his head is making me simultaneously angry and sick. I tuned out the rambling of Ethan's mind because my wolf and I need to concentrate on finding his scent under this damned fish smell.

I usually don't punish Jack for his pranks unless they cause an injury, but he's getting majorly grounded for this one. I can't smell anything but anchovies in this room.

"Con-man, ask him to talk to me for a while." I tell him leading him from the bed. "And I need you to take over on the sniffer front. Whatever is going on with his scent is still affecting me."

My Beta nods and a few seconds later, I hear Ethan more clearly with him projecting directly to me.

I'm not gonna be part of a sheik baby factory so you better find me now Alpha Asswipe!

The workings of that mind are apparently still more mysterious than the secrets of the universe. I'll have to ask him later where that thought even came from.

Little Blue, I need you to listen very closely and tell me when you hear something, okay? I feel like I'm talking to Jack. Ethan is a grown man. I need to stop thinking of him as the kid I knew.

Before I waste time apologizing, I start knocking on the walls of the closet hoping to hear a response.

Any day now, hott stuff. I hear in my head.

I guess that answers that. He's not behind the walls. In frustration, I kick out at the built-in dresser and it shifts. That is some shoddy workmanship.

OK I heard something there. Ethan sends to me excitedly. *Was I supposed to or am I on a ship to Australia to be fed to carnivorous kangaroos or something?*

I turn back towards the built in and pause for a second. Kangaroos?

I shake my head to dislodge the stream of questions that just popped in there. No time for that. The built-in dresser is somehow hiding Ethan from us.

Signaling to Connor, I also call out for the others to make sure the building is secure. It's time to open this up. Between the two of us, we can't seem to find a latch to release or move the thing easily.

After fifteen minutes of trying to find a latch, my wolf takes over and rips the whole dresser out of the wall. Underneath where it sat, is a small door in the floor that looks barely big enough to fit Jack, let alone a grown man. There's no way he's there.

All that banging I'm hearing better be you and not some dock worker. Ethan pipes up in our heads. *I don't want to be a Russian mail order bride.*

Ok he's spiraling now, but we're apparently on the right track. Wrenching the little door open, it's a chute. Is this the old laundry chute? There's no basement to this place, so where does this go? And why can he barely hear us?

"Ric, we aren't going to fit in there and I don't see him." Says Connor, stating the obvious.

"Where the hell is my brother?!" he screams as he pulls at his hair, ripping a handful out in his frustration. I'm scared for my best friend. How are we at yet another dead end when it comes to Ethan?

NINE

Ethan

Ok you guys can knock it off. I send out to them. *Connie, quit your yelling and just get me out of here before I piss myself.*

I really need to pee now. It's like the closer they get to me, the more my bladder wants to play chicken.

You really heard me? My brother is asking me.

You hear him? Ric asks at the same time.

Ugh, two at once is gonna get old fast. I can feel the headache coming on and the good juices from the drugs are wearing off.

Just get me out of here already. I send them. *My head hurts. My arms and legs are cramping. I got cotton mouth like a bitch. And my bladder isn't going to hold out much longer.*

Do they not see me? Like I know I'm blindfolded but they're obviously close, right? At least the fact that I'm hearing them with my ears and not just in my head has to mean I'm not on a ship headed for Africa to be fed to the lions.

The sound of wood splintering is happening all around me. At least I think it's all around me. Everything is still muffled really badly.

Connie? Are you listening in? It sounds like I got cotton in my ears or something.

I have to ask because the noise level is really not where it should be and the anxiety is ratcheting up again. I'm starting to think that the she-bitch and Needle Dick did something to my ears. *Did they puncture my eardrums? Did they try to make me deaf? Am I going deaf?*

I'm spiraling out. The panic is taking control. I can't stop the sob that tries to escape the gag, but then I choke. I'm choking now. This is how I get to die... tied up by a sadistic she-bitch, blindfolded and choking on a penis gag in a box that smells like little fishies... I never did have good luck.

*We hear you Little Blue. We got you. Just need to get the case out of the floor...*Ric's voice fades out as he's talking. Oh it's a suitcase, not a box. Bitch packed me up like she was going to take me on a trip to Maui. The beach sounds like a good idea right about now...

Hello darkness my old friend... he he he. I like that song. This part of dying isn't so bad.

Ric

I can hear him choking. He's panicking over some crazy scenario in his mind and now he's choking. Can he die choking on whatever is stuck in his throat? I don't know.. He said he was gagged. How did she gag him? It could be suffocating him right now and we still don't have him in sight.

"I see something," Connor says to me as we pull up even more of the floor surrounding the shaft.

There is something jutting into the shaft about four feet down. Just the barest glint of light on metal. It's a suitcase handle. Don't tell me she packed him in a suitcase! Those things are supposed to be airtight and it's been over an hour since Ethan was drugged. How long can someone last locked in a suitcase?

I let him know we see him, but the sounds of his choking are so severe, I have no clue if he can hear me, so I think it to him instead. I keep thinking at him, but the sounds of his choking fade. Is he calming down or are we too late?

Blue? Buddy?

I'm not getting a response. My wolf takes over and rips away the sides of the shaft sending splinters flying through the room. He's done waiting on our human sides to get him to Ethan. I can't say I disagree as I jump into the now much larger hole to grab the suitcase. My brain barely registers the fact that my hands and arms are bleeding, but I'm not hearing anything from the case. My mind is going to the worst possible outcome and freezes my body. I need to know for certain, but don't want to see. I can't see it if he's gone.

Connor snatches the case from me and I absently notice the blood on his face. Apparently, he wasn't able to doge some of the splinters my wolf sent flying. Rushing over to the bed, he gently sets the case down after removing the debris covered quilt. His movement snaps me back into action and I join him at the bedside. We both hold our breath as he lifts the lid to reveal Ethan.

There he is, tucked in and surrounded by a bunch of Jessica's clothing, blindfolded and gagged and tied up and... not breathing. He's not breathing at all.

My Beta collapses to the floor. I am frozen. We're too late. I gently lift Ethan out of the case and can feel a spark of electricity on my skin where it touches his.

No. No way. Ethan isn't our mate. We haven't scented him.

Scent or not, this is mate and he will NOT be dying today! My wolf growls in my head.

My hands shift to claws on their own to cut through the ropes and everything else restraining Ethan. My human mind is still in mourning for the boy I failed yet again. I'm not moving. I can only stare at the boy I can never seem to protect. I deserve to lose my mate for this. I'm not worthy of a mate.

If you don't wake up and save our mate, you will never have my strength again. My wolf warns me.

Looking at Ethan's body on the bed, I start to cut through and clear away the restraints on him. As I pull the gag away, I realize it is one of those penis shaped ones and it was definitely long enough to block his airway.

Jessica killed my boy, my mate. She will die a thousand times for this.

The thoughts of vengeance are keeping me from howling my grief while my Beta is nothing more than a lump of a man staring at nothing. We're broken.

If you won't save him, I will my wolf growls out.

Next thing I register, there are fangs in my mouth and it's biting down on the side of his neck. *What the hell are you doing?* I scream at my wolf and jump away from the bed.

Claiming what is mine, he replies as Ethan's eyes pop open and he starts coughing.

Connor shoots to his feet to look at Ethan in amazement. His tackle crushes the smaller man into the bed. As Ethan's coughing turns to laughter at his big brother's exuberant hug, my Beta looks at me with murder in his eyes. I can't say I blame him.

I just did the lupine equivalent of an elopement while my bride was unconscious.

It saved Ethan's life, but yeah. My wolf is an ass. We just took away one of the few choices Ethan had left to him, and my wolf isn't even sorry. I just hope the ass is prepared for the shitstorm that is Ethan Sinclair's temper because I'm not.

Ethan

Coming back from the dead isn't anything new to me at this point. The G Lady really kept her word in the joint, the slammer, the hellhole... all sounds better than "the lab". Waiting on that filter thing to come online again.

Anyways, back from the dead, although it usually feels much worse than this. Most of the time it takes a bit longer as well. The G Lady typically doesn't notice I've died for at least a few hours, if not days before she sends me back. This time only feels like minutes have passed. And what is this sensation? Feels all tingly. Oh wait, it's gone.

And it's back...

HOLY SHIT!

Sparks rush through my body and my eyes fly open. Is this what a defibrillator is like? Sign me up again. That was a rush. Why didn't the weasel ever mess around with the jolts for me? I kinda want to try it now.

Lungs suddenly need air, so let the resurrection coughing fit begin. At least I'm not dealing with evicting the bugs and spiders that like to crawl in while I'm out.

I can even remember the times before the docs realized I would come back. They actually buried me the first time. I don't like the taste of dirt. Hoping not to have a repeat of that one.

I start to sit up only to get tackled back down onto what I think is a bed. It's been so long since I've been in one, aside from the brief stint in the hospital. Between the bone crushing hug and the tears, I think it's safe to say it's Connie on top of me. The laughter inside me can't stay in as my coughing turns to laughter.

The hug starts to loosen as my laughing dies out. I reach up and touch my neck. It's feeling kind of funny like I got a bug bite or something. There was probably a spider up in the suitcase with me just sucking down my blood. Or maybe I really did have a bad reaction to the drugs and it's just irritated? I think that's where the needle went in, maybe?

My wolf is saying no. He's pissed. Why is he pissed?

We did not consent and he claimed us! he growls to me. *We have no mate now and he forces us to be his?!*

Hold up... Claim? Mate? I'm lost in my head and don't really notice Connie is growling at his best friend and Alpha.

The extra burst of manic laughter that escapes my mouth surprises even me. It breaks the tension, but as soon as their eyes turn on me, I can't stop. The laughter turns to sobs and I can't stop them. I can't breathe. I don't know why I feel like this. I can't stop. I want to stop. I'm scared. Why can't I stop? I'm always in control, now. Nothing controls how I feel but me. Why can't I stop?

Ric reaches out and touches my neck where it feels funny.

"Sleep," he says with a note of something more in his voice.

Strangely, I feel really tired. The sobbing slows and I fall asleep on a hiccup. Who needs sleeping pills when they can have an Alpha. Here's hoping we get to Mr. Whiskers before the night-mares start.

TEN

<u>Ethan</u>

I'm back in the cot room again. The stain on the wall keeps growing and it's sometimes fun to figure out what shapes the stain will make as time progresses. I've even added to them sometimes to try and draw. It's not exactly a picnic in here.

I hear him before I can see him. The darkness deepens as the door creaks open. He's just a man. He's just a human man. I can take him...

I can't move. Why can't I move? I'm not in the cot room. I'm on the bench. I wasn't in this room. I don't want to be in this room.

He's leaning in. I try to bite him, but he grabs my jaw. It hurts. He's not supposed to be this strong. I'm the wolf here. I'm the stronger one.

He removes the headrest. No. I won't do this. I hate this. I can't control this. My head is forced back and down as the straps come around to hold it in place. I can't move. I can't close my mouth all the way and the dental gag is shoved in. I feel the slice as the metal meets the sides of my mouth. Two teeth break and I'm forced to either swallow them or push them out with my tongue. I push them out and start to scream deep in my throat. This isn't breeding. This isn't anything to do with their experiments. This is pain.

The shadow of his body blocks out the only light in the room. I can't move. I'm screaming but it's coming out like an animal whining in distress. I don't sound human. Where is my wolf? Why isn't he coming out?

"Same time?" a voice from the darkness asks.

"Same time," says the voice from above.

I scream as the pain hits and I choke as my air is cut off. It's happening again. I just want to breathe. I want to move. I want to scream.... I want to die.

I'm screaming for what seems like forever, but I'm back in my cot room.

I wanted you to be my first, Ric. I'm sorry. I'm so sorry... I keep saying it over and over. The tears finally dry up and then the footsteps approach again.

Ric

We brought Ethan back to my house. Connor isn't happy that I insisted, but my wolf claimed him. My wolf won't let him out of our sight any time soon unless he's safe within our den. Ethan needs to be safe and my wolf needs him to be here. Putting him in my bed is pushing my Beta's limits a bit, but it's where he belongs now.

It's been about two hours since I laid him down in my room. The kid apparently still sleeps like the dead. We used to find him curled up asleep in the weirdest places when we were kids. He never even whimpered when we would move him to a more comfortable resting place. He will sleep until he's ready to wake up and then it's like a light switch getting flipped to the on position. The boy has two settings and zero chill. At least that's how he was. I'm afraid to find out how much he's changed.

I keep stopping what I'm doing to listen and make sure he's still breathing. I don't think I'll be stopping that any time soon, either. The vision of him, blue lips and eyes unseeing... never again.

I ignore my warrior on the phone for a second to listen for Ethan's breathing before tuning back into the call.

Turns out the dick in the sedan is Jessica's half-brother on her father's side. Noah Chastain is a human-wolf hybrid. His mother was apparently Mr. Chastain's side piece in the city. Jessica found out about him at the end of our junior year when they received an invitation to his high school graduation. He apparently knew all about her and what we are all along.

But the timing strikes me as funny. Didn't Jack say Ethan said they were the same guys as before? So, is Noah one of the guys from the lab? Does that mean Carl wasn't acting alone back then?

If that's the case, there is something more going on in my pack that I need to get to the bottom of. I need to know how many trai-tors I have in my pack. Since Noah was at the lab from the begin-ning when Ethan was taken, it means that all of the Chastain family is now under suspicion... along with anyone who has ever been close with them.

Dropping the phone, my wolf has us dashing through the door. I'm halfway up the stairs when it registers that Ethan is making a terrifying noise. I don't even take the time to reach for the knob. I break through the door to my bedroom to get to him. The sight of him sobbing on the bed stops my movement just inside the room. I don't know what to do and need him to give me a direction.

I need to fight something. I need to protect him. I need to comfort him. I need him to be the happy kid from my memories. I broke him when my wolf claimed him and I need to fix this. He needs to be smiling, not crying.

"I wanted you to be my first, Ric. I'm sorry. I'm so sorry" he whimpers as his sobs slow and his breath evens back out.

It was a nightmare. I sigh in relief.

No... It was a memory, I realize.

He was remembering that night. The night before the pack moved here. The night I convinced myself I was hearing things. I wasn't hearing things. Oh, Goddess, what did he go through that night? Why is he apologizing to me? Please, let it stop. Let him forget it like I did. Let him bury it, please. I don't want to know this!

As the tears fall from my suddenly blurry eyes, I know Connor heard the commotion. I know he's using his gift on me and he sees his brother laying in my bed with the sheets everywhere and tear tracks on his face. Another image burned into my memory.

It's all my fault. Three months. Three months we could have prevented this. The black hole that is my guilt is swallowing me up again, and I deserve it all. He is apologizing to me... for what was done to him. I don't deserve him. I never did.

I am aware of Connor leaving my head as my vision clears and my head feels like a woodpecker has taken up residence. Now I understand why he doesn't like using this gift of his.

I file it away for a discussion regarding limitations we need to place on its use. I've never truly had a migraine before as a wolf, but if thirty seconds of sharing my sight results in a headache worse than a six bottle bender, we're putting restrictions on its use.

One good thing is the headache seems to have done the trick to pull me from my guilt spiral. Looking down at my boy in the bed, I try to reassure myself that he's safe now.

Ethan's breathing starts getting faster again. As I step closer to the bed, he starts shaking. It almost looks like he wants to thrash and fight but he can't for some reason. I can't figure it out. A whimper starts building in his throat. It's working its way up to the inhuman sounds I heard before.

I try calling out to him, but he's not waking up. I try to use the mind speak, but he's not hearing me. However, opening my mind to him has somehow brought me into his dream. I'm hearing his screams in a way I can't in the room. I can hear what he is thinking in his dream, his memory.

My heart is breaking. My wolf is growling and gnashing his teeth. He wants to destroy someone for this, but there's no monster to fight anymore.

I'll be good! I promise! Please don't! PLEASE!

He's begging someone. He can't hear me. I'm not really here to him right now. He's completely enveloped in the memory.

Not that! I can't breathe! I'll bite it off I swear... No... You can't force me... No... NO... AHHHHHH!

There are no more words. It's like he can't form them anymore. His body is in my bed, trying to fight against invisible bonds and choking on something that isn't there. But in his mind, I'm hearing enough to figure out what is happening or at least a close enough approximation. I'm frozen in my rage and terror, watching as he thrashes on the bed, trying to escape the assault of his past.

The screams in my head go silent.

I'm sorry...

I can't hear it again. I can't hear him apologize again for something that isn't his fault. It was never his fault. It's my fault he was even there.

I snatch Ethan into my arms and use my authority to force him awake. I can't watch him relive it again. I won't have him relive that ever again.

"Little Blue, I'll still be the first to make love to you," I whisper in his ear as he wakes up mid-sob. The look he gives me is a mix of surprise, joy, and guilt.

My precious boy, you have nothing to be guilty of. It's not your fault I think towards him, and he clutches me closer.

After a few moments, Ethan pulls himself together. I can almost the wall being erected inside his mind to keep me out, to keep everyone out. My wolf whines at the thought of being pushed away, but I remind him that Ethan hasn't had anything to himself but his mind for the last eight years. He deserves this bit of ownership, and we can't take it away without hurting him more. My wolf rumbles a reluctant agreement as Connor runs past the room, barely catching himself on the doorframe.

"You're awake!" he exclaims, smiling at his little brother.

It's obvious he's ecstatic Ethan is awake, but there's wariness there. None of us know where we stand with Ethan. We haven't really had any opportunities for conversation outside since Connor brought him out of his captivity a few weeks ago.

Ethan is just staring at his brother. There's a vacant look on his face, like he's not really sure where he is or who we are. It's like he's waiting for something. There's a coldness to his features that my little boy Blue never let show before. He's a killer, or would be if given the chance, and is looking at us both as if deciding whether or not we are his prey.

None of us move or speak for some time. I refuse to set my boy down, refuse to let him go, until he asks me to. Connor doesn't seem to want to come into the room, nor is he apparently willing to leave. Ethan is just staring, sometimes at his brother, sometimes at me. We're at a standstill and no one seems to know how to break it.

ELEVEN

Ric

"OH BROTHA! I'M HOME!"

Leave it to Jack to break the tension.

Ethan starts giggling in my arms. Both mine and Connor's breaths go out in a happy sigh. My kid brother can put a smile on anyone's face. Seeing the resulting smile on Ethan's as he tries to clean up the tears and snot, I really don't think I can love my little brother more.

Max ducks his head around the corner and takes in the broken door and the state of us all. After a glare at me, he smiles. He is here to let us know he and Jack are setting up a sundae bar in the kitchen and that we should clean up and join per *the fabulous master Jack*'s instructions. That brings another giggle out of Ethan. Max smiles at him and heads back downstairs. I've never seen Max that soft with someone other than Jack. My wolf doesn't like it.

"Bathroom?" Ethan asks, interrupting my thoughts. I point to the door to his left. He jumps out of my arms and almost face-plants on the floor in his rush to get there. Luckily, his foot catches in the blankets and it swings him to his butt instead. Another giggle sounds as the door closes behind him.

Connor turns his gaze from the closed door to me and levels me with *the look*.

"You hurt him, I hurt you. I don't care if you're my Alpha," he snaps at me. "I will die for you if I have to. I will kill for him, and not have a second of guilt over it."

It's a good big brother speech. My wolf sees it as a challenge but holds himself back from reacting. Connor is our mate's family and he's talking about protecting our mate. Anything that protects our mate is apparently alright with my wolf. I can't help but agree.

"Back the fuck off, Connie!" comes the voice from the bathroom, "Only one dishing out pain around here will be me!" There's a sound of a flush followed by running water.

We both hear him sigh, "I don't need you or anyone else to avenge me. I'm going to do that myself."

The water shuts off and he walks back into the bedroom. "Now what was that about sundaes?"

I head out of the room to give the brothers some privacy. Connor looks like he needs to have a minute alone with Ethan, and I need to get downstairs to make sure my kitchen, and my little brother, aren't full of just sugar and ice cream.

Walking into the kitchen, I see Jack sitting at the island, spoon in hand, waiting. It's adorable that he's waiting for us, but I want to prepare him in case Ethan isn't up for being social. He basically threw a tantrum when Connor pushed the talking issue instead of getting out of the way for ice cream.

"Jackie, remember the guy Ethan you told us about?" I ask him. I'm trying to bring it up gently and feel my way through it all. I mean, I gotta tell my little brother that I married the guy who saved him, but he doesn't know it yet and hell... I need a drink for this.

"Dude, I know all about Ethan. Maxie told me about him." Jack replies as I stare at him in shock. Max shouldn't be telling a seven-year-old about Ethan. Wait, Max doesn't know about Ethan except he's alive though.

"Ethan is Brother Connor's little brother like I'm your little brother," he says in a matter of fact tone, like he's reciting an answer in the classroom. "Bad people hurt him and took him away from you guys, but now he's back. Right?"

He looks so proud to remember that. It's an oversimplification and I need to prepare him for the possible rejection from our new family member, but then I hear the man himself speak behind me.

"That's right, kid," Ethan says as he walks around me. "The guy chasing you was one of those bad people, but I'm here and he's not so let's call it a good day and eat our body weight in ice cream. How's that sound?"

The smile on my brother's face when he lays eyes on Ethan could light up the eastern seaboard. My wolf starts grumbling in jealousy as Jackie abandons his ice cream mountain to drag Ethan to the counter.

Jealous of a seven-year-old? I ask my wolf.

He hasn't claimed us back yet, so any male aside from his brother can take him away from us. I get in response.

Lifting my eyes to the counter, I realize Ethan was not kidding about the whole eating their weight in ice cream. I should be the responsible one and put a stop to this, but I don't want to dim either of their smiles here.

Max comes in with the save, carrying takeout that smells like a burgers and fries. My stomach is grumbling at the aromas coming out of the bag.

Ethan perks his head up sniffing the air, spoonful of coffee ice cream and gummy bears forgotten halfway to his mouth.

"Please say that's for me?" he begs as he gives the puppy dog eyes to my warrior.

Max's grumbling laugh is the only answer given, but he hands one of the containers over to Ethan and the other to me. "Connor took his into the living room if you want to join him there. I can watch the kiddos, make sure they eat."

"I'm not a kid." Is said in stereo both from Ethan and Jack.

That made us all laugh, and the boys at the island started going in on the food Max brought. It's only a matter of time before the fries meet the ice cream, so I obligingly take my meal to the living room. This will give Ethan and Jack a chance to bond without any kind of interference from me.

I need Ethan to have a reason to stay here. I'm not too proud to use my little brother as the leverage needed to keep my mate under my roof. My wolf growls in approval.

As long as he doesn't leave us and it doesn't harm him, I'll accept anything.

Me, too. I'll fight dirty if I have to.

Ethan

I love this smell. I missed this smell. Grease and cheese and meat and yummy yummy goodness. I snatch the container from Max's hand as he says something or another to Ric. I'm trying to ignore him and his wolf. My wolf is certainly not happy with him.

Barbecue sauce and pickles...

You remembered, I think in Max's direction.

The dude jumps about twenty feet in the air and does this nifty little spinning move to turn and face me wide-eyed and jaw dropped.

Oops.

I forgot he doesn't know about my mind speak thing yet. Well better late than never.

"Did you just speak in my head, Ethan?" he asked incredulously.

"You don't have to answer out loud. Just think it," came the voice from beside me.

"Yep. That's right, kid. You remembered." I praise him and he responds with an ice cream drippy smile.

It's disgusting and adorable and I love it. This kid is now my official little brother. I'm adopting him. No one can say otherwise. I'll steal him from Ric if I have to. I only need to find out his name somehow. It feels weird asking at this point.

Since when can you speak into other people's minds and can you read minds as well? Max cuts into my musings.

Out loud, I say to the room, and for the benefit of the ones in the living room, "I've been able to do this since my wolf woke up and talked to me the first time. I didn't have it when you knew me before. As for the mind reading thing, it's hit or miss. I have to really be focused on the person, usually in the same room, and they need to be thinking loudly, if that makes sense."

I'm glad no one seems to have picked up on how I worded that. Bad enough I'm omega. Add onto that the fact that I was gone for so long. Then add on the freaky mind speak thing. I'm weird enough without anyone knowing that my wolf and I didn't talk until days after our first shift.

Usually, it happens in the months leading up to the shift. I thought there was something wrong with me. I was so afraid I wouldn't even be able to shift on my birthday. And then to do it without a wolf's guidance? That was terrifying.

I'm a freak of nature. I knew that as soon as I shifted and saw Mom's look of horror. Yeah, I tell myself it was surprise, shock, whatever... but she was scared. Dad never did get the chance to tell me what was wrong with my wolf. I guess that's just another thing to add to the list of things I'll never know from them. Safe sex, pregnancy, driving, freaky wolf thing, love, kindness... the usual parent stuff.

I guess I'm making a face or something because Max is looking at me funny, like he heard all of that.

You didn't hear all of that, did you? I send to him because that would be mortifying.

He shakes his head and gives me a soft smile. *No I didn't hear anything, but your face showed a lot. Might want to save the heavy thoughts until you're alone, kid.*

I give him a smile in thanks while I bite into my burger. Oh, this is a heaven that I forgot existed.

Grease is the word alright. I hate that movie, but damn it applies. Clog my arteries and call it a day, I love this!

I swear it only takes three bites to finish the burger. The fries are even better. Salty and crisp and perfect for dunking. I have nothing to dunk them in though.

Suddenly a divided cup with ketchup on one side and ranch

on the other appears in front of me. The kid's got a proud smile on his face next to me.

"I didn't know which one you like, so I gave you both. I like both" he says as he's dipping some nuggets in a cup of his own.

Man, I kinda wish I had nuggets. Maybe the dino ones and we could have them fight and the loser gets eaten... Definitely bringing that up with Maxie for the next time he grabs the takeout.

And now my fries are gone, too. I guess I'm a bottomless pit because I'm still not done eating. It's back to my ice cream tower, which now resembles gummy bear soup. I still eat it though. I'm not missing out on anything now. I missed too much.

A finger is suddenly pushing up my brows. Someone managed to sneak up on me.

I jump back off the stool and find myself in the corner with a knife before it even registers. The kid is looking at me in horror. Max is surprised. Connor and Ric race into the kitchen looking like they're ready to go to war.

I stand up straight and put the knife back in the block. Then I casually stroll back upstairs.

Keep it together. Keep it together. No one will see once we're alone. No one is hurting us again. We can run away now. Keep it together. We aren't there anymore. We're not there. Keep it together.

I keep the mantra going in my head until I can shut and lock the door to the bathroom. I turn on the shower and let myself fall to the floor. Just ten minutes. I can fall apart for ten minutes and they'll never know. The shower hides the tears. I learned that a long time ago. Just ten minutes.

The first tear falls and I feel myself slipping away

Ric

It is a strained silence filling the living room at first. Neither Connor nor I want to be the one to break the it, so we just eat our food. It all tastes like ash anyways. Ethan doesn't want to be anywhere near either of us right now. I can't blame him. He didn't ask for anything he's been through.

My mind keeps replaying what he said in his nightmare. The desperation in his voice. The pleading.

I could hear the helplessness. I could hear the sound of the hope draining out of him.

I can't force another bite after hearing Ethan explain his gift to Max. The rest of my food sits untouched in my lap. He saw Max the day before we left. If he didn't have his gift when Max knew him before and he got it when his wolf woke up, that means he didn't have his wolf with him for his first shift. How in the hell did this kid survive that on his own?

A loud clatter cuts the silence and Jackie's frightened "eep" sends both me and Connor vaulting over furniture to get to the kitchen. I freeze in the doorway, stopping Connor along with me. Ethan is in the corner next to the fridge, crouched like a wild animal with a knife in is hand. There's no sign of recognition in his eyes that are darting around the room.

Max is frozen, half in front of Jack. His positioning shows no aggression towards Ethan, but he'll be able to block any attack that may head that direction. Connor looks how I feel. How do we protect him from something that isn't here? There's no enemy to fight, no monster to kill.

As the light returns to his face, Ethan takes a deep breath. I can see the moment he registers what just happened. He doesn't say a word, but just puts the knife away and walks out of the room. He looks like he doesn't have a care in the world.

I hear him in my head. As I look around the room at the others, I realize they hear him too. My baby boy is broadcasting and none of us know what to do.

"Ric, what the hell happened to him, man?" Max asks as Jack starts crying into his shoulder.

Connor shakes his head and I clench my fists...

"You really don't want to know." I say as my eyes raise to the ceiling while I listen for the shower to turn off.

TWELVE

Ric

Ice cream is forgotten after Ethan's little freak out. Jackie wanted me to make sure his new brother is alright, so I'm knocking on the bathroom door in my bedroom.

"Little Blue? You doing alright? Jackie-boy is a little freaked out and wants to make sure you're ok," I call out to him. "He says your gummy bears all drowned but they'll make great fossils when you freeze your lake of coffee."

I decide to give him the full message to see if it will get a response. He didn't respond to Connor at all when he tried to talk a few minutes ago.

I hear a soft giggle followed by a hiccup. It's a start.

"Should l tell him you want the fossils or do you want to come out for ice cream soup?" I ask as I hear him shuffling toward me.

The door unlocks and opens to reveal Ethan, completely nude, and not completely grown up if I'm being honest. There's an inno-cence in those eyes that I still see sometimes in Jack. The Ethan in front of me is not the adult or even the teen I remember. This Ethan is just a little boy, so I adjust my tactics.

"So, ice cream soup or fossilized gummy bears? Your choice." I crouch down a bit so my head is below his. I'm going on instinct here, but the small smile on his face says I'm on the right track.

"Want snuggles. Mr. Whisker gives bestest snuggles. He keep bad men out of dreamland," he mumbles through a yawn.

Apparently, Ethan is much younger in his mind right now than I thought. He hasn't had that much broken English ever in the time I've known him and I first met Connor in kindergarten. I think Jackie grew out of that around four years old. I'm in some uncharted territory, but I'm hoping my instincts will carry me.

"How about we put on some jammies and I'll snuggle with you until Mr. Whiskers gets back from his very important mission with Connor? Sound good?" I ask him as I shoot a text to my Beta to bring the teddy bear to my room.

I'm hoping this works because I remember the toddler tantrums from just a few years ago with Jack. I learned then that I'm a sucker and no match for a pair of puppy dog eyes full of tears.

Luckily, Ethan seems to be more tired than anything, and he nods after bringing his thumb to his mouth. He doesn't seem to know where to go or what to do so I gather him up in my arms like I used to with Jack.

He clings to me like I'm his life-size teddy bear. I guess I did just volunteer for the job, but having a naked Ethan hanging off me is really testing my control.

Before I do anything I may later regret...again, I snag a t-shirt from my fun shirt drawer. It's the drawer I keep all of the shirts that Jackie has gotten me over the years. I'm glad for my choice when I see the smile bloom on Ethan's face around his thumb.

Getting him changed with the thumb stuck in his mouth

becomes a game and his giggles echo down the hallway. I want to hear that sound as much as possible. The sound seems to be some sort of a signal and suddenly there's a pajama clad Jack bouncing into the room, followed by an apologetic looking Max.

"I tried to hold him back, Boss-man." Max says, trying not to laugh at the sight in front of him.

Jack has climbed up onto my bed next to Ethan, and Ethan is just admiring Jack's pajamas. There's a moment where Jack looks completely confused but then he shrugs and lays down.

"Puppy pile snuggles?" Jack asks with a smirk on his face.

Again, the thumb breaks up the smile on Ethan's face, but I will do almost anything to keep bringing that smile back... even snuggle with Max if I have to. And apparently, I have to.

Laughing, Max climbs onto my bed next to Jack, who snuggles into Ethan. Ethan snuggles Jack like a stuffed animal but looks to me with pleading eyes as he asks, "Keep the bad men out?"

"We'll keep the bad men out," I tell him as I climb in on the other side of him. The look he gives me makes me think I can save the world.

I don't need to save the world. I just need to keep him safe.

I'm not sure how long we have been laying here, but a soft knock on the door frame makes me look up from my sleeping boys to see Connor smirking at the sight.

"Delivery of Mr. Whiskers as promised," he whispers holding up the ratty old bear.

"Fanky CunCun," Ethan murmurs in his sleep.

"Well, that's unexpected," he whispers in surprise as he hands off the bear to his brother who resumes his soft snoring, clutching Mr. Whiskers to his chest.

I nod to Max and he nods back. I need to go talk to my Beta about this latest development. The boys will be fine with him while we have this talk.

I tuck the blankets in around Ethan after I get up. He barely even registers me moving. I have to say that's kind of disappointing, but it's not even a whole day since we got him back.

We have forever, I hear in my head.

My wolf really is becoming an optimist here, but I want to hope right along with him.

I don't even realize I leaned down to kiss Ethan's cheek until after I've already done it and see the look on Connor's face as I turn toward the door. I grab him on my way out of the door and we head to my office downstairs. I need to do some research on this, and I think I need to ask Connor more about Ethan as a kid.

THIRTEEN

Ric

After a while, we seem to have figured out the answer in our research... Age regression.. Finding this out really seems to help Connor feel a bit better about what he saw. He only heard the toddler version of his brother. He didn't get to see the whole thing. It was both adorable and terrifying seeing it without any knowledge on what it was and what was coming next.

Having read psychological reports that state regression can be part of the healing process for trauma is a good start for Connor to accept that his little brother is more little than he thought. Speaking of little, that's another thing we found in our dive into research.

Sometimes age regression is a part of a subsect of BDSM called age play. In this case, regression is more of an escape from adult thoughts and responsibilities. It's a way to de-stress and give up control to a caregiver. It requires a lot of trust, and part of me is hoping that Ethan's regression is this and not trauma based.

The alarm on Connor's phone pulls us both out of our research deep dive on the internet. He is looking up the psychology of it all. I got caught up in shopping for the perfect pacifier for my little Blue.

"Three A.M., Ric. You should get back to bed in case he has another nightmare," Connor tells me with a yawn. "Mr. Whiskers might have lost his touch over the years."

It's nice to know that my Beta has rediscovered his sense of humor sometime in the last four hours. Maybe it's just sleep deprivation talking. I'm not going to pass up his blessing on getting into bed with my mate for the rest of the night.

We part ways at the stairs. Connor has the guest suite downstairs whenever he needs it. I'm pretty sure that he's moving in for good now that Ethan will be here with me.

It's difficult not to run up to my room. There's no rush to get to sleep, but I don't want to waste another second being away from my boy.

Entering the room, I see Max lift his head to acknowledge it is me in the doorway. As I climb into the bed, Max is lifting Jack into his arms.

"I'll take him back to his room and give you two some privacy," he whispers on his way to the door. "He should only be waking up to his Daddy in bed with him after a regression like that."

I do a double take on that one. So apparently my head warrior is familiar with age play and recognized the signs in Ethan before any of us ever did. I'm pretty sure the questions in my head are obvious on my face when he adds, "We can talk after breakfast. Let's find out which Ethan wakes up next to you before we get into it. Little or Big, Ethan is going to need you to take care of him in the morning."

I chuckle softly and shake my head as he carries Jack out the door. That kid will sleep through anything and everything until he gets his full ten hours, just like Ethan was at that age. Hoping that Ethan sleeps just as peacefully now, I let my eyes close and I join him in sleep.

<u>Ethan</u>

Opening my eyes only to make contact with the soulless black beads of Mr. Whiskers is a terrific way to start the day. I know it's really him and not some replacement bought off the internet because I can feel the extra weight of Stabby, the blade Max gave me a long time ago.

Mr. Whiskers holds onto Stabby for me since it's generally frowned upon to be carrying a switch blade. And I have plans for Stabby. I made a list over the last eight years and will be adding onto it once I can get my secret papers back. I have some maiming to do.

Movement behind me has me tensing up. Mr. Whiskers is ready, so I need to be too. I start reaching for the hole only me and Mr. Whiskers know is there to grab Stabby.

Easy Blue. It's just me, Ric speaks into my head.

My body relaxes, but my mind starts racing. The memories of last night are coming back. The kitchen, the knife, my shower, my thumb, Connie... or should I say Cun Cun.

Oh man, I haven't dropped like that in a long time. Usually, I'm alone when I let my mind go, so I don't know how to deal with these kinds of awkward situations. Last time I wasn't alone was when I was first brought to the lab. Either they didn't notice it or they actually liked that I basically turned into a toddler in my head. Doesn't matter. I never let go that much in that place after that.

I can't believe that I managed to fall away so much with Ric of all people seeing it. On the other hand, waking up next to someone is a new experience as well. Perhaps I can play it off that I'm embarrassed about that instead?

"Let's get dressed and get some breakfast," Ric says as I feel him getting out of the bed. "Jack and Max should be up pretty soon, and I know my boy is gonna be wanting his building block waffles. Those take a bit longer to make than regular ones."

Building block waffles? What are those?

Nope. Can't go back under again. I have to stay as adult as I can right now. Staring at Ric's naked backside as he pulls up his boxers is definitely helping me stay grown up. Maybe a bit too adult as the t-shirt I'm wearing seems to be riding up on its own.

Damn morning wood. Yeah, I'm going with that and not a reaction to Ric bending over to pick up the sleep pants from the bottom drawer of the dresser. I kinda feel like I wanna bite it.

Oh crap! He can see me in the mirror. His smirk tells me he is totally aware of the real reason I grab a pillow to cover my lap.

"Mr. Whiskers needed a seat." I tell him defiantly and he actually chuckles at that. I don't think I'm fooling him.

Mr. Whiskers can take a seat elsewhere for now. It's time to get dressed, my little Blue. He's getting good at the mind speak.

I agree it's a good idea to just get dressed, so I jump out of bed and run to the bathroom, slamming the door behind me. The only clothes I have are still on the floor in here. Ugh, they smell terrible. There's not a chance I'm putting them back on now that I've gotten out of them.

Any chance you got something in the size not jolly green giant that I can borrow until I can get back to my own clothing? I ask.

There is a knock on the door in response. I open it to see no one there. Well, that's kind of disappointing. Looking down, I see a pile of clothing. Yeah, it's another one of his million XL shirts, but there's also a pair of superhero sleep pants that appear to be about my size. I'm not going to complain about clean clothes, but my wolf grumbles in my head.

What's your problem? I ask him.

Wants us to be mate but has another man's clothes. He continues his grumbling.

I laugh out loud at his jealousy. Just last night he was pissed at being claimed as a mate. Now he's pissed because Ric has clothes that are obviously not his nor Jack's.

Did you neglect to notice the tags are still on the pants? They're brand new. I chide my wolf.

Cue more grumbling, only this time he's embarrassed. That should keep him for a while.

I'm a bit ashamed to admit it takes me way too long to leave the bedroom. Without having the frustration of an argument with my brother to propel me, I'm finding it rather anxiety inducing to cross the threshold. This freedom thing is going to take a lot of getting used to.

Sneaking down the hall is easy. I don't even hear anyone else on this floor. There's no one to even notice me practically hugging the wall and jumping past each doorway so the light shining under won't be broken by my steps. There's no one to notice how much I slow down as I approach the next obstacle... the stairs.

The stairs are scary. I can't see the bottom. I don't know who or what is down there. I don't like not knowing. I'm ready to turn back around. Surely, someone will just bring me up a plate or something, right? I mean it's not like they're going to starve me if I don't come down. I'm sure of it... pretty sure anyways.

Oh, but it smells so good. I want to go down but my foot won't move. It's like my brain doesn't remember how to do stairs. I'm a grown up. I can do stairs. I've been doing them my whole life for Goddess sake. But I can't take that first step. There's no going down and there's no going back to the bedroom, so I sit.

I just need to wait out my brain. Eventually it will come online and remember basic instructions like how to use stairs.

Ethan, baby? It's time for breakfast. Are you coming down? Ric asks in my head.

I flinch at the voice in my head. This isn't like me. I don't even know where it's coming from.

I need help. I whine back at him.

I feel pathetic and useless. I didn't even remember that I could call out for help. I just froze and let myself be stupid. I'm just a dumb kid who doesn't know anything. I shouldn't even be here.

I don't even remember putting my head down, but next thing I know, Ric is in front of me gently lifting my face to see him.

"What's wrong, Baby?" he asks gently. "Why are you sitting at the top of the steps? Do you not want to come down?"

"I forgets how to stairs," I tell him. Oh yeah, I'm going under again....."Forgot" I try to correct myself. It's a losing battle and I can see him switching gears.

"Well, if you can't do them on your own, do you want me to carry you down? Or hold hands?" he asks as he stands back up and holds out his hand.

I grab his big hand like it's a lifeline. "Handsies," I tell him, and the thumb goes in my mouth.

Thumb out, Little Blue. He says into my head. I give him a look that basically says he's not the boss of me. Not sure how well that translates with a thumb in my mouth, but it makes him chuckle.

"You need to hold the banister and my hand. You only have two, so thumb out for now," he says out loud this time.

Ok yeah, that makes sense. With a nod, I pop the thumb out and grab the railing as we start going down the steps. We take them one at a time because steps are tricksy, and I don't want to fall down. I don't want to get hurt. I don't like hurting.

"Hop up," Ric says as he helps me up on the same stool I sat on last night.

"OK, Daddy," I mumble as I clamber up onto the stool. Why are chairs being difficult today, too?

Wait? Daddy? I mean Ric. Ric is helping me, not Daddy. I wish I had a Daddy like him. My Daddy ended up in heaven trying to stop the bad men. I don't want a new Daddy if it means he will go to heaven too. The bad men are still out there, and Ric is too important to go to heaven.

It's ok Little Blue. Go ahead and eat breakfast and we'll talk later. No need to think about the grown up stuff now. he says into my head.

I must be doing that face thing Max talked about last night. No one else seems to have noticed what is going on inside my head except for him. I don't know what to call Ric right now. He's not my big brother. He's not my Alpha. He's not quite Ric and yet so much more. I'm so confused.

Pushing away the thoughts is easier when I have something else to focus on, so I stare at the food on my plate. Now I get what he was talking about with the waffles. I kinda wanna build a tower and then dump the syrup on it and drown the townspeople who are hiding in there. They hide instead of help.

I want to, so I do. The villagers of the sausage town hole up inside the tower of waffle seeking to hide from their responsibilities to the syrup kids. The syrup kids just want to be needed and wanted, but the sausage people only care about protecting themselves. No one wants to help the syrup kids, so it falls to me to dismantle the tower in the only way a werewolf should. I bite it down piece by piece.

By the time the sausage people are exposed, it's too late. I have to finish them off. They abandoned the syrup kids. I didn't abandon them. I will never abandon them. I will never forget them. The sausage people will all pay for what they've done.

As I look up, I see Connie giving me a funny look. I don't even remember him coming into the kitchen.

"Is there something on my face?" I ask out loud. Getting the weird look seems to be enough for me to grown up again.

"Just a bit," I hear through the giggles to my left. Hey, the kid is here too. Jack, not kid. Last night he was a bigger kid than I was for a while.

I feel around my face and just feel sticky. The giggles get louder and I realize it too late. I'm just spreading the syrup around because my hands are apparently coated in the stuff.

Oops.

Before I can get up to get clean, Ric puts a wet paper towel into my hand while he uses another to wipe off my face. Yeah, it's something I expect to be done for a toddler, but it's kind of nice to be taken care of like this for once. But I'm a grown up now, so I frown at the jerk's smiling face.

I think I like this game.

Once everyone has finished their breakfast, Max takes Jack upstairs to get ready for school. Man, I miss school. Those were some fun times. Not the teachers, or at least not most of them, but the seeing friends and learning stuff... that was fun.

"I guess I'm too old to go back to school, huh?" I ask mostly to myself, but Ric answers me anyways.

"Well, we can work on getting your GED," he tells me, "and then in the spring if you want we can get you set up with classes at the local university. It's in another pack's territory, but the Alpha there lets our pack go to school there if our people want to stay close to home."

College? Me? I only just finished eighth grade, but I'm supposed to do college? That's a lot. It's too much, too fast. I got things to take care of and I can't go under again. Twice in twenty-four hours is enough.

FOURTEEN

Ric

He's been slipping in and out of being little all morning. Max and I had a full-blown conversation this morning while I was making breakfast. Jack spent that time watching tv while we worked in the kitchen. Max explained that he's pretty sure I'm what is referred to as a Daddy Dom. I need to have someone to take care of, someone to rely on me to take control. That control freely given relaxes me. Even though the burdens of being Alpha stress me out, taking care of Ethan last night was probably the most relaxed I've been in the past decade.

So, we've figured out I'm a Daddy and Ethan is what is called a little. His age regression doesn't seem to be trauma related as much as it seems to be escapism. This falls more in line with the age play stuff I found last night. Little Ethan seems to just need reassurances and clear instructions. I'm happy to give him all of that. I want to give all of Ethan that, big or little. I don't want him to ever have to wonder again.

His reaction to the idea of school makes me wonder if he's about to slip back into being little. According to Max and the late-night research session, the fact that Ethan is slipping so easily is a good sign. It means he feels safe with us. My wolf is still preening over that. But school is apparently too much for him, so I decide to change the subject.

"School can wait for now," I tell him. "Jack is almost done for the year, so what do you think of taking a vacation somewhere?" I ask and his face lights up.

"Can we go to that park with the Superhero rides?" he asks as he's bouncing in his place on the floor.

Racking my brain, I am having trouble placing what park he's talking about. I'm even trying to think back to eight years ago to see if anything hits. Superhero rides are more common now, but he's been gone for so long it's going to be tough for me to narrow it down.

"You talking Six Flags or Universal, Kiddo?" comes Connor's voice from the doorway.

Ethan looks up and purses his lips like he's thinking really hard before he says, "Can we do both? I can't decide."

He turns to me and looks so hopeful. I really am a sucker for the puppy eyes, so I tell him, "Six Flags in the summer and we'll do Universal for Christmas if you'd like. I'd rather not do Florida in the summer."

This time, I'm kind of glad I'm a pushover as I find myself with a lap full of my baby boy and him squeezing me like there's no tomorrow. I'd give so much more than the cost of a couple trips to theme parks if I can get more of this.

I'm guessing my thoughts are pretty clear on my face when Connor clears his throat and gives me a look that is a mix between a smirk and a scowl. I'd like to think I'd get the same look from his dad if he was still around. Mr. Sinclair was a great man.

I'm kind of surprised Ethan is still in my lap as Connor takes a seat on the sofa next to us. Ehtan's face is turned toward Connor, but I'm surprised he doesn't say anything.

"And he's out," Connor chuckles as he reaches for the remote on the coffee table.

At my look, he starts to explain, "When Ethan was a baby, like infant baby, he refused to fall asleep unless he was in someone's arms. As he got bigger, he still needed it. It's why Mr. Whiskers came about initially. He was getting too big to be held to go to sleep every night, so the story of Mr. Whiskers the nightmare hunter was born."

OK that makes a lot of sense why the stuffed animal is so important again, but it doesn't explain why I have a hundred and fifty pound dead weight in the form of my sleeping mate on my lap.

"Back to the sleep thing," Connor continues after seeing my confusion, "because he was used to being held to go to sleep, as a toddler especially, he would pass out in a lap if he was there for longer than thirty seconds. We were able to mostly break him of it by the time he started school, but when he got stressed, it seemed to still work. Still does, it seems."

Makes me wonder. Is this because his little side is a toddler or is it because he's stressed out? I hope it's the first option. I don't want him to be stressed.

"Thanks for the explanation and the not judging," I tell him as I settle in to get more comfortable. "you here just to hang or is there something we need to talk about?"

"Just a social call mostly," He responds. "You know you can put him down now and he'll be out for at least thirty minutes. Just in case you want to keep circulation in your legs and all."

His chuckles are joined by Max's as he walks back in.

And there goes my good mood... "Why aren't you at school with Jack?" I demand before he can even sit down.

"Jack is fine. I got three of my best watching him: two on the outside of the school patrolling and my cousin inside the classroom with him. He gets so much as a splinter, and they are all going to feel my wrath and they know it."

"Not if I beat you to it," a muffled voice growls.

Was that mumbling coming from the sleeping boy in my lap?

"What was that, Ethan?" Connor asks. So, he heard it too.

The sleepy boy's head lifts from my shoulder as he levels Max with a severe look and says, "Anyone causes harm to that precious skittles cloud and me and Mr. Whiskers are breaking out Stabby and going to town."

I'm still trying to work out all the parts of that sentence as Max bursts into a full on belly laugh.

Ethan

The short nap apparently did the trick to reset me to grown-up mode. Waking up, I hear that Max left other people in charge of protecting Jack. I don't like the thought of that so I decide share it with the class.

At the mention of Stabby making a showing, Max laughs as if it's the funniest joke on the planet. I don't know if he's laughing at the name I gave his knife or at the thought of me stabbing someone. Either way, I'm starting to get mad.

Why is it that everyone expects me to just lay down and take whatever happens to me? Since when does the stamp of omega mean pushover? I'm an adult... ish. I'm fully capable of kicking ass and protecting my own. I was doing just fine in my cave. The only reason I even got caught again was because I allowed myself be caught. I can take whatever comes at me. Jack will never face what I did. No kid in this pack will suffer what I did ever again, not if I have anything to say about it.

I push myself off Ric's lap and plant my ass on the floor as far away from everyone else as possible. I might be sitting lower than they are, but they have no clue how much more rage I feel than they do, how much more damage I can do, both physically and mentally.

You might be able to kill, but I can destroy. The Goddess might have tightened my collar but she gave me a long ass leash. I project to the sky. I'm so used to no one being around to listen that I keep forgetting not to blast out my frustrations.

"What was that, Ethan? What's this about a collar?" Max asks. "Sounds kinky," He adds, trying to be a smartass. I'm not in the mood.

"You want to know about the collar the G Lady slapped on me while I was in the clink?" I ask the room. I'm thoroughly pissed now. They don't know the hell of being shackled in any way, let alone the chains I bound on myself in my youthful stupidity.

They don't really want to know, but it's time they understand why I was even still there at the end for them to find. It's time they come to terms with the fact that I died so many more times than just that time they got to witness at the bitch's house.

"Buckle up, boys. It's story time," I tell them as I open my mind so they can feel it all with me.

FIFTEEN

Ethan

"OK G Lady let's make a deal. I don't have to be a baby factory and you get my promise not to kill, right?"

The Goddess is staring at me with a mixture of awe and pity. I guess no one ever speaks to her like this, but I'm just a kid who is sick of being torn apart all the time. I just want it to be over and she can help me get out of here.

"My child, I will assist you in here," she starts, "You will not die, no matter how much damage to your body. I will send you back if your soul should try to cross and your body will suffer no lasting physical harm. You will not be able to get pregnant by any other than your true mate as determined by the fates. None other can open your womb." She pauses for effect, but I don't need it. It's all sounding pretty good to me so far. I just hope she gets to the part where I get out of here already.

"In exchange, you cannot kill. You cannot kill at all: not another person, shifter, or animal... not unless you are acting to save a true innocent life. And I am the judge of innocence. To break this covenant will cost you the life of ones you hold dear."

Well, that's an easy trade-off. I'm alone in the world obviously. I mean no one has come for me so far, so it must mean they're gone too. Has to be, right? They wouldn't leave me like this.

No way. They loved me. I know it... Yeah, they have to be dead and gone. Oh wait, she's ready to continue. This is a lot to remember, but I'm sure she won't let me forget this.

"The last of the bargain is that you and your mate will not be able to scent one another. You will have no way to seek each other out. Unless the fates decree you meet by chance, the only way you will know you've met your mate is if he gets you with child. Bear that child and give it breath and our covenant shall be fulfilled and all will return as it should."

This sounds like a pretty good deal. I get out. I become basically an immortal. I get permanent birth control, not that I'm thinking of EVER doing anything like that by choice... not after what I've already experienced up to today.

"Sign me up G Lady. Sign on the dotted line and all," I tell her.

Has anyone else ever heard a Goddess giggle? I kinda like that I'm hearing it now.

"Child, I need you to give your name and say you accept the terms for it to be valid. I would hate to be called a cheat over a miscommunication."

Well, I feel like an ass now.

"I, Ethan Lewis Sinclair, accept the terms of our deal

and vow not to kill until I pop out a kid. That work?" I ask honestly.

"Very good, my child. Remember, you cannot kill, not even yourself, or the lives of your brother and mate will be forfeit. You still have years of suffering to endure, but I have faith in you. You can rest easy that you won't bring a child into this wretched place." She says all of this as she fades away and leaves me alone in my cot room once again.

Hold up! What did she say?! Does that mean I'm not getting out of here yet?

Fuck that, what was that about my brother?! Connie is alive... He didn't die that day.

Connie is alive. He's looking for me, of course. He's just not that good at finding me. He's shit at finding me. That's all it is. He's looking. I know he is. He has to be.

Has to be. No way would he leave me behind. He hasn't forgotten me. He's still looking. He's looking.... At least I know he's alive, right?

Footsteps down the hall coming closer. Ready for round one million four hundred thirty five thousand something. I should stop counting now. Four years tomorrow... how many more do I have to go? Happy Birthday, Ethan. You get a Goddess screwing you over and the magical birth control so they can strap you to the fucking bench every fucking day now. Happy Birthday to me...

As I shut down the link between us, they're all staring at me. Max looks sick. Oh yeah, I forgot he didn't know anything about what happened cuz he's been with Jack the whole time since I've been out.

Ric looks like someone kicked his puppy. I guess someone did.

I am technically his since that he put that bite on my neck. Now that I think of it, we really need to talk about that because I don't know how this bite is gonna work with the G Lady's deal. I kinda like the idea of not being able to have kids, but that would also mean Ric doesn't get to be a dad. I already think of him as a Daddy, but he really should be a dad and I don't want to keep him from that. He'd be a great dad, much better than his own.

Connie looks the worst of the three. I kinda forgot that I didn't know he was alive for a while there. Yeah, it hurt to find out he was alive, but I was also happy about it. I didn't want my big brother to be dead. I really am happy he didn't die back then. But there's a difference between hope not existing because there's no one to look for you, and hope slowly dying because the people who you know should be looking aren't finding you.

They don't even know how many times I died in those last four years; how many times I wished I would stay dead. The first time wasn't the worst. That experience, while terrifying crawling out of a shallow grave in the basement, was still kind of awesome. Each subsequent time was a little less awesome. Every time coming back felt like the walls were getting closer, the noose was getting tighter.

I had no escape. I stopped fighting back. I stopped wanting to fight back. There was no more hope. Physical death might not release me, so I wished that I would mentally die and never come back. I wished for any release I could get. I still crave it, even now...

Looking around the room again, I realize. I wasn't as closed off as I thought I was. There's horror on all of their faces. I guess they didn't get that far in their thought processes regarding the deal. Oops.

I'm not supposed to be this emotional. It only hurts me more later. But it looks like I'm hurting them. I don't want to hurt them. They aren't the ones I want to hurt. I don't want to see their faces anymore. I can't look at them anymore.

No one stops me as I run from the room. No one stops me as I rip off the clothes Ric left for me. No one stops me as I open the front door and shift. I jump the gate at the end of the drive and hear no sign of any pursuit. Even if they tried, they won't catch me. No one is faster than my wolf.

There is no one, not since the vampire left me alone in that place. He was the only one who could keep up with me. They said he ran, but I'm not dumb. None of us ran. The only reason I'm still here is the G Lady's deal. The rest of them are still in the base-ment...or I should say, under the basement. I smelled a lot of them down there. I was the only one who ever left.

I reach the edge of the pack lands only running into a few people along the way. To almost everyone, I'm just a silver and blue blur. I'm too fast for them to see and what they do see is just light reflection and some freaky glowy thing my eyes do when I'm going super fast. I think it's an omega thing cuz the betas I met couldn't do it and they never knew of any alphas who could.

My wolf is starting to drag a bit, so I slow down to a normal run speed. I can't keep going full throttle, but I'm already in the neutral zone. Heh. Star Trek reference. Dad would be proud. I wonder if this weird speed and eye thing is what he wanted to talk about. Or maybe it's the silver fur? I mean, Mom didn't even see me run like this, so I don't know.

I'm starting to get pretty deep into the woods now, so I guess I should head on back to my cave. I don't want anyone to find it by following my scent, so I loop back towards the pack. No one should be anywhere near my trail yet so I might as well take advantage of the delay to hide the way to my home.

At the border, I make sure there's no one around and then I scale a tree right on the line. From here, it's a bit slower going to jump from tree to tree, but at least this way, I know no one will be able to follow me.

When I go back...

No.

If I go back, I'll have to point out to Ric and Max that they need to remind their warriors to look and scent up if they're going to do any good at protecting the kids. The old fucks can go die in a fire.

Climbing down the cliff to the entrance of my home, it hits me. I forgot Mr. Whiskers.

He's going to hate me. I really hope he will forgive me. I mean I'm going back... eventually. I just need a little bit of time to get back under control. Apparently, this freedom thing really fucks with my emotions.

With my mind made up, I kick the squirrels out of my sleeping bag and curl up with the other stuffies.

"You guys aren't Mr. Whiskers, but I hope you can help me out in his absence. I'll bring you to him when I go back and he can give you all official training for fighting the nightmares." I tell them all. "For now, just do your best."

Yawning, I allow myself to close my eyes and attempt to relax. Only way to shut the guys out completely if they get close enough is to be asleep. I just need my space for now. Sleep is a great escape and I can always use more. More sleep and less judgy faces.

More sleep and less waking up would be better.

SIXTEEN

Ric

He died?

And not just once, either by what he let slip out. He was buried. He crawled from a grave after being buried. How many more tortures did my baby have to endure in that place?

"He said four years, right?" Max asked. "Or thought it, whatever... but he said four, not eight, right?"

We both look at him and nod. I wonder where he's going with this.

"So, if the Goddess only had this deal with him for the last four years, how in the hell did he survive the first four?" he asks us both. "Based on what he showed us, he already was being cut open. He was already being..."

"Shut the fuck up!" Connor screams as he punches a hole in my wall.

I can't say I blame him for being upset. I mean it's not every day that you see the memory of your little brother finding out you're alive and feeling the hope bloom in him. He had another four years for that hope to die out. Four years of dying apparently.

Fuck!

I need to go give my boy a hug and never let go. I race from the room only to slip on something in the hall.

Why is there a pile of clothing in the hallway... These are the clothes I gave to Ethan this morning. I listen for the sound of the shower or him in the bedroom or anywhere in the house and.... I don't hear him.

"FUCK!"

I run to the front entryway and the door is wide open. He's shifted and gone. He's in the middle of the territory and no one knows his wolf. *I* don't even know his wolf. The only people who have seen him in that form are dead.

I'll have to kill anyone who hurts him even though they'll be doing the right thing stopping an unfamiliar wolf inside the territory. I need to get the word out. I don't even know if half a claim will show up in wolf form, so I can't even rely on that. My wolf is trying to take over and force a shift, but I'm struggling to hold onto my human side. I need a plan, not claws for this.

"I'm guessing you didn't undress the little dude and open the door," Max states dryly.

"Thank you, Captain Obvious," I snap back. "Get word to the warriors that they need to call with any strange wolf sightings and they are NOT to approach."

"Right, no scaring off the mate who still doesn't know he's your mate," he replies with a smirk.

At least someone isn't freaking out.

"How are you so calm?" Connor asks holding the sleep pants Ethan was wearing earlier. "You saw and heard what we did. You know what he went through now. How can you stand there and not want to protect him from everything out there?"

Max levels us both with a look that says he's seen more than we ever have and ever will. When the hell did Max have to go through something that would give a man that look in his eyes. Ethan has that look.

"Your little brother went through more shit in one month of that hellhole than you guys have ever experienced in your entire lives. He went through more fear and pain than you both can imagine... before he was even taken." He says to us with his anger starting to rise.

What the hell did Ethan suffer before he was taken? What is Max talking about?

"Did either of you even know that Ethan was nearly beaten to death on the way to school when he was ten? Did either of you know that he was teaching himself self-defense from watching movies because of the bullying he went through? Did either of you know the reason he keeps that damned stuffed animal with him isn't just because he likes the snuggle?"

He lets that sink in for a bit to see if either of us are showing signs of any recognition. I don't even need to look over at Connor to know he's just as clueless as I am. With a sorrowful sigh, Max continues,

"He hides a switchblade inside that bear. He'd even used it a few times. I helped him clean it up after. Only right, since I gave him the blade. He calls it his Stabby. He knows how to use it right and he knows how to keep it hidden."

Ethan's need for his bear is making more sense now. With that thought on my mind, I race up the steps to my room. There in the middle of the bed sits Mr. Whiskers. Ethan didn't take him. I still have a chance to see him again at least. A breath of relief flows out of my body as I grab up the ratty bear and clutch him to my chest.

Max and Connor come into the room after me. My Beta is staring at the bear like it's the first time he's ever seen it. All the time that Ethan was sleeping with it under his pillow... how long was the knife in there?

"When did he get the knife from you?" Connor finally asks Max.

"It was right after he was jumped at ten," he says. "I was walking by and ran the punks off before they could do more damage, but they had already broken a couple ribs and split his head open. I'd seen full grown men be down for the count with injuries like that, but that little dude popped right up. His only worry was that he'd get in trouble for getting blood on his shirt."

Max has a sad smile on his face as he continues, "I remember thinking to myself how bad is this kid's home life that a bloodstain is worse than getting his ass beat in the dirt. So, I took him home and cleaned him up, gave him a clean shirt and all. By the time I wiped the blood from his head, I couldn't find a wound. He had already healed the cut."

At this pause, both Connor and I look at each other. We know what Max isn't saying. Only powerful adult wolves should be healing that fast. We need our wolves to heal fast. At ten, Ethan didn't have a wolf. The only other way to speed up healing in our kind is cumulative healing, but that is a very slow building process. How many times was Ethan injured that his healing was that quick at ten? Or is it how powerful is Ethan that he was strong even back then? Either one is a scary thought.

Max continues on once he sees we got his point, "So before I send him on his way, I ask him if he knows how to protect himself if it happens again. That's when he told me about the movies. There's just something about the kid I felt I needed to protect, so I gave him my favorite blade. I showed him how to use it, how to hide it. I told him to find me after he uses it so I can show him how to clean up after himself. Took a little less than two weeks for him to find me. It was messy, but the kid learned quick."

I'm finding myself rethinking almost every interaction with Ethan. We were constantly chasing him off. We thought he was just an annoying little brother who was hanging around trying to be a big kid. What if he was hanging on because he needed the safety of being around the older kids, the safety of being around the future Beta and Alpha? Did we cause him more harm back then by running him off?

"You guys know the physical stuff wasn't the worst for him, right? He's never been afraid of physical pain, just so you know. He's got this way of zoning out of it and going total Zen if he has to. It's pretty wicked. He tried to show me how once upon a time, but my angry little ass couldn't manage it back then. I've gotten pretty good at it now, though" Max just keeps going on, showing us how much better he knew Ethan back then.

"It's the unknown and fear of disappointment that bothers him the most," he tells us. "He is so freaking terrified of disappointing people that he never considers his own needs. I mean, you were both heading off to check out schools on his birthday, but he never complained. Hell, he didn't even tell you that he hadn't heard his wolf yet."

That bomb hits as intended. My warrior is really pissed at both of us and rightly so. We went off to Pittsburgh and even took his safety net away from him. It doesn't matter that we had no clue that he didn't even know if his wolf was going to show up. Thirteen is a special birthday to a wolf, and we left him alone in a pack that apparently was abusing him.

"I didn't even know if he ever heard his wolf until he explained last night," he continues. "I'm guessing he showed up for him when they shifted, but the way little dude said it, I've got the feeling it's not the case," Max is on a roll now so I'm letting him go. We need to hear this. We need to know this before we go bring Ethan back home.

"From what I'm gathering, he was alone, thinking y'all were dead for four years in there," he's trying to convey something to us both, something we're not getting.

"It's easier to take what they dish out when you don't have hope. If you don't have hope, they don't have leverage," he breathes out through the emotion suddenly choking his throat.

Sounds like he's speaking from experience. This is a side of my warrior that I don't know about. I signal Connor to stay quiet when it looks like he's going to interrupt.

"Take away their leverage, they can't break your mind," Max continues. "See, Ethan could heal his body even before his wolf showed up. As long as they didn't break his mind, he was able to withstand everything. I'm thinking that's why he didn't die in those first four years. They couldn't break him because he didn't have anything to live for except sticking it to them. And we all know how much he lived for pissing off the people who crossed him."

We all share a sad smile at the memories of Ethan's pranks, but then Max continues,

"But then the Goddess shows up and strikes this deal with him. He thinks he's getting out. He's excited. She gave him hope. He was so happy for about thirty seconds. The bitch gave him thirty seconds of joy followed by four years of an even worse hell than before," he sobs out and tries to get control back.

"She broke his mind and heart before they ever could when she revealed to him that you were alive, Con. *She* did that. It wasn't the docs or the dicks that assaulted him. It was her... *She made him want to die after making sure he couldn't.* That's why he ran. That's why he's broken."

Although it's completely blasphemous to speak it out loud, Max is speaking the truth. The Goddess betrayed him by making this deal. She increased his suffering for no apparent reason when she could have easily gotten him out of there. She appeared to him, so why couldn't she appear to us and let us find hm?

The need to find my boy has increased, but I'm not as worried as I had been for his physical safety. Now, I'm kind of worried for the safety of my pack if someone comes across him. Then it hits me, why hasn't anyone alerted us about a strange wolf? There's no way he could have been running loose in the pack for this long and no one has spotted him. He's always been good at sneaking, but it's been too long for there to be no one who noticed him.

"Max, thank you for the much needed history on our boy, but we need to refocus unfortunately" I say while clutching Mr. Whiskers to my chest. I can feel the outline of the knife, and I'm dreading the day I roll over onto this thing.

"Why hasn't anyone spotted his wolf or him?" I point out to them both. "It's been at least an hour and it would take him at least two to get to the closest border even at a full sprint. Someone had to have seen him by now, but nothing has been brought up yet. And the thing with that dick, Noah. There's a severe lack of security in our pack."

Max is busy typing away on his phone. I'm pretty sure he's got all of his warriors in a group chat for pack wide announcements. He tried to add me into it once upon a time, but I have enough going on with my phone that I don't need to be a part of the warrior group chat.

"So apparently no one has seen a wolf or Ethan, naked or otherwise. Also, nothing about any unfamiliar wolf," Max says without looking up. "However... there were apparently multiple sightings almost an hour ago of a silver or blue blur between here and the border to the neutral territory. If we want to assume that the blur is Ethan's wolf, that means he made it to the border in about fifteen minutes and crossed into neutral territory about forty five minutes ago."

Connor and I are both staring at him. I know my jaw is dropped at the thought of him being able to travel over twenty miles in fifteen minutes while dodging around people and buildings. And no one saw anything but a silver or blue blur?

"Max, did you get to see his wolf on his birthday?" Connor asks. "You're the only one who was around on that day who isn't dead. No offense, but it's the truth."

"No offense taken, but no. I only got a glimpse," Max answers. "He was damn fast back then so before I could get to where I heard him, he was already gone. I promised I was going to be there and well my personal shit made me late."

There's that note of something in his voice again. I never asked about his personal life. Max just kinda hung out with us when he could and just wasn't around the rest of the time. It never bothered me then and well after the fire, I rarely cared about anything until Jackie came along.

"But yeah, the silver tracks with what I remember," he says, lost in thought. "There was something like a muzzle flash in the woods where I was supposed to meet him, but no sound. It freaked me out bad until I saw him later in the day talking to his dad on the porch."

And my warrior is back to all business. He's focused on his phone again.

Now that I know he's left the territory, I'm a bit more worried. I need my boy to come back to me. Setting Mr. Whiskers down on the bed, I pull out a pair of shoes.

"Let's go bring our stabby boy back home," I say. They both follow me downstairs and out the door.

SEVENTEEN

Ric

We end up splitting up. Some of my warriors had tried to follow Ethan's scent into the woods. It just keeps looping around through the trees and back to our border where it disappears again.

He's a master at hiding from us, but now we know his little trick with the mind speak. I know he'll hear if I reach out.

Ethan? You ok, baby?

No response.

I'm not too worried yet. We could be too far from where he is holed up. He might be sleeping. He might just be ignoring me. No matter the reason, I know he'll at least come back to us eventually.

"Any luck?" I ask Connor as he comes to where I am from the west.

"Looks like he went into the woods like before. Maybe he went back to that cave he found. I don't know."

My Beta looks like he's aged ten years in the last month.

Max comes at us from the east and says "What I want to know is how he does this trick of his with hiding his scent trails. If it's not an omega thing, I need to be able to teach our warriors how to do it, or at least how to defend against it. It's a liability... and not one I like."

I look out to the woods to the south. I swear we've scoured every inch of these woods between here and the hospital by now. There is no scent of him anywhere beyond a mile or so in, or at least that's what everyone is telling me.

Trying to track him this time is a lesson in futility. I can't scent him. The only way I can track him now is by the claiming bite, but it's not complete. I can feel he's alive and not physically hurt, but that's it.

I wonder how long it will take him to connect the dots and realize we're fated. The details of his deal made everything click into place for me. Between the sparks, my wolf's possessiveness, and the lack of scent, I'm pretty certain Ethan is mine by right of fate. I just need him to believe.

To my right, the last rays of sunlight are filtering through the trees. We've been out here all day. He's not going to be found if he doesn't want to be.

"Let's go home first. Jackie will be getting nervous if none of us is there," I say to the men gathered around me. "We'll pick it up in the morning."

I leave an extra patrol on for the night with the orders to alert all three of us if ANYTHING strange happens or is seen. I'm not taking chances, not with him.

Walking back through the front door without Ethan is probably one of the hardest things I've been forced to do in the last five years. My wolf is pushing me to go back out there, to not stop until we have our boy in our arms. But I know the man better. He won't come back until it's on his own terms.

Jack is watching television in the living room as we walk past. The excitement on his face falls as he notices Ethan isn't with us.

"Where's Ethan?" he asks in concern. "Is he alright? He said he's going to show me some things from when he was my age. He's coming back, right?"

The adults in the room all look at each other with pity. Who is going to be the one to break the kid's heart? We're the ones to blame for Ethan leaving.

Jack's gaze flits over all of us and settles on me as tears start to gather in his eyes. He knows who is really to blame.

"Brother Ethan promised me. He promised and he said he never breaks a promise, so why isn't he here?" he is practically begging us to produce Ethan from thin air. And I would if I could. Not just for me, but for this boy in front of me. He needs Ethan just as much as I do, and he's only had one day to get attached.

The hurt on Jack's face is gutting me, and I try to come up with anything I can say to make it even marginally better.

"Never mind. We'll just play later," he says with a smile on his face.

The adults in the room all look at each other in confusion and then it hits us. Ethan reached out to Jack. He didn't go too far away after all. He just doesn't want to be around any of us but Jack.

I can work with that. I just have to make sure I'm never away from my little brother until my baby boy comes back to us.

Ethan

How come after one night in a bed, I can't sleep at night in a sleeping bag anymore? Eight years naked on a cot. Two weeks in this luxurious cave. One night in a bed with jammies and I'm spoiled forever.

The bad dreams came back as soon as the sun went to bed today, so I think the stuffie army really needs to get some training from Mr. Whiskers. Or maybe I need Daddy Ric to keep the bad men out of dreamland. I'm not totally sure, but I do know that I'm getting hungry.

The cookies and chips stacked in the corner look to be demolished by the squirrels that snuck in here while I was gone. They didn't touch the snack cakes, though so I rip into a couple of those while I wait for my brain to finish booting up and getting closer to grown up thinking.

Where are you, Bro? You're supposed to show me how to pick on Max, but you aren't here!

Oh, crap! In my rush to get away from the guys, I forgot about Jack. I know how it feels to be abandoned, and I never meant to do it to him.

So sorry, kiddo, but the grown ups, and I use that term loosely for those three, made me mad and I had to jet for a bit. I'll be back soon to show you how to prank all of them. I tell him while I finish my dinner and grab a juice box to wash it down.

Never mind! We'll just play later. He says back to me a moment later.

I get the feeling he's not alone because I get the sensation of two minds knocking for entrance, and one trying to kick down the damn door.

Gotta go kiddo, but do me a favor? Tell your asswipe of a big brother that if he doesn't knock it off, he'll learn how it feels to be castrated. I'm sure Stabby and Mr. Whiskers are up for it.

The pushing on my mind stops about a minute later. I wouldn't really castrate him. I don't think. I mean it would grow back eventually. I speak from experience and all. But I'm kinda liking the thought of all those bits on Ric. He's the only guy that has ever made me feel all tingly down there. I never got any kind of reaction down there, except when thinking of him. Even the docs were confused by it. I know I still am.

Looking out of the cave entrance, I can see we're only a few days from the full moon. That means my heat will be coming again soon. My wolf tells me this one will be special. When I ask why, he shuts up. Only thing he keeps repeating is something about our true mate and it's time. He's still pissed about Ric's wolf biting us. Something about blocking us from sensing our fated mate or something.

I really don't care. If we never find our mate, I never get pregnant. I never die. I won't have to worry about having someone else to lose. Only person I have to worry about is Jackie and even with their track record, those guys will keep him safe. They actually *see* him. They never saw the real me.

The moon in the sky is mocking me. She's always done that. All the other wolves get her love and feel her warmth as she grows in the sky. I just feel empty. The closer to full she gets, the harder it is to hide the pain. Her light shines too bright, the shadows inside me shrink, and I fall apart. There's not enough super glue left to put me back together anymore, so I leave the pieces behind in the moonlight.

I think she's collecting them. Pretty soon she'll have a whole boy to start over with. She'll have the perfect little boy who can make his parents proud, who won't ever have to question if he's loved. The perfect son who does his homework and chores and doesn't embarrass everyone by showing up late or dirty. The perfect brother who doesn't need to secretly follow along just to feel included. He'll be invited and carried and get piggy back rides because he's such a good boy.

He'll have friends who will run with him and play with him and invite him over for sleepovers. He'll have parties thrown *for him*, not for the connections. He'll be listened to and loved. Those are the pieces the moon has taken from me. She's taken the best of me since I'm too broken. I give her those pieces so that the next boy can be happy and not end up like me, scared and angry all the time.

I look up again and she's mocking me. She isn't holding those pieces. She threw them out like trash, because they came from me. The pieces I gave up, the parts that would make the best boy, are gone because the moon knows my worth. I have none, except to make sure they all pay. I need to pay Uncle Carl a little visit first.

Actually, first things first, I need to figure out where the hell I even am. Then I can go after Carl, and the docs, and fucking Needle Dick, and the voice on the phone. I'm saving him for last. I don't doubt that I can find him. I can't die. I have forever to find him.

As I turn my face to the sky yet again, this is the first time since I was very very young that I remember smiling into the moonlight. I finally have a purpose... and it's to destroy them all.

Remember our deal, my child, flits through on the breeze.

Oh, I remember G Lady. I remember all right. I don't have to kill them to destroy them. In fact, it's so much more fun this way.

EIGHTEEN

Ric

It took us a week to find the cave. When we found it, Max said he could tell Ethan had been living there but left a day or two before we found it. The evidence of how he was living there was obvious. Snack cake, cookie, and potato chip wrappers were everywhere. Empty juice boxes were all over the place. It's obvious where he had his sleeping area set up because it was the only piece of floor in the cave not covered in debris.

He might be twenty one, but he still lives like a kid.

I guess that's the only way he knows, though. No one ever showed him how to cook or shop or anything else. I mean he figured some of it out judging by the tags on the floor. At least he has some changes of clothes now.

I wish I would've gotten the opportunity to give him the ID, cell phone, and credit card I got set up for him. At least then, we could track him through those.

Right now, we are absolutely clueless on where he could be.

He has a full day's head start on us to wherever he has decided to run off to.

Climbing back up to the top of the cliff, I wonder yet again how in the hell he managed to do this while carrying all of the stuff he had in there. I've struggled carrying groceries from the car into the house with only a few steps.

How did he manage to do this climb with cases of stuff to carry?

Clearing the top of the cliff, we all sit and catch our breath for a bit. Our little Blue is a beast, doing this day in and day out after all he was healing from. And with the rain and wind? Holy hell he makes me feel old and it's only a five year gap.

Jack's ringtone plays from my pocket as I snatch up my phone.

"Hey little man, what's up?" I answer before he says anything. He asks every day if we've found Ethan. He's getting used to the disappointment.

"I can't find Mr. Whiskers," he says.

"He should be in my room on the bed. He might have fallen off, but I didn't move him," I tell him and listen to his little footsteps pound up the stairs.

"He's not here!" he cries. "I have to find him! If he's gone, it means Brother Ethan isn't coming back and he has to come back!"

"We'll find Mr. Whiskers, buddy," I try to console him as the guys look over at me in alarm. "Maybe I put him somewhere else when I was half asleep this morning. I'll come home to help you look, okay?"

"Ok," he sniffled through the phone. He really needs to blow his nose. "We can't lose him! We just can't!"

At this point, I'm not sure if he's talking about the bear or Ethan, so I just give him some comforting words and promise to head straight home now. School is officially done for the year and he's back to being all alone except for us grown ups. He really needs someone who can spend time with him and relate on his level. I need to look into some summer camps or something.

"Where's the bear?" asks Max as I put my phone away.

"Was my brother in the house?" asks my Beta at the same time.

"Let's go back and take a look," I say. "The bear is likely under the bed and Jack is too upset to really look. He just wants Ethan back home, like we all do."

The hike back to our territory doesn't take us all that long. I don't understand how it took us a whole week to find his hideout when it was less than a mile from the border. I keep getting thrown by my boy's smarts and I smile at the thought of having it keep happening for the rest of our lives.

Rolling up to the garage, Jack is standing there with a new stuffed animal in his hands. This one is a tiger. He always wanted a tiger stuffie, but I could never find one that seemed to fit. This one definitely seems to by the way he's clinging to it. The sight punches a hole in my gut.

"Where'd the new friend come from?" I ask him as I get out of the car, nodding to the warrior who is keeping an eye on Jack in our absence.

"He was on your bed," he tells me with tears in his eyes. "Right in Mr. Whisker's spot."

So my gut is right.

Ethan came for his teddy and left a friend behind for Jack. He left the cave two days ago, but only did the swap today. I know I put Mr. Whiskers in place this morning before I left. The damn thing never left my bedroom unless Jack needed him, but he always went back to his spot on the bed.

"Your new friend have a name?" Max asked. "Does he have a message to tell us?"

Jack shakes his head, staring at the ground. Only mumbles came out between the sniffles.

"Speak up, buddy." I say. "We can't understand if you're mumbling."

"I *said*, " he starts with anger. I like anger better than the tears honestly. "There was a note but I'm scared to read it." The tears are coming back and he's clutching the tiger even tighter. "What if he says goodbye? What if he's not coming back?" he asks us looking at each of us in turn.

"Wasn't I a good boy? Why doesn't he want to stay with me?" Jack is crying like he has never cried before. I scoop him up in my arms and squeeze him tight while he sobs out his fears.

I hate Ethan a little bit right now.

Carrying Jack back into the house, I see the letter on the kitchen counter. He put it next to the waffle iron, the building block waffle iron.

I know I put that away. It hasn't come out since that morning when Ethan took off. I'm just as scared as Jack, so I stare at it while rubbing circles on his back. I want to go back to four hours ago, when we still had hope of him coming back to us.

"I got one, too." Connor says from the hallway. "It was left on my bed."

"Me as well," Max chimes in, coming into the kitchen from the living room.

Jack motions for me to put him down, so I set him on his stool at the island and watch as he pulls a letter out of his back pocket.

He hands it to Max and asks him, "Can you read it for me? I'm still not good with all the big words and Ethan knows a lot of them."

So we all got one. How long was he preparing to leave us all behind?

Max solemnly takes Jack's letter and nods to him before opening it to read out loud to all of us:

Hey Kiddo,

Sorry to take off on you like this. You need to know it's got nothing to do with me not wanting to be your brother or any bullshit like that.

I know I shouldn't say bullshit in a letter to a seven-year-old, almost eight which is practically a teenager though so it's OK in my book.

Jack lets out a little giggle at that. It's good to see the smiles coming back to him.

You are a bright ray of sunshine in my otherwise dark world. You give me hope of a better future and I'm going to make the world a safer place for you. I know you don't understand it now, but you will in about six years.

My wolf says you're special like us. In my experience, special means a target, so I'm making sure nothing out there can hit yours.

Special? Like Ethan is?
Connor and I lock eyes while Max takes a pause in reading. Jack will always be protected.

Since I'm going to need Mr. Whiskers for my mission, I'm leaving you with my pal Tony. He's not as good at being a nightmare hunter as Mr. Whiskers, but he's got Stabby Junior to back him up.

Make sure to take good care of Tony and I'm sure Max will show you how to take care of Junior. Give the big oaf a hug for me and I'll be back once I take care of a few loose ends.

Love ya, Kiddo.
Ethan

All of our eyes lock on to the tiger in my brother's arms. Ethan gave my seven-year-old brother a switchblade hidden in a stuffed animal. I'm going to have to spank him so much for that one. My boy's got a lot to answer for with that one.

Connor rips his letter open next and after skimming through, he looks at us all before reading:

Connie,
Big Brother,
Jerk-face,

Pick your name. They all apply. I asked around a bit about you over the last week. People in town think you're awesome, but quiet. The people at the hospital think you're too serious. The people in this pack, though? They know you're too sad. You need to cheer up, Dude.

When did Ethan get to talk to people in the pack? Why did no one bring up talking to him with any of the warriors or guards? Or us...

It wasn't your fault I was taken. You were eighteen. What could you have done? They would have killed you too. They wanted me because I am an omega. They wanted a thirteen-year-old boy because they didn't want someone who could fight them off. They wanted me because I was weak.

My wolf let out a growl hearing that. Ethan has never been weak. I reign my wolf back in so I can listen while Connor continues to read.

You have always been strong, so much stronger than me. They killed Dad. I heard it all and thought it was a dream. I remember now. They killed him. They killed Mom when she tried to save Dad. I thought they were going to kill me, but instead they did much worse. They would have killed both you and Ric, so quit beating yourself up over it.

I don't know how to feel hearing that he doesn't blame us. He believes that had we been there, we'd have died as well. Connor and I meet each other's gaze. He feels like I do, still.

We would have made a difference. Despite Ethan's beliefs regarding that night, we both know that three adult alpha wolves would have been victorious.

Shaking his head, Connor continues,

I used to be mad that you were alive out there and I was trapped with the monsters. Turns out if you spend enough time with monsters you become one yourself. But you stayed the hero, my hero. You rescued me from that place. Do I wish it happened sooner? Of course. But after meeting your new little brother, I understand. You couldn't risk him. I'd never ask you to.

So this is why I have to leave. You have to make his world safe in the pack. Be his hero now. I can't be the hero, but maybe I can be an antihero. You taught me about them, remember? I don't need to be good anymore. Just protect our little brother, OK?

Love always,
Ethan

We all glance at Jack. He's clutching onto Tony like it's the only thing holding him in one piece. Maybe it is. Maybe it's the only thing holding us all together.

Max looks at us all next and opens his letter to read:

Heya Maxi-pad!

Maximillian,

Yeah I remember your REAL name. Thanks for all the help when I was a kid. And thanks for keeping my secrets. You were one of the very few who got to see the real me and you didn't treat me any different. That means a lot to me. You'll always be my honorary big bro no matter where my mission takes me.

He chokes up at that. I've never seen Max show any emotions except for anger or amusement. Just how close was he to Ethan before?

As he continues, he has a sad smile on his face. He really does know and love my mate.

YOUR mission, if you choose to accept it... and you

fucking better... is to teach Jack what you taught me. Show him the stabby stuff. Show him the fighting stuff. But show him that he's strong. Show him that he's not alone. Show him that the world is still good even when it's filled with shit people.

You saved me long before I got sprung from the hell I was taken to. Teach him to save himself.

Seriously though. Take care of him.

Your Little Dude,
Ethan

Max hides his face as he finishes reading. I can tell he's trying to put his mask back up, so I don't say anything. This is hitting us hard. These letters are a goodbye. It doesn't sound like he's planning on returning in any of these.

My letter is the last. I'm still afraid. The others are all in tears looking at me, expecting me to read mine aloud just like they did. I just want to take it to my office so I can break down when it happens. Jack's glassy eyes seal my fate though, and I open my letter and read:

Alpha Alaric Jameson,

Sorry I never learned your middle name. Seems like the kind of thing you should have shared before claiming me, right? Not like I had a say in that or anything.

I have to take a breath and pause. I knew that was coming at some point, but it's still a gut punch and my wolf is hanging his head in shame.

My wolf tells me you robbed us of our true mate. He's pissed, but I want to say thanks.

Thanks? Wait... he's glad I claimed him? I continue reading.

Because of my deal, my mate and I can't scent each other. Your claim apparently took away the other signals that my body might give me when meeting my fated mate. Since I have no desire to have a baby or do anything that could ever result in a baby, your claim keeps the deal intact.

This means I won't die in my mission. I can keep Jack safe for you. I'm going to take care of the people who hurt me, so they won't hurt him. They will want him. I can see the special in him. So can my wolf. We need to protect him.

Just know this isn't for you. It's for him. I'm glad you got him in your life. I'm sorry about your mom though. I never got the story on that, maybe someday.

I hate that I made him so mad at me. I hate that he thinks it's his job to protect my little brother. I hate that we've been so busy with one crisis after another that he hasn't even gotten any information on what has happened with us while he was gone.

I can't keep focusing on the what ifs running through my head, so I continue reading.

I'll be back someday, when I know the people who hurt me can't get to Jack through me. See, I have a list. Now that I know where I'm starting, I can go back and take care of them all. Did you know that you can make someone wish they're dead, but not kill? Max told me when I was a kid but I didn't believe him. Then, I experienced it. Now they will. They all will.

    You are their Alpha. You need to take care of them all. If the bad men get any of them, I'll make YOU wish you were dead.

                              Sincerely,
                      Your Little Psycho

I stop reading aloud as there is a post script that is obviously not for others to know. We all need to digest what we just read. I send a warrior out for some takeout and the others take Jack into the living room for some time in front of the TV. No one is really watching the screen, but the noise keeps the quiet from being suffocating.

Leaving them to the cartoon, I try not to race up the stairs as I recall the post script on my letter.

P.S. – I never really asked how you felt about me going under and turning into a toddler all of those times, but I want you to know you would make a great Daddy. I'm sorry you won't get to be a dad because of me. But if you want to be my Daddy, there's another letter in our special place where I started to feel safe and snuggly for the first time in a very long time.

Tearing apart my bedroom, I'm trying to think of where he could have hidden this letter. It's not on the bed. It's not under the bed. Ripping the bedding away and pulling all of the furniture away from the walls yields no results. Then it hits me.

I stumble into my bathroom and there is the letter sitting in the drawer where I had stashed a superhero toothbrush for him as a surprise. He took the toothbrush with him but left this letter behind.

I rip open the letter and perch on the end of the bare and crooked bed to read:

Dear Daddy Ric,

I really hope you don't just throw this letter out. See, I always wanted a Daddy. I had a dad, but he died. He was killed protecting the house. I want to think he was protecting me, but I have no way of knowing. Here's the thing... they said they loved me. They always said it. Everyone says it all the time. But their love didn't protect me. Their love didn't heal me.

I know it sounds pretentious saying their love wasn't enough when they died that night and blah blah blah. I'm not talking about that night or the eight years that followed. I mean the ignoring the five year old at his own party because the Alpha is showing off his son's admission to an exclusive summer camp. I mean the never realizing the eight-year-old had a split lip and broken wrist and only seeing the grass stains on his pants and making him change so the neighbors won't see.

In my world it was more important to be perfect in the eyes of others than to show any genuine affection to their child.

I knew they were strict with Ethan, but I never realized the extent of it before. I always looked up to Mr. Sinclair, now I'm feeling not so much admiration as anger towards the man.

I have to continue before I get too worked up...

> So, I don't know if they loved me, Daddy. But I know you always did. You held my hand to show me the fishies in the pond at my birthday party instead of getting congratulations on your achievements. You picked me up when I fell off my bike trying to keep up with you and Connor. You ordered me chocolate shakes at the diner when I snuck in after you even though it grosses you out that I would dip my fries in them. You showed me in so many ways that you loved me.
>
> You loved me enough to give me a new name. I'm your Little Boy Blue. You called me that on my fifth birthday. You said it was because I was blue head to toe, from my eyes to my clothes to my feelings. You changed one of those things that day, but I was still and will always be your Blue.

I stop to wipe the tears away from my eyes. I forgot the reason I named him Blue. I was a ten year old kid who was just trying to escape his father's bragging and came across this little boy hiding at the edge of the party. I didn't realize at first that it was Connor's brother. When I did, I wondered why he was sad on his birthday. I took him to the pond to see him smile. The smile he gave me that day changed my life.

I'm almost done with the letter now. I pick it back up to finish reading.

I don't know where this leaves us as far as my going under and not being a grown up at times or if you want to be my Daddy after I'm done with everything. I just needed to make sure you know that you showed me the best love in the world and I'll try to bring back your good boy when I'm done, if you want him. I have to go hurt the bad men to bring him back. Good boys shouldn't have to fear the bad men.

I love you, Daddy.

He didn't sign it. He didn't end it. He wants me to keep loving him and by Goddess I will never stop. Reading this letter, it's obvious I have always loved him. Baby or no baby, Ethan is mine and he is coming home. He wants to get his revenge. He is not doing it alone.

"Connor! Max!" I shout down the stairs. "Pack your shit! We're going after him!"

I can hear Jack's excitement from up here. We're bringing his new brother home again. This time he's going to know he's not only loved and wanted, but he's also needed here.

I run down the stairs and into my office to gather what we'll need on the road. I need to grab the stuff I prepared for Ethan. If he's going to be out there, I want him with some protections from the human authorities.

Digging through my desk, I can't find the box I had his stuff in. I searched the whole office for the next half hour. A knock at the door shows me that Connor and Max are packed and ready to go.

"I think we can track him," I tell them with a smile. My little Blue found his gifts this morning and we can follow his trail.

NINETEEN

Ric

Another week has gone by while we chase after Ethan. At first, I wasn't sure if he was actually the one who took the stuff from my office. The phone didn't turn on and the card wasn't used. When the card was finally used after two days, it showed a purchase in Atlanta. We thought he would have headed north back toward Ohio.

The credit card alert showed a purchase at a coffee shop. Connor did a quick peek while we all crossed our fingers that Ethan was in a safe situation. He saw the coffee shop's logo on the cup in Ethan's hand, so we headed south.

We were an hour north of Atlanta when there was another alert on the credit card. This time for a plane ticket to Pittsburgh. We couldn't figure out why he was headed there of all places, but I dropped Max off at a metro station to catch a flight to Pittsburgh. The thought was maybe he could catch up while Connor and I took the car and started on the almost twelve hour drive up there.

We met Max outside of the movie theater at the Waterfront complex just south of the city. There had been a couple of charges at the theater and at least a deposit paid at the hotel down the road. When Max checked the hotel, they hadn't seen him, and the reservation had been made online.

The next charge was at a place called Kennywood. After looking it up, it seems the little shit snuck into an amusement park. My wolf wanted to go in after him, but between the lights and the sounds and the smells, it would be impossible to locate him in an amusement park.

We stayed in the area for a few days, but the next alert wasn't coming through. Either he lost the card, or he found a way to get some cash. Not knowing where he was heading to next, Connor started to listen in for clues.

And that's where we are today, sitting in a parking lot in Youngstown, Ohio waiting for a clue on the direction we need to head next.

"He's on a bus to St. Louis. Why is he going to St. Louis?" Connor pipes up from the backseat.

"Maybe his stop is along the way," Max answers while pulling out of the lot to head in the direction of the interstate. "Have either of you made the connection yet that we're heading toward home?"

I look up from my phone. The small town on the Ohio border with Indiana hasn't been home since Ethan was taken. Home is where Jackie is, and he's never been there. But, of course, that was the only home Ethan knew.

"Why would he go there if it's his mission to get all the bad men?" Connor asks us both. Max shrugs as he merges onto the interstate heading west. I almost say I don't know when a thought occurs to me.

"Do you think he knew about Carl?" I asked Connor, turning to face him.

His look of shock kinda answers the question for me.

"Carl is dead, right? Why would the kid go looking for a dead man?" Max asks while my Beta and I stare at each other.

"Did anyone tell Ethan that Carl died?" I ask slowly.

The silence in the car is telling. Well, I guess we know where he's heading now. Max picks up the speed. Here's hoping we can get there before Ethan realizes there's no one left alive to hurt... before anyone who might still be there realizes that our boy is not only alive but looking for them as well.

Ethan

Buses are boring. I much prefer planes for long distances. The ride from Atlanta to Pittsburgh was a bit bumpy, but the kid in the seat next to me shared his coloring books and we had a great time. His mom thanked me for keeping him occupied or something like that. She's just lucky I didn't swipe one of the books. The kid seriously got some awesome coloring books. He did let me keep the blue crayon though. He thought it was cool that I told him my name is Blue.

Yep. I'm going by Blue right now so that I don't set off any flags or alerts to the guys back home. I know they're following me. I felt Connor jump in for a look at the coffee shop. That's why I flew up here. The original plan was to catch a flight to Dayton or Cincinnati, but I had to improvise. Pittsburgh was the closest I could get without it being totally obvious where I was heading, at least on short notice. The guys might not be the only ones trying to follow along.

Getting off the plane in Pittsburgh was crazy though. I got in a rideshare using an app on the phone I swiped from Ric's office. I also found an ID for me and a credit card with my name. Fair game and all, so I took them figuring I'll need them to get around now. Any who, the driver was cool and took me to this place called the Waterfront when we left the airport.

I decided to watch a couple of movies at the mega theater there. The place even had some arcade games in the lobby to play while waiting for the movie times. I had also booked a hotel room down the road and was planning on checking in after my third movie, but when I was walking toward the hotel, I saw Max heading into the lobby.

I didn't want him to stop me, so I hid until he was gone. I found another place that didn't need a credit card across the river.

The area seemed a bit rougher around the edges, but the people were still really nice. I took a few days in Pittsburgh to test how close the guys were to me and find out how they were tracking me. They managed to show up wherever the card was used in under an hour, so I'm pretty sure that's how they're doing it.

It kinda sucks that they took away my ability to use the card, but I'm not going back. I won't go back until I take care of the bad people. Trading my shoes for some cash, I managed to get a bus ticket to Saint Louis from Youngstown. Rideshare took me to Youngstown. I figure the hour and a half from the amusement park to the bus depot should be long enough for me to make a clean getaway on the bus.

I'm trying to not look at any signs or anything just in case Connie tries his sight thing again with me. The headaches aren't so bad anymore, but the multi-vision thing is a bit annoying. It's kind of like having a screen in front of each eye and your brain is trying to decide which one is real. Seeing Ric's hopeful looks when Connie pulls it off is starting to get to me.

The bus pulls away from Columbus and the next stop is Dayton. That is where I'm getting off. The old house is about an hour drive from Dayton. If I shift, I can make it in about ten minutes, but I kind of don't want to rush it. I don't know what I'm heading into. I mean, what if there are people living there now? I think it would be a bit weird having to explain the hidden room in the basement.

Getting off the bus, the driver reminds everyone that they need to be back in an hour or else we're stuck in Dayton. I'm tempted to shift and run out to the old place, take care of Carl, and come back so I have an alibi. What do the humans care anyways? They turn away. They don't look. Otherwise, they'd have known that their own kind was doing those things to us in there. They call us monsters. They're the real monsters.

Walking along the streets, my mood continues to plummet. It's been an hour at least and I'm just now leaving the city. As the sun starts to dip lower, I grab my phone to order up a rideshare. And the damn thing won't turn on. I guess I forgot to charge it enough last time. Or maybe I forgot to turn it off after the rideshare dropped me at the bus depot in Youngstown. I don't know.

I'm tired. I'm sweaty. I'm hungry.

I want my Daddy.

But he's not here. He has to take care of Jack. It's been over a week since they started chasing me. He should be back home by now. Jack shouldn't be left alone for this long.

I pull Mr. Whiskers from my backpack. *It's going to be a long night of walking,* I think as my left thumb pops between my lips.

TWENTY

Ethan

Sitting up, it takes a couple minutes to remember where I am. Oh yeah, I stopped in at a Waffle House for some food. I got wonderfully greasy food, cooked by a big dude named Stan who noticed me nodding off over my plate of scrambled eggs. He came out and yelled at the drunks in the corner to leave me be and made me lay down in the booth. He reminded me of Daddy so much that it wasn't difficult to listen to him.

Looking around for Stan to thank him, I see a note on the table.

DON'T WORRY ABOUT THE MEAL, KID. GET YOUR ASS BACK HOME TO YOUR DADDY. TRUST ME, HE NEEDS YOU MORE THAN YOU NEED HIM. BE A GOOD BOY AND DON'T GET INTO ANY SITUATIONS.

—STAN

Wiping the tears from my face, I throw a five on the table for the server who needs to clean up my mess. Racing out the door, I turn in a circle. Which way is west again?

The sun is to my left, so I think I should go to the right. Sun rising in the east and all that, right?

Once the highway has dense enough woods running next to it, I duck behind the trees and strip down. These woods almost smell like home. I'm close now.

Letting my wolf take over for a bit, we zoom through the trees, blurring past everything in the early morning light. Recognizing the pond where Ric showed me the fish, my wolf stops for a drink. I take back over since we're so close to the house and drop the backpack from my mouth. Pulling on my pants, I remind my wolf that this isn't pack anymore. The scents are all stale, so we have to watch out for humans here, maybe even something else.

Before we were taken to that place, I didn't know there was anything else out there except us wolves, vampires, and humans. The other things I heard and smelled in that place made me realize we aren't the biggest and baddest out there. There are much worse things to fear in this world than supposedly bloodthirsty vampires. The ignorance of the pack I grew up in still astounds me. Although, there's a good chance they knew and just didn't bother to tell me.

So what if I took a little longer to get dressed? I haven't been here in eight years, and I didn't exactly leave on good terms. I don't even know what happened at the house that night. I just know I heard Dad die and I was carried out. I kind of remember hearing Uncle Carl talking about money and omega and getting more money. Then it was that place when I fully woke up.

What am I supposed to say to the people living there now?

"Hey there! I used to live here until my parents were murdered and my evil uncle kidnapped me and sold me as a lab rat where I was operated on while I was awake for the last eight years." I mumble to myself as I finish tying my shoes.

Laughing at the absurdity of it, I start down the trail that leads to the backyard.

Clearing the last of the trees, I freeze. Dropping to my knees, I start to weep. There is no house anymore. It's just a burnt-out husk. All the memories, good and bad... that's all they can be. The dents in the walls... The corners where I would hide away to take naps... The fort in the attic Connie and I built... My secret hidey holes... gone.

My hidey holes... There's one that might still be here. It holds a super special thing that I need to have.

Racing for the wreckage, I don't even care that I'm getting covered in almost a decade of soot and dirt and grime. I'm digging for the baseboards of what should be the kitchen....

There. I see my mark.

The wood is charred but not burnt through. Holding my breath, I pry the wood away from what is left of the floor and wall... and out drops a key. *It's still here.* I let out the breath I was holding and start to cry again. This time it's not despair. It's joy. This is the key to my past and my future. This is the key to keeping Jack safe.

Ric

We lost him just outside of Dayton. We managed to make good time getting back to our hometown only to change course when his cry for his Daddy blasted in our minds. We searched the bus station and the city all night long. He wasn't at any of the hotels or motels and none of the people on the streets could recall seeing him.

Heading back after that disappointment was hard, but now we're heading back towards our hometown. Max is getting edgier the closer we get. Come to think of it, we never really knew Max beyond the surface level of the lovable goof until we moved away. I'm starting to think our hometown was only ever a happy place for me.

As we pull into the driveway of the old pack house, it strikes me that it's horribly pretentious to maintain the properties here since we're never coming back. This isn't home anymore. In the past, my wolf would rage against any suggestion of giving up this land and these buildings. Today he's silent.

Before, we had to keep them in case mate came home. My wolf tells me.

This means, he held onto hope all this time. He knew Ethan was out there and we did nothing?

Didn't know. Only hoped. He replies. *Hurt too much to think otherwise.*

OK I can understand that one.

When we climb from the car, we're all exhausted. We need sleep after spending the entire night searching the city. The sun coming up over the trees really is a beautiful sight, but the bed is calling my name. Any bed will do. We have our pick in the town. Almost all the houses are mine.

Falling face down on the bed, it doesn't take long for sleep to claim me, but it's only about an hour later that I'm being woken up by an excited Connor.

"He's here!" he says before I can even fully open my eyes. "He was at the house... well what is still there anyways."

Oh, my baby boy must be hurting from seeing that. His home is nothing but piles of burnt wood and scorched earth now.

"How do you know he was there?" I ask blearily. Sleep is not letting me go easily this morning. I have never been a morning person.

He turns his phone to show me a picture and I have to laugh at the absurdity of what I'm seeing. Right there on the driveway in front of the charred remains, he wrote "Ethan was here" followed by a drawing of what I can only imagine is a penis wearing a cape.

"At least the little dude still has his style," Max chuckles from the doorway.

"I'm guessing he's not in the immediate area since you're here and he's not?" I confirm with my Beta.

"Yeah, he did whatever he does with his scent as soon as I hit the trees," he replies, still staring at his phone screen.

At least we know he's alright and his spirit isn't crushed by seeing the house in ruins. My baby boy is so strong, but I'm still going to be there for him. I need to be there for him.

While we all load up on the caffeine so we can stay awake, my phone alerts me to a motion detector going off in the basement. Curious, I pull up the camera feed on my phone to see what kind of critter got in this time. Last time it was a skunk who thankfully I watched make its way back out again. I never realized before today that I kept the camera subscription and alerts all this time in case Ethan returned.

This time, the camera is showing my boy. Ethan is downstairs creeping through the basement, not twenty feet below us. And we wouldn't even know if not for this technology. None of us heard or smelled anything. Has he always been this stealthy? I remember a bumbling kid who crashed into things constantly. Where did this ninja expert come from?

Max glances over my shoulder and asks, "What building is that? I can get over there in under five minutes."

I look up at him and tell him with a smile, "You're already here. He's downstairs right now."

Before Max can leave the room, I add, "I don't want to scare him off, so let's just watch."

I feel like we're back in high school using a phone to watch porn in the locker room with how close they're crowding me to see the screen. It's a little weird, but I can't stop smiling at the screen.

My boy is safe.

We watch in silence as he creeps along to the wall that housed the old vault. Dad had the thing removed after some pups locked a schoolmate in there and almost killed him.

Come to think of it, Dad never told us who the kid was that was locked in. I just remember the adults freaking out that their pups were going to be in trouble. They should have been. No one really said anything about the kid who was locked in.

Going back to the screen, I have to resist running down into the basement to gather him into my arms. He's obviously fighting back panic, but he pushes through it. I'm so proud of him.

Then it hits me why he would panic. *He* was the kid who almost died... and there was no justice. No punishment for the offenders. No comfort or counseling. Everyone just pretended it didn't happen and the vault door was removed like it was the problem.

We all watch as Ethan climbs up into the darkness of the old vault and is out of sight for a while. I turn on the audio and we hear his soft snores. I don't understand how he can manage to fall asleep in the place he almost died, but that's not important at this moment. He's napping now, so we can make a plan while we know he's safe.

TWENTY-ONE

Ric

Sitting in my father's old office, I'm seeing a lot of examples where we all failed Ethan. There are photos everywhere of me on the desk and my achievements line the walls. At the Beta's desk, there are pictures of Connor, of me and Connor, of Connor and his parents, and only one of Connor with Ethan. The calendar on the desk has multiple dates highlighted and written on for Connor's college visits and graduation and business meetings and even the neighboring pack leader's daughter's birthday... but no mark for Ethan except to say dinner at five with Alpha on the day that was to be his party.

After reading the letter that was left by my Blue, I want to destroy this place for all the pain they put on him as a little boy. All the pain they ignored. All the pain they hid from us on purpose. This whole pack abused my boy and when we get back, they're all going to pay the price.

The growls coming from my throat finally bring the attention of my Beta and warrior away from the video feed and to where I'm looking.

"I miss our folks, too, Man." Connor says as he puts a hand on my shoulder.

I shake him off and turn to him in rage.

"Do you really?" I demand. "Do you really miss the people who emotionally abused and scared a little kid because he couldn't keep up appearances? Do you really miss the people who covered up the fact that he was locked in a vault by his peers because they didn't want the negative attention of having a pup being somewhere he shouldn't?"

I was trying to keep my voice down so it wouldn't carry and wake up Ethan in the basement. I don't know how much he would hear down there and don't want him running from us again.

"Do you miss the way they adored you and ignored him? Did you even notice what they put him through?" I ask watching his face for any sign of recognition, any signal that he saw what I didn't. "Did you ever notice how he couldn't be dirty, or loud, or speak at all in front of the adults? Did you notice how his birthdays were more about us than him?"

We are both in tears as he is looking at his father's desk and the reality sinks in.

"Can you remember him ever getting a present after Mr. Whiskers?" I ask in a whisper, "Honestly, man. I'm asking. Because I can't."

"I saw when you didn't," Max pipes up from behind my father's desk. "The old Alpha saw too."

My dad knew a pup was being mistreated and did nothing? No, that's not my dad. He would never turn a blind eye. He would've fixed it, right? I look at Max practically begging him to say my dad was fixing it or had a plan or something, but he crushes me with his next words.

"Hell, most of the pack saw it. It was most of us older kids who didn't see it," he says to us as he starts going through the drawers of my father's desk. "The younger pups noticed, and it made him more of a target. The adults turned their backs to every single abuse inflicted on him. The younger pups were even encouraged by some of their parents to continue the abuse."

He looks up at us as he closes the last drawer and growls, "I saw it all."

Max is fighting his own tears now.

"What the hell did you see that we didn't? How did you know to help him? Why didn't you tell us about it? We could have helped him!" I spit at him. "Your silence kept it going! We would have stopped it!"

"You couldn't stop it," he says dejectedly, "it was on the order of the Beta and his wife."

"Only the Alpha could've stopped it, but I have no clue why he let it continue," he tells me.

He looks directly at Connor and says, "I don't know why your parents loved you and hated him, Conman...."

"I don't know why parents insist on having kids and not loving them," he mumbles under his breath.

Those last words hang in the air, and we hear a whimper through the phone. We hold our breaths until we hear the soft snoring resume.

"You want to know why I saw it and you didn't?" he asks after some time.

Connor and I both nod our heads at him. I don't know about Connor, but I need to know how in the hell I was so completely blind to it all. I need to know why I needed a letter to literally spell it out for me to understand that I was unknowingly complicit.

"Sometimes in order to see the abuse happening, you have to know what it's like to be abused." He says to us. "My Ma was a right nasty bitch. I saw the abuse because I'd been there. I also knew thanks to my Da what it feels like to have people ignore what's right in front of them. I couldn't subject another kid to that."

"And that's why you taught him what you did..." Connor finishes for him.

Max nods and says, "I learned long ago that no one was going to protect me. I wanted Ethan to be able to protect himself in case I wasn't able to be around."

As we're all letting the morning's discoveries settle, the sound of a car door outside pulls my wolf to the surface.

Who the hell is trespassing on my territory?! he snarls in my head. I have to agree. Whoever came here just now must be looking to die.

TWENTY-TWO

<u>Ethan</u>

Sneaking into the packhouse and climbing into this hole again is something I hate to have to do. Every time I've done it since that day when I was six is like reliving it all over again. So far, so good. The panic that hits every time I am here will recede in a moment. Even after they tried to kill me, this was still my secret place. I'm honestly amazed they never bothered to get the lock on the window fixed after all this time, though.

I climb into the hole once the panic dies down and curl up to nap. This is the only place I know that no one will look for me. I mean, what kind of idiot can fall asleep in the place where they were almost murdered? The kind that spent eight years sleeping in the place where they were repeatedly murdered, that's who.

Grabbing Mr. Whiskers from my bag, I curl up into a ball and let the dreamworld take me. I hope for blessed oblivion, but the memory of that day eventually comes back. Looks like the memory gods decided this one doesn't get to be locked away. I guess it's time to remember it after all.

The kids from school are following me down here and watching me climb inside. They don't know about the secret room behind the vault. No one does because the only people who came down here are the stuffy old men talking about heritage and history and hysterectomies or some other H words. They're no fun.

I come down here to hide my secrets in the secret room. That's where I keep my journals. That's where I drew my story on the wall like the cavemen. That's where I put that big folder with my name on it. It had a bunch of mumbo jumbo and big words all over it, so I also brought down a dictionary.

Regeneration is a cool word, means to grow something back. It's in the folder a lot of times, so I know it's important to remember. Some lizards can even regrow like an arm or a leg or a tail. Sounds like what Deadpool can do. Connor showed me a Deadpool comic once, but Mom went nuts over it being in my room. I think I may even still have the scar from the belt on my ass from that one...

Ass... he he.

I can swear here too. No one ever hears me down here so I can say what I want. I start giggling at the thought of all the words that I get to say finally.

I jump when there's a big bang and the room shakes. The whirring and clicking noises that follow are sounds I've never heard before. I crack open the door to my secret room to look out and all I see is darkness. It's pitch black. The only light I have is my little number birthday candle I use to light my secret room. The six is almost gone now. it looks like a zero and it just keeps melting down.

I don't like the dark.

"HELLO?" I yell out and the echo in the small space hurts my ears.

I hear a slight thudding from the darkness. Is someone knocking? If I can hear them, they can hear me, right? In my rush to lock my secret room, I drop my candle, and it goes out.

It's so dark. I'm so scared.

I'm screaming as loud as I can.

I'm pounding on every wall.

I don't even know where the door is anymore. I've been screaming for so long. Why can't anyone hear me? Why won't anyone come get me?

I keep screaming long after sound stops coming out.

I keep pounding long after I feel the bones in my hands cracking and breaking.

I keep at it long after feeling the wetness of something sliding up my arms as I keep raising my fists to pound.

It's getting harder to breathe, but I keep screaming. Someone will find me. I know someone will.

Even if they don't care about me, Mom and Dad will care that I'm not home for dinner. I'll take the belt again. I'll take whatever Mom gives me for a punishment. I just want to go home.

I can't lift my arms anymore. My screams have turned to coughing. It's getting harder to even do that.

Connie will come find me. Even if Mom and Dad decide not to, Connie will come....

Connie has a game tonight; I realize as my brain gets really fuzzy. My chest is starting to really hurt. The coughing has turned to gasping.

No one is looking for me. Connie has a game... I'm going to be in so much trouble for missing it...

Ric

As I get ready to rip this intruder a new asshole, I'm brought to my knees by a memory from Ethan. I can hear his soft snores coming from my phone's speaker, so I know he's sharing his dream with me.

Connor and Max rush over to me and start looking around for something to fight.

"Connor, take care of whoever it is," I tell him.

"Max, I need you here to keep watch," I tell my warrior. "Ethan is sending me something in his sleep and I don't know how much this is going to incapacitate me."

Connor looks like he wants to argue, but at my look of pain, he acquiesces. I don't think he can handle knowing more about what his brother went through right now. I don't even think I can handle it, but my boy isn't giving me a choice.

"Let's get you in the chair, Ric." Max says as he leads me to my father's chair. Hopefully this is something quick so that we can go get my boy before he disappears on us again.

Connor is able to get rid of our uninvited guest pretty quickly. It was a nosey human who drives past on his way to work and was curious as to why there was a car here. No one had been here in so many years, so it probably would stand out. Max doesn't buy it and neither do I. It doesn't matter how curious you might be, unless you own the property or know who does, there's no reason to be knocking on any door in this territory.

Right now, I'm focusing on this memory Ethan is sharing with me. We're two hours into it now and I'm inconsolable. I'm living the horror of that night with him. Two hours he was down in that vault screaming until he had no voice, turning his hands into mincemeat, suffocating... and his only worry was that he was going to be in trouble for missing dinner.

I can tell we're getting to the end of the memory. He's having trouble breathing. He's stopped moving...

I'm amazed at his unwavering faith in his big brother. He truly never questioned whether Connor would look for him. The unyielding faith... Is this how Jack sees me?

Any minute now, I'm going to see my father open the door. I know my father saved him. I know he didn't die that day. Any minute...

I slide out of the chair to the floor as I feel his anguish at realizing Connor isn't coming. Connor couldn't come. That was the night of the championship game for our middle school basketball tournament. We were all in the gym winning the trophy while Ethan was down there alone and screaming into the darkness.

Any second, my dad will open the door... Any second...

The memory cuts off with no sign of rescue and I fall facedown on the floor sobbing.

How did he survive? There was no sound of the door being opened at all. There was no noise at all except his final rattling breath and then nothing. How long was he not breathing before the door was opened? Who would even be alive who could know? I have to know how we all failed this boy so much!

"What is it, Boss-Man?" Max asks me as I sit back up and raise my head to the ceiling. "What did he share with you?"

"He actually stopped breathing before the door was opened," I say and get shocked looks in return. "He didn't even know he was dying. He..." I can't even say it.

"He what?" Connor asks. "What, Ric? I didn't even know my little brother was the one locked in down there and you're telling me he stopped breathing in that hole. He *what?!*"

I can't look at them. I stare out the window that faces the front of the house. The blue sky reminds me of the color of Ethan's eyes.

"He believed you would save him when he missed dinner. He had hope..." I whisper to the room.

I steady myself and look Connor in the eyes, so he understands just how much we all let him down.

"He had hope," I start again. "Until he remembered we had the basketball game."

I have to choke back my own sobs to continue, "And he accepted that your game, *our* game, was more important than his life... how in the hell does a six-year-old get so mistreated that a basketball game is more important than their life, even to them?"

We're all looking a little wet in the eyes when my phone alerts me to movement at the back of the house.

"If Ethan is moving on, we need to follow," I say as I switch the phone to viewing the back yard.

It's not Ethan. The camera is picking up about five to seven humans in tactical gear with weapons.

"Looks like the visitor was the welcoming committee," Max says with a sadistic smile. "Let's fuck some shit up!"

My wolf and I agree as we head toward the back staircase. My mate is in this house and he's been through more than enough. It's time to get a little stress relief while my baby boy finishes his nap.

TWENTY-THREE

<u>Ethan</u>

The trip down memory lane is not what I wanted to experience. Waking up again in this place almost sent me into a full-on spiral down into thumb sucking, but I'm holding it together, barely. Judging by the amount of light coming in through the window, it's about time for me to move on.

Opening up my secret room, there's just enough light to find everything I want to take with me. I stuff everything I can into my backpack, but it won't close. I forgot how much stuff I gathered in here over the years. I spent a lot of time snatching up every piece of paper I could find with my name on it. I'm not leaving it behind before I get a chance to go through everything.

I ignore the blankets and things I can replace out in the world when I'm on my mission. What I take are the files I stole from Alpha's office and my dad's home office over the years. I take my real birth certificate, not the one that was peddled out to the rest of the pack. I take the file that turns out contains my medical records up to age five, when I stopped going to the doctor. I take the journals I stole from my mom's filing cabinets. I take the weapons I made for my protection. I take my journals to help me understand the clues I missed back then.

I grab so much that the backpack still can't seem to hold everything, so I dump it all out. I take the stuff from my secret room, my superhero toothbrush, and Mr. Whiskers. His head has to poke out the top, but I get it all to fit, finally. I leave behind my changes of clothes and the picture book I took from Jack's room. I'll replace that once I'm on the road.

I turn on the phone to see what day it is and there's a message on the screen from a number I don't know. Not surprising considering I don't know any numbers. I'm kind of glad I found the outlet in the park bathroom to charge my phone up a bit.

> **Alpha Daddy**
> Stay put in the hole, Little Blue. We got
> company and it's going to get messy.

Daddy found me!

I don't know if I'm happy or want to run away again. But Daddy says to stay put, so I'll stay put for now. I sit at the edge of the vault and let my legs dangle down and wait for him to come down and get me when he's done with the company.

They must be watching an action movie because that sounds an awful lot like gunshots. Max must have picked out the movie for them to watch.

"Mr. Whiskers, do you think we should go back with Daddy?" I look at my bear seriously. "I think he just wants to help us, right? I mean he hasn't tried to force us back at all and he could have just taken us back while we were napping."

Of course, Mr. Whiskers agrees with me. He's smart like that.

The sounds of the movie are getting louder. Is Max trying to go deaf?

I didn't react to the sound of the breaking glass, but I *did* react to the blood dripping over my left eye.

Not a movie then as I turn to see the bullet hole in the wall next to my head. Reaching up to wipe away the blood, I realize it's just a cut. Funny enough, they never shot me in the lab. I'm not sure how my body will heal from an actual bullet, but I'm sure better equipped to handle getting shot than the rest of them, with the whole not able to die thing and all.

"Come on Mr. Whiskers. It's time for me and Stabby to get to work." I say as I pull the blade from the neck of my teddy.

I can't hold in the excitement anymore. Time to take what I've learned and put it into action. I just have to remember...

No killing... No killing... No killing.

TWENTY-FOUR

Ethan

Sneaking back out through the window is a bit easier with the glass removed. At least I didn't need to worry about it squeaking again. Not that anyone would notice. It's a freaking war zone out here. There's already about a dozen humans down for the count and there's three more trucks pulling into the yard now. I can see Connor and Ric fighting half a dozen each in their wolf forms.

After glancing around at the carnage, I spot Max. Where did Max get a rocket launcher?!

Oops. Better duck.

One of the three approaching trucks goes boom and I feel a piece of shrapnel lodge in my upper thigh.

"Well, that hurt," I mutter as yank the rusty metal out and watch the hole start to shrink. The blood loss is going to suck, but after about a month of regular food and water, I'm able to heal a lot faster now.

Blue, get your ass back in the house! Daddy yells in my head.

Silly, Daddy, I tell him while I shake my head and open up Stabby. *It's not fair to take all my fun away. Let me play, please?*

I purposely turn toward him to give him the puppy dog eyes. He's wavering. He's going to give in to me. I just know it. His eyes hold a look of indulgence before it morphs into a look of terror. I want to hurt whoever is causing that look on his face. Before I can seek out the asshole who is scaring my Daddy, fire races down my back. When I turn around, I feel it on my front, too. The howls of the wolves behind me hold rage and grief and it registers...

Dude pulled a sword on me?

As he lines up for the next strike, I send Stabby into his right armpit to cut the tendons and the sword clatters to the ground. Stabby then swings down to sever some more in his right leg. While the guy is trying to balance on one leg and I think grab for a gun, I slice into his left forearm so he can't make with the grabby hands. I follow it up by dropping to the ground and severing the Achilles tendon in his left leg.

The dude drops to the ground like a sack of potatoes, and I wish I could spend more time with him, but there's more people out here that want to hurt my Daddy. Picking up the sword, it's decided. Stabby just got himself a big brother.

My cackles of glee echo across the yard as the wolves rend and Max keeps finding ways to blow shit up. Stabby and his big brother Slash are getting a workout. There's a lot of moaning and groaning around me, but no one is in danger of dying. I can't break my word to the G Lady, after all.

It doesn't take long for the only sounds to be heard are the groans of the guys on the ground around me. Slash and Stabby are tired just like I am. The guys are making too much noise. It's time for their naps. I'm ready for another nap myself.

Daddy, I'm tired. Make them be quiet so I can nap. I send over to Ric as he's wandering around the yard looking for something.

He looks up at me yells in my head, *Get that thumb away from your mouth until I clean it. It's covered and their blood and we don't know where they've been.*

I giggle and his responding smile tells me he's not really angry. Daddy is playing with me. I haven't been this happy since he showed me the little fishies. Max comes over with a big grin on his face and hands me a wet wipe. I don't know where he got it, but I appreciate it. I know my thumb is going to head back toward my mouth soon enough.

"Where'd you get the rocket launcher?" I ask him after I get my hands clean enough and reach for another wipe to clean my face.

He looks at me and winks. "Same place you got your new sword."

One by one, the moaning is getting cut off. I don't really care. As long as I don't kill them, the G Lady cannot hold me responsible. And every single one of them hurt me first.

I walk away from Max while he's admiring my handiwork to head towards Daddy and Connie finishing up on the other side of the yard. Daddy has someone cornered by the pack house. It smells like they pissed themselves. Daddy is good at making people do that. Connie told me he did it to Jessica too.

My thumb pops back out of my mouth when I smell him. I knew my thumb would end up in my mouth, but this smell pulls me completely back to being a grown up. There's no mistaking that stench. I can understand why neither of their wolves wanted to take a bite. I know from experience that it takes about a week's effort to feel even remotely clean again after coming into contact with him. I haven't felt truly clean in over eight years thanks to the subpar specimen of the human race crouching in front of my brother.

Connor's wolf is standing guard over Petey boy as close as he can get and Ric is struggling to get closer due to the smell. I know the feeling. You really can't get any closer without wanting to retch. They're already struggling with it. I spent eight years in close quarters with the smell and even I'm still struggling with keeping my breakfast from Stan down.

I stalk closer and wait for old Paint Peeler to see me before I speak. His eyes widen as zeroes in on me across the yard, stalking him like the prey he is.

He smiles. The dumbass actually thinks my being here means he will escape this. Even though I wish I had nose plugs, I harden my eyes and smile back at him and continue my approach.

Ric and Connie back away as I reach where they are. Max comes closer to see what the fuss is.

"What the fuck is that smell?" Max asks as he pulls up short, holding his nose and dry heaving about a dozen yards behind me. I keep moving towards Pete.

"It's worse up close," Ric chimes in breathing through his mouth as he stares incredulously at me being seemingly unaffected. "My wolf forced the shift back to human. He couldn't take it anymore."

Who is this guy to you, baby bro? Connie asks in my head. I shake my head at them.

"This one is mine," I growl in a commanding tone. "I'm taking him somewhere alone. You can do what you want when I'm done."

"You'll go nowhere with him alone!" Ric yells, but his authority rolls right off of me.

"This is eight years in the making," I reply coldly. "Not even you get to take this from me, Alpha."

He will feel pain for every single thing he did to me. He will know what it means to be helpless. He will know what it means to want to die and have it just out of reach. He will know how it feels to be violated again and again and again...

I realize my thoughts are leaking again as the trio of growls register behind me.

"Max, I need to borrow some stuff," I call back to him.

"Whatcha need, little dude?" he growls out. "Name it and I'll get it."

"I'll think of more later, but can you get me a blowtorch?" I ask. "Oh, and something with a handle like a broom"

His grin is wicked as he tells us, "Let me check the trucks."

Grab the jack while you're at it. I think at him. I don't know what I might want it for, but I plan on keeping my options open.

The dumbass is still smiling as I reach him.

"Come on blue eyes, you know you don't want to hurt old Petey. Remember what happened last time? You sure you want a repeat?" he says, completely ignoring all four of our wolves growling at him. "You get me out of here, I'll make sure to make it real good for you next time, just like that first time, right?"

Before any of the other three can react, I knock him out with a single punch. They would kill him. I don't want him dead, not yet. He needs to suffer first....

Actually no, first he needs a damn bath.

"Hey Max?" I ask while they're all still trying to calm their wolves. "Can you do me a HUGE favor?"

"Anything," he says.

"Can you tie him up and drop him in the pond a few times. I am going to be around him for a while to take care of my business, but I don't want to destroy my nose permanently while I'm at it."

"I'll grab the rope," says my brother laughing all the way to the shed at the side of the yard.

"Where do you want him when you're done?" Max asks me while Connie is grabbing supplies.

"The basement of the old Beta house," I tell him.

"There was no basement at the house," Connie tells him returning with the rope. "Just a small wine cellar."

"There's a basement." I say to my brother. "They just didn't let you see it...what they did to me down there."

That place has everything I'll need and more. And best part is, the fire didn't touch it because of the stupid measures Mom took to soundproof it.

"Can we have a minute?" Connor asks the others and they both look to me for my approval. I nod to them to let them know I'm ok with it. It's time to let Connor know just what kind of people his parents really were.

Max hogties the unconscious Pete and literally drags him toward the pond, gagging the whole way. The poor fishies.

Ric meets my eyes trying to convey something.

I'm just a thought away if you need me, Blue, he sends to me with a small smile before following Max at a considerable distance.

Once they're out of earshot, Connor turns on me.

"How do you know about this basement and I don't?" Connor asks me, trying to intimidate me.

I'll be honest, when I was a kid, he could do it. He's my big brother. He was my rock, the only thing I could ever count on in the hellscape of my childhood. But it won't work on me. I've been through too much to worry about disappointing him now.

"You don't know about a lot of things, Connie," I say under my breath while trying to decide how much he should know. The look on his face tells me that he heard me, but he's not pushing. Connor never pushes. That's why he's the golden boy. That's why he's the one that needs to stay pure and strong and good.

I'm the one who has always been shrouded in emptiness and filth. I can't even say darkness because at least the dark can hide things. It was always empty around me, unless Connor was around. He's the only reason I know what light and happiness really are.

"What did you see in there?" Connor asks me.

There's hope in his eyes that I only had to witness things down there or that it was some sort of timeout. I can see it in his eyes. He knows deep down, but he's fighting it.

Mom and Dad truly did love him with all of their hearts. I can't say the same for me, though. Dad tried in his own way. He'd never win father of the year, but he didn't ever physically hurt me. He even stopped Mom on a few occasions, not many but it was at least something. He also did what he could to isolate me from the pack to save me from the bullies. I like to think he didn't know that he was hurting me with that, too.

I start to explain to my big brother, "Dad tried his best to help."

Connor's eyes start turning a bit glassy. I can't do this if he's going to cry.

"If you're going to bawl like a baby, then get the hell out of my sight!" I yell.

I don't mean to be mad at him, but if this is enough to set him off, the he needs to get the fuck away from me before I hurt him. I never want to hurt my big brother, my hero. He gets to be happy. I went through everything I did so he could be happy. He needs to be happy. That's what I've always been told. It's always been all for him. Why doesn't he understand that?

Connor wipes at his eyes and straightens his posture. "I'm good, Ethan," he tells me evenly. "I need to know."

Turning my back to him, I continue the trip down memory lane. I can't look at him if I'm going to get through this.

TWENTY-FIVE

<u>*Ethan*</u>

"It started just before my fifth birthday," I start. I decide to switch to mind speak because these things don't need to be overheard.

I was excited because you were almost done with school for the year and I'd get to play with you and Ric all day again. I ran too fast around the corner from the kitchen and wiped out on the floor right next to the dining room table.

Apparently, I hit my head on something when I went down and got a gash on my forehead. Mom started to yell at me for getting blood on the rug but then she stopped all of a sudden. She looked confused for a second when I sat up and then she got REALLY angry.

Next thing I knew, I was being locked in my room. I don't know why she didn't just take me to the emergency room, but I was laying in bed with Mr. Whiskers when the doctor came in. She didn't even pick out clean clothes for me or let me clean up the mess. *I always had to clean up my messes or else I didn't get to eat until dinner, you know.*

I glance back at Connor and he's got a very confused look on his face. Surely, this isn't the first time he's heard of this kind of thing regarding me. That rule was in effect as long as I could remember. Most days when he was at school, I didn't eat between breakfast and dinner.

I can't look at him anymore, so I face the wall of trees in the distance and continue.

So, the doc sat down and used one of those weird smelling wipes to clean away the blood from my wound. But apparently there was no wound. He told Mom it was all some prank and that she shouldn't be wasting his time and that I should be punished for wasting his time as well. He slammed the door on his way out.

Mom was really really mad at that. You know she never liked being talked down to. I don't think she ever let you see just how much it bothered her, but this time was apparently her breaking point. She grabbed my arm so hard it snapped the bone. I screamed that she was hurting me, but she didn't care. There was no one else around to hear me.

She dragged me to the wine cellar that you knew existed and lifted a bottle on the top shelf... and the wall opened up.

It was just a mostly empty office back then. There was a desk, some chains in the corner, other odds and ends sort of just thrown in for storage, and a wall of filing cabinets... nothing like the mad scientist lair it would become later.

She threw me to the floor as soon as we were in the room and told me to get my ass up on the desk. I'd never seen her so mad, so I did my best to try and do it. I could barely reach the top of it and my arm hurt so much. But I pulled myself up somehow.

Mom screamed in rage when she looked at my arm. It didn't hurt as much, but that apparently made her even more mad.

She used the chains to hold me down on the desk and left me in the room. There were no windows, so I was alone in the dark for a long time. Or at least it felt like a long time. I was only four at the time, so it could have been five minutes. Five minutes felt like forever back then.

I can smell the salt from his tears. I need to finish telling this before I end up crying with him, for him. I don't want to hurt my big brother, but he needs to know this, even if it's not everything. Giving him this should stop him from digging further. He doesn't need to know it all.

She came back after a while. I had stopped crying long before the door opened back up. As she flicked on the light in the room, I noticed a file in her hand. She put it in one of the drawers of the filing cabinet as I watched.

She kept mumbling things about evil spawn and how unfair her life was and how much of a mistake it was for me even existing. I didn't understand it at the time but didn't really get a chance to think on it either before the wooden baton started connecting with my body. I don't even know where she got it to be honest.

The gasp from behind me is one of surprise. Yeah, Connie was Mom's pride and joy. She never let him see the worst parts of her. Thank every deity in existence that the only thing he got from her is looks. He got his eyes from his dad, though. I don't think I could handle looking into her eyes again.

I go on so that we can be done with this. It's almost over and I can tell Ric and Max are ready for me.

I don't know how long she beat me. I felt bones breaking everywhere. To be honest, I don't know what hurt more. Was it the physical pain of my body getting shattered piece by piece? Or was it the pain of my four-year-old heart knowing this was my mommy doing this to me? I could never decide.

I feel arms wrap around me. Connor is sweet for trying to

comfort me now... or perhaps he's seeking comfort. Either way, I can't stay strong with him touching me, so I shrug him off.

After I finished healing and she finished writing something in a journal, she unchained me and threw some clean clothes at me. Mom always picked my clothes out for me. Otherwise, I'd be an embarrassment to the family, she used to say.

When we got back upstairs, she set me to the task of cleaning up the blood from earlier. I had to hurry because you would be getting home from school soon and Mom said if you saw the blood you'd be scared, and I'd have to go back to the room behind the wine.

I finally turned back to face my brother. He's kneeling with his head bowed. I watch each tear fall and join the puddle that has formed on the ground in front of him. He can never know how much worse it got if this is how broken he is after just one story. This was only the first time she took me to the basement.

I grab his chin and raise his face to mine. He has to understand this one final point and then let it go. I don't get to dwell in it, so neither does he.

"That wasn't my only trip to the basement," I tell him. "There were many more and for various reasons."

"Sometimes it was because I upset her," I explain. "Others were because she wanted to test a theory on me."

"But she always found a way to get me into that room... and I let her," I whisper. "I let her because she was Mom and I didn't know back then that Mom was a monster."

I let go of his chin and head toward the stairs in the charred remains, fighting my own tears. That woman got the last of my tears a long time ago. I stopped crying for her the day I realized she would never love me back.

I feel a tear roll down my cheek as I reach up to lift the bottle that would open the door. Wiping it away, I let the cold surround my heart.

I open the door to my nightmare, only this time I get to be the monster. I watch as Max and Ric toss their bundle on the table in the center of the room. I flick on the switch as I enter. The hum of the overhead lights sends a shiver down my spine from the memories.

I lead Max and Ric outside before I slam the door on them and throw the lock.

"Hello Petey..." I sneer at the man on the table. "Let's have some fun, shall we?"

TWENTY-SIX

Ric

After depositing the putrid smelling human in the basement, we got locked out. The look on Ethan's face is that of a killer. My wolf is demanding we kill the bastard and save our mate's innocence, but we're way too late for that. The little bombshells he keeps dropping mean we've always been too late for that.

The lab set up in the basement of the old house reminded me of those old horror films with the mad scientists. Is that what his parents were to him? Was he just an experiment to them? How often was he down there? And why is Connor so shocked that the house has a basement?

My Beta is looking a little green sitting in the bed of the truck we confiscated from the humans. I wasn't putting that smelly dude in my car to bring him over here and neither I nor Max was willing to carry him over. The open bed of one of the trucks solved our problem.

I don't ask him what they talked about while we were gone. I have the feeling I already know after seeing the lab set up. Connor just found out his parents experimented on his little brother and none of us knew. I want to be here for him, but at the same time I want to punch him. How in the hell did he live under the same roof as them, under the same roof where it was happening, and not know a thing? But judging by the look on his face, he's beating himself up enough for both of us.

We all learned a bit more about Ethan's history here... more than we wanted to know. I hate that he's locked in with this guy, especially after the little they let slip about their time together. My wolf wants to disembowel the guy and choke him out with his own intestines. I can't say it sounds like a bad idea, but this is Ethan's chance at closure. We all let too much get taken from him already. He gets to have this.

We've been sitting for hours outside the charred remains of the old Beta house. Connor is practically catatonic, and Max occasionally goes off to take something else down to Ethan. I don't want to know why Ethan wanted a cheese grater. He should be coming back up soon, I hope.

Looking up at a commotion from the remains, I see Max running for the bushes... and he's blowing chunks. I don't want to know what he saw to cause that. He's the guy I go to for torture when it is needed. I'm better off not knowing. Apparently, Connor doesn't take the hint and uses his ability... and now he's running for the bushes.

Blue? Maybe start to clean up a bit? The guys are out here losing their lunch with what they're seeing. I send out to him in an attempt to start to bring him back. It's been over six hours already and I want to get us away from here while it's still dark out.

Sorry Daddy. I'm almost done. I just have to finish my necklace and I'll be ready.

Necklace? Oh, my little psychopath is going to need a lot of snuggles once we get him all cleaned up. I'm thinking Mr. Whiskers is going to need some help with the nightmare defense when we all go to sleep after this.

Although, something tells me my Beta and my warrior won't be able to sleep well after seeing what they've seen. I give a little head shake as I continue to hear their retching in the background.

Another hour or so passes and the sun is starting to creep onto the eastern horizon.

Ok baby, time's up. Put your toys away now. It's time for a bath and bed. The moon is going to sleep, and we need to as well. I send out to him

I'm not sure why I'm talking to him like he's little right now. It just seems to fit the situation better.

OK Daddy. I'm done. Want me to rinse off down here while Max and Connie clean up my mess? Or do you want me to come straight to you? He asks me. I can feel him slipping further into his little self now that he's done with what he set out to do.

I need to see him at his worst, so I tell him to come straight to me. Before my boy gets within earshot, I tell Max, "If you still have any grenades left, blow the basement to bits. That fucker doesn't get to live another day."

Max goes a little green and swallows hard before saying, "As long as I don't have to look in there, sure thing. It was bad enough hours ago. I don't want to see, especially knowing the piece of shit is still alive."

Connor chimes in with a whisper, "No one who hurt Ethan deserves pity. Us included."

Can't say I disagree, brother. We're all silent while we watch with fascination as Ethan rises from the ruins of the house, completely soaked in blood, with the sun behind him. He's like a little avenging angel, or demon depending on what side you're on. My little phoenix rising from the ashes. My little bluebird.

Nodding to Max, I go get my boy.

"Come on little bluebird," I say as I take his arm. "Let's have a dip in the pond first and then we'll go to a hotel."

"Ok Daddy," he sighs happily as his thumb inches towards his face. Before I can even try to stop him, his nose wrinkles and his thumb goes back down.

"Daddy, I need soap. Lots and lots of soaps... and bubbles. Make sure I have bubbles," he tells me seriously as we arrive at the pond.

"All the bubbles in the world, baby," I smile at him. "We'll rinse off here and then get you squeaky clean at the hotel with lots of bubbles in the bathtub," I tell him.

As he smiles up at me, his bright blue eyes are almost glowing out of the mask of blood and hair and other things that I don't want to know what they are that are on his face.

TWENTY-SEVEN

Ric

Ethan ended up falling asleep as I carried him back to the truck, so we had to reconfigure how we were doing this. Connor went back to the pack house to gather our stuff and load up my car. Max drove me and Ethan in the truck to a motel just outside the old pack borders. He woke up just long enough for me to scrub the stench off of him in the shower and pick all of the bits of Pete out of his hair, but Ethan was zonked out again as soon as he was dried off.

Connor met us at the motel, and we all took the time to scrub off ourselves and put on clean clothes. We didn't have any more clean clothes for Ethan. His backpack only had a bunch of books, files, and papers along with some interesting looking items that I can only assume were weapons he made. There was nothing else in the bag except the phone charger and the superhero toothbrush.

Now that we are all dressed and not smelling like a decaying corpse, I don't want to stick around the area any longer. We decide to put him in one of my shirts and a pair of Connor's shorts that happen to have a drawstring. Even at the tightest, they won't stay up if he's really moving around, but for in the car it should work.

Once everyone is dressed, we load up and head for home. It's been almost two weeks, and we need to get back to Jackie. He needs to see his big brothers for himself. And my wolf needs to take care of the members of my pack that thought it was appropriate to abuse a child. Jessica isn't going to be the only one being judged at the next full moon. The whole pack might be going down as well.

As we cross the border from Ohio to Kentucky, Ethan cuddles closer to me more in the backseat.

I love you, Daddy. I hear him sigh in my head.

Daddy loves you, Little Blue. So very very much. I think back to him. He wiggles a bit more and his snores fill the silence of the car.

Daddy will make them pay. My thoughts continue even though he's out cold.

Don't take away all of my fun. I hear him pouting in my head. I chuckle in response and just pull him closer to join him in a quick nap.

My phone blaring over the speakers wakes us up. Connor answers it by hitting the screen in the console.

"Everything ok back home, Jack?" He asks in concern.

There's a sound of rustling and a thump and everyone but Ethan sits up a bit straighter.

"oomph!" is the only response we get from the little guy and my wolf is starting to wake up as well.

"Answer us, little man," Max warns him with the start of a growl.

We don't generally talk to Jack like that, but we're all keyed up and this call isn't starting off putting us at ease.

"Sorry. Sorry." He says and we all let out a breath. "Dropped the phone under the bed when you picked up." He explains. "When are you guys coming home? When is Ethan coming home? Tony misses him and Junior misses him too."

Oh Goddess, I forgot about the knife that my mate gave my seven-year-old brother.

Max laughs at that and says, "Keep Junior tucked away until we get home, you little scamp."

Jackie laughs, but he definitely caught that his questions weren't answered.

"You guys gotta come home soon. You promised we'd go on our trip this summer for my birthday! I need all of you there."

Oh crap. We've been so caught up in finding Ethan, I forgot all about our trip planning.

"Do you really think we'd miss your birthday trip?" Connor answers for us all.

Ethan flinches at that and I'm thrust into another memory as he relives it in his sleep. I'm glad I'm not driving.

Coming out of that memory, I'm gutted. Hearing my own voice and knowing how it made him feel at the time is probably the most shocking part of that whole memory. Knowing he didn't blame us and was looking forward to seeing us the next morning does a lot to help alleviate some of my guilt, but not nearly enough.

Glancing at the console, I realize about an hour has passed and the phone call with Jackie is long over. I look down at Ethan's peaceful face as he continues to snore against my side.

"What the hell was that?" Connor asks me to pull my attention back to the front of the vehicle. I can see now that they've switched seats. "You were in like a trance there. I had to tell Jackie you fell asleep on us."

"He did that before in the office," Max breaks in before I can say anything. "When he had the breakdown, remember?"

As Connor looks over to his left, Max continues while keeping his eyes glued to the stretch of highway in front of him.

"He didn't freak out for nothing," he tells my Beta. "Apparently, little dude there is reliving some stuff in his sleep based on what's going on around him and our Alpha is picking up the wavelength or whatever when it happens."

That's actually a pretty accurate description of what's been going on. I'm kind of surprised that Max got all of that without even talking to me about what I'm seeing or what's happening.

"How'd you figure it out?" I ask him, again making sure Ethan is still sleeping.

"Before, in the office, you knew things that I know our little dude didn't share," he says to us both.

"I'm not the sharing kind of guy" Ethan groans as he goes to sit up. I miss the contact but let him stretch as much as he can. "Where are we now? I thought I was getting a bubble bath?" He winks at me.

"Just left Tennessee. We should be home in about two hours give or take," Max replies tapping the GPS showing on the console screen.

"Have we been going straight through?" I ask them both.

None of us got any sleep the night before we got to the old town, and we haven't slept since. I think I might have dozed off a bit here in the backseat, but neither of the guys up front has slept.

"We've been switching off driving every three hours so the other can nap," Connor explains. At least that makes me feel a little better about the fact that they've done all the driving since we left the motel.

Ethan suddenly starts looking around like he's about to cry. He's starting to panic as he's not seeing what he expects to see.

"What are you needing, baby boy?" I asked him while combing my fingers through his hair to calm him. "Tell us and we'll look too."

"My backpack. I need my backpack," he says as he's starting to hyperventilate. "Mr. Whiskers is in there. And my journals. And the reports. And the stories. And the secret files. And Mr. Whiskers. Did I mention him? He's mostest important. I need Mr. Whiskers. Where is he?"

He's nearly hysterical now. Max has already pulled over and Connor races to the back of the car to dig out the backpack. I'm just holding him to my chest, letting him hear my heartbeat as he's screaming through the sobs for Mr. Whiskers.

Max meets my eyes in the rearview. They are all going to pay for what they did to our boy. Connor dives back into the car and thrusts the bear into the backseat, smacking me in the face in the process. My reaction to the small injury was apparently funny to the little boy in my lap. His giggle as he grabbed the teddy got us all to relax again.

Connor hands me the backpack more gently than the teddy bear and I put it between my feet. If what is in here is that important to my boy, It will be guarded from here on out. It won't be leaving our sight.

"Did we remember Slash?" Ethan mumbles in Max's direction as he pulls us back onto the highway.

"What's slash buddy?" Connor asks him turning around in his seat to look at us.

"He's Stabby's big brother. Big brothers and little brothers shouldn't be separated once they find each other again," he explains, putting weight to the words for Connor to figure out. This is directed at him and somehow this blade represents Connor to him, and I really need to pick up a psychology book when we get home.

"Your sword is in the back with the rest of the weapons," Max explains while the rest of us are still puzzling out what the hell my boy is talking about. "I'll get you a good quality scabbard so that you can have both Slash and Stabby with you when you go out. Sound good?"

Just how armed is my warrior going to make my mate for daily excursions? Then again, after everything that's happened, I wouldn't object to getting him a rocket launcher if we could figure out a way to conceal it... and for it to not be lethal. This no killing thing is quite difficult to plan around and still give him the tools to keep himself safe.

"Mmmmhmm," Ethan mumbles around his thumb as he nuzzles back into my side.

"And he's back asleep," says Connor with a smile. "When he's peaceful like this, I can almost think what I found out in the last few days is all just bad dreams."

Max snorts in response to that but keeps his mouth shut.

"Care to share with the class?" I asked him.

"You guys think finding out you were coddled is a bad dream. I lived worse than your worst nightmares. And that boy there? He lived through hell itself," Max spits out as he takes the exit that will bring us to the highway through town next to the hospital. "Better wise up and accept your *bad dreams* before that beautiful kid back there starts to think he's too broken to be around you anymore. Cuz I guarantee that's where he's headed if you don't pull your heads out of your asses."

TWENTY-EIGHT

<u>Ethan</u>

Max is right. I am too broken to be around good guys like my brother and Ric. I can't even bring myself to call him Daddy anymore. He doesn't deserve to be stuck with someone as broken as I am. He made himself stuck with me by claiming me, but I can fix that. I just need to reject him and claim someone else, right?

My wolf growls at that. *Only mate we will ever take will be fated mate. No claiming.*

But how do we set Daddy free if you won't claim someone else? I don't want to hurt him anymore, I tell my wolf.

Heat will fix. Heat comes soon. When no babe comes, he'll recall claim. Wolf wants fated mate. My wolf replies.

So, I just have to go through my heat with Ric. He's going to do that stuff to me and there won't be a baby and he'll revoke his claim and then he'll let us go. We can go finish our mission and save Jack. No more claim, no more confusion.

And no more Daddy...

I manage to keep still and quiet, but I can see the drops of my tears hitting my borrowed shirt sleeve and the wet spot just grows as the ride goes on.

When my heat ends, I'll go far away. I'll go in search of Mr. Weird Voice and save Jackie. I'll be like Deadpool. They can keep killing me. I'll keep coming back. I'll die a million times if it means they don't get to touch a hair on Jack's head ever again...

Pulling into the garage, I pretend to still be asleep. Ric and Connie are fooled, but Max isn't. I hear his chuckle as Ric lifts me into his arms.

"You're going to spoil him," Max says to the Alpha.

"He deserves to be spoiled today and every day from here on out," Daddy replies. Not Daddy, Ric. I have to remember to call him Ric. He's not going to be Daddy once my heat is over and there's no baby.

Ric carries me into the house and up the steps to his bedroom. After he lays me in the bed, he kisses my forehead and goes to leave the room. I feel another hand brush my hair off my face... Connor.

"Does he feel warm to you?" Connie asks the rest of the room.

Max places his big oaf hand on my forehead and sighs.

"He's going into heat," he says "I started smelling it in the car and yeah this confirms it."

Ric walks back into the room carrying a cup of water with a lid on it. "Confirms what?" he asks. "I wasn't listening. I had to side-track Jack who wants to see Ethan like yesterday."

"He's going into heat," Max is explaining to Da... Ric. "Connor and Jack are the only ones safe around him. You and I wouldn't have any control."

I need to quit pretending to sleep now. They all need to know something if this is how they're determining how I spend my heat.

"Connie can't stay," I tell them, opening my eyes.

"Listen, kid, I know it's embarrassing that your brother would see you like that but our nature won't abide incest, especially as close as siblings, "Max explains to me like I'm stupid.

"Hey fuckface," I interrupt his alphasplaining. "I remember eighth grade biology thank you very much. Considering it's the last year of classes I had, I remember most of them pretty damn well."

They're all looking at me like I grew another head. Good. Maybe I can piss them off enough that they don't follow next time I leave.

"Connie can't stay because we aren't brothers," I start to explain, but Connor interrupts like the alpha-hole he is.

"I was there when they brought you home from the hospital," he tells me. "We looked exactly alike except for hair and eye color until we each hit puberty. I think I would know..." I cut him off the same way I did with Max.

"YOU *DON'T* KNOW!" I yell at him. "None of you know! Those people you called my parents never conceived me. The man you call my father had zero blood ties to me, but he at least didn't actively treat me like I was a bug under his shoes. The woman you call my mother was my aunt. She was saddled with me because the Alpha couldn't afford to have a werewolf baby end up in the human foster care system. I was put in that family to hide the fact that a sixteen-year-old hybrid half-sister of the Beta's wife died during childbirth after telling no one who the father was."

I have to take a breath and try to calm down. I have to remember that even I didn't know this before yesterday. I only read a few pages from the journals, but they were definitely enlightening.

"I am the unwanted bastard child of a wolf-less hybrid of a distinguished but disgraced family line who was only kept alive because it would look bad if I wasn't," I finish as the tears finally start to fall.

Ric tries to climb in next to me to hold me, but I push him out of the bed. Hell, I managed to send him flying into the dresser. I'm not in the mood to be held. I just want to be alone.

With a look, Max gets the memo and starts ushering them both out of the room.

Want me to lock the place up and stay on guard until it passes? Max sends to me as he's herding everyone back downstairs.

Ric can stay. I told him. *We need to prove he's not my mate so he'll free us.*

How in the hell does the Alpha staying through your heat get you free of his claim? He growls back at me.

Pretty sure the only way I'll ever have sex again is my heat. I hear him stutter on his steps heading to the kitchen. *If it needs to happen, I'd rather not be fully aware, and Ric is too good to ever attempt it without an outside force pushing him.*

I can hear some murmuring from downstairs, but I just curl up and try to calm down in preparation for what I'm about to endure for the next forty-eight to seventy-two hours. I hope the books are right and I won't remember anything beyond the first few hours until it's over. I already remember too much from the other times.

"He wants WHAT?!" Ric's voice rings through the house as the tears start to fall again.

I just want to set him free. I'll do it again one more time. I won't even cry or whine or even move. I'll even let him strap me down. I can't hold him back. He's got a pack to run and I'm just a bastard with a death wish who can't die.

I can hear Ric stomping up the stairs, so I try to prepare myself for convincing him that I want him to fuck me. I mean, I want him. I always did ever since the first time I realized that two boys could actually be together. But I'm broken that way now. So, I have to pretend. I can't be afraid. I have to be strong. I have to be strong enough to do this for him... to free him.

TWENTY-NINE

Ric

Max stumbles as we come into the kitchen. I mean, yeah who could have seen that revelation coming? I figure we have about two hours or so until Ethan's heat really kicks in, so I'm going to cook up some food to leave here for him before we all vacate the house for the next three days.

"He's not my little brother?" Connor asks into the quiet of the room while I start a few soups on the stove. I need to make sure there's nutritious and quick to reheat foods available for my boy for the next three days.

"He's the same kid you grew up with. Why the hell does everyone get hung up on this DNA bullshit?" Max growls at us. "That kid is more your brother than he is a son to any of the people who had any claim to be his parents."

"Speaking of parents and DNA, your ass came from two of the worst specimens of our kind that I've ever seen and yeah that's saying something," he continues to Connor, "But you are one of the best people I know regardless of your species. You care, dude. That's not DNA. That's love and you and the little dude have it."

I nod and hum an agreement as I throw more veggies into various pots on the stove. "Still doesn't mean any of us are staying through his heat," I add in. "The love might be there, but without the DNA to back it up, we can't risk it. We don't need him having nightmares of his big brother trying to do that with him."

Connor looks relieved that I'm making the call and putting my foot down as the Alpha. I think Ethan would recover if it happened. Connor wouldn't.

"Actually, Alpha," Max cuts in. He only calls me Alpha when he knows it's something I'm not going to want to hear.

"Spit it out, Max."

"Ethan says he wants you here," he rushes to get it out. "He wants you to be here so you can take him during his heat so he won't want to say no and so you can't be honorable and stop if he does change his mind..."

I explode. My wolf is uncharacteristically silent on this one. Usually when something threatens to harm our mate, he is the first to jump in. But this time? Radio silence.

I'm pacing the kitchen so that I don't reach out and decapitate my head warrior. I know he is just relaying the message from Ethan but damn it. I can't hurt my boy. Even if I was completely mindless in a rut, I would stop if he was afraid. I wouldn't touch him if he didn't want it.

His wolf wants us. Mate has accepted deal with wolf. My wolf tries explaining it to me, but I don't care what kind of deal he has with his wolf. I won't hurt my boy.

I stomp up the stairs and force myself to be calm before I enter the bedroom. It's time to explain to him that he's going to be alone in the house for the next three days and there's nothing he can do to change my mind.

I step into the room and freeze. He's sitting in the bed appearing poised and collected, two things no one would ever associate with Ethan Sinclair. It's his eyes that stop me, though. Those eyes that shine like the perfect summer sky are now dull and lifeless. He's shutting himself off from me, from all of us. I can still see the tear tracks on his face. This is destroying him, and I refuse be a part of it.

"There's food in the kitchen for you. We're all leaving in about an hour," I tell him before he can say anything. "If you need anything just send us a message and we'll drop it through the garage. The house is equipped as a panic room from the inside so no one can get in until you release it. I'll show you the controls."

I turn from the room and head toward my office. It's the location of the controls for the house, of course. It's the only room in the house that truly needs to be able to be secured in the event of an attack. My father was nothing if not paranoid. The old house wasn't like this, so I guess what happened to his Beta scared him. I never really thought about why we got the panic house before. I really was a self-absorbed little prick, wasn't I?

Ethan follows me into my office, but I notice him place Mr. Whiskers outside the door looking towards the window. He takes the time to make sure the teddy stays in place exactly where he wants before he closes the door behind him, leaving the bear as sentry. It's obvious that he's still affected by everything.

I look at him as he wanders around, admiring the artwork. If it wasn't for the bear, I would think he's just fine and that my wolf and I could stay in the house. We could put him in here, past the secondary defense and take care of him.

"The controls to the house are in this drawer," I tell him as I pull out the middle-left drawer of the desk. "The code to unlock them is zero five two three."

He spins around so fast, he almost loses his balance. Grabbing the back of a chair, he steadies himself and looks at me in surprise. "My birthday?" he squeaks.

I nod in response.

"I changed it after my parents passed and I took over the pack with Connor." I told him. "Only a handful of the pack know where the controls are. Fewer know my code. Of the pack, only me, Jack, Connor, and Max know the code to the controls."

"and me" he whispers to himself with a smile.

I nod, feeling he's not quite all together right now. His cheeks are flushed, and I can tell he's breathing heavier. His heat is coming on faster than expected, so it's time to speed this up.

"We're going to get out of the house now. Once the garage closes, use the code and lock us out." I tell him as he leans over to see the control panel. It's pretty straightforward and all the switches are labeled.

"What happens if I hit a wrong button?" he asks, turning to me.

His face is right next to mine and it's taking an extraordinary measure of self-control to keep my wolf from trying to finish the claiming process.

"If the wrong code is entered, a warning will sound, and you have thirty seconds to enter the correct code or the room will lock down," I explain. "If the room locks down, it can only be opened from the outside. Only myself and Connor know where that control is," I finish as he resumes his perusal of the art on the walls. There's not much on the walls so it doesn't take this long to see everything. I'm pretty sure he's trying to delay being left alone.

"So theoretically, I can lock everyone out of the house and then lock myself in here so I can't get out even if I open the house back up?" he asks me without looking away from the family portrait on the wall from when Jackie was an infant. I wonder if he's thinking about his own family pictures. I don't recall seeing any after he was born in the Beta house.

"Yep. That's right," says Max from the doorway as he opens it up and steps in. "This room also cancels out cell phone signals when triggered like that so the intruder can't call out for help or warn any co-conspirators." He winks towards Ethan and gives a sad smile.

My wolf's grumbling at the whole situation stops and his ear perks up like he's heard something he likes.

I walk over to the door to follow Max out now that I've shown Ethan where everything is, but Ethan calls me back to the desk.

"This is the switch for the house, right?" he asks me, pointing to the one labeled as house controls.

I think it's pretty obvious what controls what, but I go over everything with him again. My wolf is getting restless and excited, so I start to head to the door.

"I'll leave you to it then and we'll get out of your way for the next few days," I say as I reach for the door.

The warning alarm starts going off as I turn to Ethan and see a look of triumph on his face. My wolf is jumping for joy inside me as he realizes what our mate's plan is.

I grabbed the door handle and ty to yank it open. It only pulls open about an inch before it's slammed back shut. I try again and can't pull it free. I hear someone grunting on the other side of the door. There's less than ten seconds before I'm locked in with an omega going into heat and I have to get out. I can't risk hurting my boy.

I grab a chair and hurl it at the window. The force is enough to crack the glass that I should be able to jump through now. Before I can take a step, I'm taken to the ground by a silver wolf with the eyes of a summer sky. Ethan's wolf stopped me. And the shutters slam into place on my office.

I'm trapped in this room with an omega in heat and the only one who can call for help to get us out is the one who trapped us in here.

Ethan

Are you sure about this, little dude? Max is asking me for the millionth time. My body keeps getting hotter and I really don't want to spend the next three days alone, horny and in pain, trapped with the memories of the heats I've already gone through.

If you don't figure out how to make sure he stays, I will remove every appendage from your body, joint by joint until you're a torso with a head and a dick and make you watch as I remove it and stuff it in your mouth. I growl at him.

I'm tired of being treated as a fragile thing. No one in my life has ever seen me as valuable. It's like my whole life was a game to try and break me. I even died a few times, more than a few, but I'm still here. I'm still standing. I'm not some wilting flower. I'm a fucking jagger bush, thorn bush, bramble weed. I cause damage to those who hurt me.

Just checking! I'd like to keep all my bits, thank you very much. He says to me as he knocks on the door to the office. I hear the conversation, but it's turning to white noise. I have to get Ric stuck in here. He thinks he's being honorable and noble by leaving me alone. He's just going to cause me more pain if he leaves, but I don't have time to fight with him on that. He's getting ready to go out the door! I have to stop him! It's now or never.

"Is this the switch for the house?" I ask him as he turns back to me.

Of course, it's the switch for the house. The damn label says HOUSE. Playing dumb is frustrating, but I have to give Max a chance to secure the door.

You better keep that door shut if you value your extremities. I growl out to Max while Ric is finishing going over the panel again.

As Ric reaches the door, I hit the number pad. I don't even know what numbers I punch in, but I know they are wrong as the warning alarm starts going off in the room. Ric stares at me in horror. I can see the moment it clicks that this was intentional. I stand between him and the control panel, so he doesn't even try to get to it like I expected. He goes straight for the door and tries to get it open.

It opens about an inch before Max manages to get it closed again. Ric looks like he's not sure whether to be angry or surprised that someone else is helping me in my plans. He tries the door again and can't budge it. Whatever Max managed to come up with, it's working. My plan worked. He's stuck with me in here and we can take care of this mate business once and for all.

The panel reads eight seconds when I hear the cracking of glass. He threw a chair at the window? I thought it was bulletproof glass?! He's about to run himself through it to get outside, but I can't let him. Three seconds left. I can't go through this heat alone! I can't be alone!

I'm frozen, but my wolf is not. He shifts us and tackles Ric to the ground. He's staring up at us in shock as the shutters slam shut. The panic recedes along with my fur. Now it's time to face his wrath.

THIRTY

<u>Ethan</u>

Is Connie outside already? I ask Max with my mind speak. I'm pretty sure I can still call out even if the phones don't work.

He's asking about the office shutters and where Ric is. If you don't want him to get to the release, you got about 30 seconds to flip that switch. Max tells me.

With Ric still prone on the ground, I race around to the desk and flip the switch on the house before slamming the drawer shut. We're trapped in this room for the next three days and no one can get us out, even if we wanted them to.

Shock shifts to disbelief and then to anger on Ric's face as he stands up and looks at me. I'm back to standing behind the desk, only naked now thanks to the assistance from my wolf in keeping him here.

My mind is starting to go fuzzy again. I know I don't have much time before my body starts doing things I know I won't like with him. I need to go to my safe space in my head, but I need to make sure he's going to do what needs done.

"I'm ready for you, Daddy," I force out of my suddenly dry throat. I have to hide the fear. Everything down there is working as it should. I can feel the slick leaking out of me. I can see the arousal on him. I can really see it. I guess being the Alpha has its perks.

And Noah got package envy from me... he'd die on the spot seeing what Ric has been carrying around all this time. Wow.

Clearing his throat brings my eyes back to my Alpha's face. He's smirking at me. Why is he smirking?

Huh, I guess I should probably close my mouth, I realize as a spot of drool drips down my chin.

The fuzzy feeling is getting more intense and is pushing the fear further away as Ric stops in front of me. He's still fully clothed. Why are his clothes still on? Why did he stop? I don't want him to stop. I want him to be naked on the couch with me on top and...

I jerk back from him at the thoughts that just popped into my head. I can't want this, right? I mean I know I have to do this, but it's a mission. It's a task to complete. It's a necessary torment to finish up this mate business.

There's no pleasure in this for me. Theres' no fun. It's only ever been pain having someone else inside me. I thought I was being ripped in two by Noah, who I call Needle Dick for a very accurate reason. There's no way this won't be excruciating pain with Ric.

I just have to withstand it for a few days and then it will be done. That's all.

I look up to see the hurt and fear on Ric's face. He doesn't want to do this with me either. I'm forcing him the same way they forced me all those years. I can't do this to him! I've changed my mind!

Max! Max! I call out desperately. *I changed my mind! I don't want to do this. You gotta let him out of here! Send Connie in to get him out. PLEASE!*

I'm screaming it to him over and over, *Get him out! Save him!* But the door isn't opening. The house stays silent.

As I drop to my knees in tears, fighting the white noise of my heat rushing through my body, I can barely make out what Max is saying over my screams and sobs... *The controls on the outside aren't working! Ric must have set the timer. We can't get into the house until the timer runs out. Connie can't get to the switch for the office. I'm sorry, Ethan. I'm so sorry. Everything will work out, I promise...*

With the last of my hope gone, I look at Ric and realize I've become the monster I feared in the dark.

"Forgive me, Daddy" I whisper before the world grays out and instinct takes over.

Ric

The look Ethan gave me upon initially realizing I was locked in here was proof enough that he planned this with Max. Knowing Max, he went along with it thinking I'd just open the house back up and Connor could release us, and it meant Ethan was indulged but no harm...

I didn't tell my Beta or my warrior that I set the timer for three days. I didn't tell them I changed the override command. I was stupid for that.

I was thinking about the fact that going through heat alone is painful for an omega and Ethan would likely call out for help. Since none of us are immune to him in this state, having the ability to open the house back up could have been disastrous, so I changed the override. I mean, a part of me figured he'd try to get me to stay in the house while the house locked down, but I didn't expect him to completely trap us in here.

I'm strangely ok with it now that I can see the interest and hunger on his face. I stalk closer to him, needing to touch him, taste him...

Before my fingers can make contact, he wrenches himself away from me. He's pacing now. The tension in his body keeps increasing with each turn of the floor.

When he stops moving, his eyes meet mine in horror.

He drops to the floor grabbing his knees and starts rocking back and forth. I've never seen this before. He's never done this with us. I don't even think he's aware of what he's doing as he starts clutching his head and whining like an animal in distress. I'm frozen. I don't know what to do for him. I'm afraid anything I say or do is going to make it worse, so I stand there and stare like the coward I am.

The rocking stops. The whining stops. His head lifts and his tear-filled eyes meet mine as he whispers something about forgiveness. Why does he need to be forgiven for a panic attack?

I don't even get a chance to even think of any possibilities before my arms are full of a very determined Ethan attempting to rip my clothes off.

Now, I understand. His full heat has hit him. He's barely more than an animal acting on instinct. My own instincts are demanding I meet his efforts, but I'm surprisingly in control. The alpha in me should have already taken him to the floor to mount him, but instead I'm rocking him and soothing him. I'm attempting to somewhat calm the storm of arousal he's drowning in right now. The no scent thing appears to be helping me keep sane.

He keeps pulling at my clothes. I remove my shirt as quickly as I can manage with him still clinging on to me. Once he is skin to skin, he seems to settle a bit.

All.... Skin... Empty... Hurts... His thoughts are leaking out to me, but they're barely coherent.

He's struggling to stay with me, to have some control. Instinct is driving him and my being here without doing what nature intends of us is only hurting him.

"I'm going to help you through this, Blue." I whisper in his ear, and he relaxes into me again.

Removing the rest of my clothing is a little easier than my shirt was since he refuses to let go of my neck. It's like his arms are a collar and he's the decoration. The image of him in a collar causes me to stumble on my way over to the couch. My wolf rumbles an agreement through my chest. *Even humans know Mate is ours with collar.*

So, my wolf is a kinky little fucker, huh? Who knew?

Sitting down naked on the couch with a lap full of horny and squirmy Ethan is not how I saw today going. Maybe a movie. Cooking dinner. Ice cream with Jack. Bubble bath and story time...

yeah that's how I saw it going. This is too fast for us, but Goddess only knows why he had to get his heat now.

My lower half is ready and waiting for Ethan to figure out positioning, but my arms are holding him tight to my chest, so he can't mount me and hurt himself. Slick or not, it will hurt him to just jump on with no prep.

"Are you sure, little bluebird?" I ask him over and over while I look for recognition in his eyes.

I don't want to be a monster, Daddy. He says into my head. *Don't let me be a monster too. Save me, Daddy!*

His fear is breaking my heart. He's not afraid for himself. He's afraid he's becoming a monster? Did what happened in that basement break him? It's true we just swept past it, but does he really regret doing that?

"If you're a monster, then so am I for letting you go in that basement," I tell him. "I should have been the one to handle that man, not you. You should have been safe, always."

He starts shaking his head faster and faster.

"No. No. No. No," he keeps repeating as tries to grab for his hair.

I crush him to my chest to stop the shaking and rising pitch of his voice. The restriction of his movement seems to cause an even worse reaction as he starts screaming into my chest. Immediately, my arms fall away and I try to move him off of me.

Instead of getting away, he grabs at me, holding on like to let go means his death. Tears are freely falling from my eyes as I can't seem to understand what my boy needs right now. He's hurting and I don't know how to fix this.

"Tell me what to do, Ethan," I sobbed into his hair. "Take whatever you need. Do whatever you want."

He's still shaking and grabbing at me. I know I'm going to have bruises and he's broken the skin in a few places, but I'll never make him let go.

"You're not a monster," I tell him softly and feel the tightening of his grip. "And if you ever become one, that's fine."

"It's not ok," he whispers into my chest. "If I'm a monster, I'll hurt people. I'll *like* hurting people."

I chuckle a bit at that remembering how happy he was cutting his way across the battle the other day.

"Sweetheart," I get him to look up at me. "You already like hurting people. You like hurting the ones that hurt you and threated us."

He shakes his head and buries himself back into my chest. I can barely hear his response as it's muffled by my own muscles, "They weren't people. They were monsters. It's ok to hurt the monsters."

I chuckle again and he looks up at me with a clarity surprising me considering his heat is riding him hard.

"Monsters don't care about people. Monsters take and take and only give back hurt. Monsters don't care if you're in pain or tired or scared. Monsters force you to do things you don't want. Monsters take their pleasure and leave you tied up for hours unable to fight back...."

Now I understand... He changed his mind, but because of my override he can't fix it. I am such an ass.

"Baby, look at me," I tell him when he buries himself back into my chest.

"You are not a monster," I say as his eyes meet mine. He shakes his head, but I continue, "You will never be like those bastards in the lab. You will never be like the abusers everyone called your parents. You will never inflict pain on anyone who hasn't earned it."

I can see the fight behind his eyes as he tries to reconcile what he's hearing with what he's thinking, all while his body is screaming at him to get relief.

"You will never be that kind of a monster." I tell him, but the fear is still in his eyes. "If you ever become a monster, you will be Daddy's monster, my little psycho who enjoys his playtime rearranging the bad guys' insides while keeping them alive..."

His resulting giggle tells me I'm on the right track.

"I know I didn't plan on being here with you. I know you may think you're forcing me now because I didn't want to be in here." I tell him as his frightened eyes meet my own. "But Goddess knows I want you so don't worry that you're forcing me. The reason I didn't want to be in here is I don't want to hurt you or cause you to remember painful things."

The relief on his face is like seeing the sun after a storm. It brings a matching smile to my face before I see his eyes cloud over with arousal. It looks like our reprieve is over and I'm going to have to take care of my boy in the other way now.

I clutch him to my chest with one arm again so that my other can reach around to start stretching him out. I'm not going to be bringing him anything but pleasure over the next few days.

Ethan's reaction to my fingers inside of him is one of surprise. He tenses at the intrusion but quickly relaxes into it. I can smell the spicy scent of fear for half a second until it fades away. I'm usually noseblind around him, so it causes me to freeze up for a moment. Ethan notices me stop and tries to pull away as a result.

"I'm sorry. I'm sorry. I'm sorry," he keeps repeating as he's fighting to get away from me.

"Shhh, little one." I try and calm him while keeping him tight against my chest. "I smelled your fear, and it surprised me is all. I still want you. I still want this" I keep murmuring assurances to him and feel him relax again. I hold him for a few minutes, not moving at all before he starts to squirm again.

Taking that as my cue, I go back to prepping him. It takes a while, but I'd take forever getting him ready if it means I don't have to see pain in his eyes while we make love.

He's lost in a fog of lust as I remove my fingers and replace them with the head of my penis. Slowly, I start to lower him down, allowing his body to adjust to the new intrusion. Ethan has his eyes screwed tight, and I know he's not exactly comfortable with this.

I can't keep going. I can't do this to him. As amazing as this feels for me, I can't take seeing the pain in his body. I'm going to pull out and find other ways to help him through the next few days.

As I start to lift him off of me, Ethan's eyes fly open. He levels me with a look that is a mix of rage and shock. I knew it. I hurt him. I begin to lift him off more gently and look away from those glowing blue orbs.

"Don't you fucking DARE stop," he growls at me, removing my hands from his hips and slamming himself down my entire length in one go.

We both freeze. I can't believe he did that. I'm conflicted as I see the tears escape his eyes and the grimace on his face, but he voiced his needs to me. I don't want to cause him pain, but he doesn't want to stop.

"Little Blue," I gasp out, "If you want this to continue, you have to do it. I can't see you in pain and keep going."

I make it a point to close my eyes and place my palms flat along the back of the sofa so that I'm not touching him at all.

"You are in total control of what happens here," I tell him with my eyes shut tight. "Use me how you need to. You are mine and I am yours. You have me however you want me, now and forever."

I can feel the tears falling on my bare chest, but I keep myself still. I keep my eyes closed.

I don't know how much time passes, but I feel him shift in my lap. His sharp intake of breath doesn't sound like pain that time. My wolf preens in my head at the sound.

Take your pleasure, Mate he says, and I hear Ethan gasp in surprise. Apparently, my wolf has figured out how to mindspeak to Ethan now. Who knew?

That permission is apparently what Ethan needs because he starts moving, building a rhythm and momentum until he spasms and I feel wetness on my stomach. I open my eyes to see him start to tilt backwards, so I reach out and catch him before he falls.

Lifting him off me, I lay him down on the couch as he comes down from his orgasm and grab a towel from the closet to clean us up a bit. I'll take him into the attached bathroom when I'm sure the first wave of his heat has passed, but I'm pretty sure this is just a brief reprieve, not long enough to take a shower.

"What the fuck was that?" Ethan mumbles, staring at the ceiling in amazement.

"What do you mean?" I ask him, pausing as I'm wiping up his release from my body. "never blown a load that quick before?" I add a bit of a joking tone to it. I don't want him to be embarrassed at orgasming that quickly.

Shaking his head, he lets out a dark chuckle. "Never blown a load from having a dick in my ass."

He glances over at me as I drop the towel in shock. Never?

He looks away in shame and whispers, "Kinda hard to get off when you're tied down and in pain... well when you don't want to be anyways. I've heard some kinky fuckers like that shit."

His smirk tells me he is defaulting to humor to hide what he's just revealed. His eyes are questioning. Is he asking if I'm into bondage and sadism? I mean, I like the idea of some of it, but not like what he's gone through.

"Only pain you'll ever get from me is a red ass if you want a spanking." I tell him honestly.

His look of relief shifts into the haze of arousal as he notices my dick is still standing at attention.

Licking his lips, he marvels, "You didn't get off. Why did you stop if you didn't get off?" His confusion is pulling him back from the haze. "Am I broken inside now? Now that the baby bits are gone, I can't give you what you need?"

He's starting to cry again. Sinking to the floor next to the couch, I pull his head to my shoulder, positioning him to be able to scent my neck. I keep forgetting we can't scent each other, but it's what the instinct demands.

I keep pondering what he's talking about with his baby bits as he's curling himself around me completely.

For the next few minutes, hours, whatever length of time, I just let him cling to me and cry it out. The tears have apparently exhausted him enough that he's asleep.

Pulling out a blanket from the closet, I cover him up on the sofa while I go sit at my desk to wonder what he's talking about. He's not going to be this coherent when he wakes up, so I write a note to remind myself to ask Connor about it when we get out of here.

A whimper from the sofa cuts through the silence as I look up. Ethan is sleeping fitfully, but he's still asleep. I let him lay there and get his rest. It's going to be a long couple of days.

THIRTY-ONE

<u>Ethan</u>

Coming out of the fog that is my heat is always more abrupt than the textbooks stated back in school. The books all say that it's a "gradual regaining of the senses with the decline of the hormones" or some bullshit like that. That has never been my experience. For me, it's pretty much immediate. Hormones stop, brain comes online. Panic ensues first, followed closely by pain, humiliation, and rage. Memory takes some time to recover.

My brain just kicked back online, so I hightail it to the corner of the room I'm in. I hear a noise from the direction of where I ran from and see a man start walking towards me. Looking around, I don't see anything I can use as a weapon. I don't see anything I recognize either. Did they take me somewhere else? Or is this a new room in my hell?

Knowing this is going to hurt, I duck down to cover the vulnerable areas and hope he's one of the nicer ones. I kinda don't hate the nice ones who will only lift me back to the bench to strap me in to finish.

The footsteps stop and I try to make myself smaller. I know I'll heal it, but I don't want to feel pain right now. Goddess only knows what depraved things he's made me do during my heat. I must have been pretty into it since he untied me. I only get untied if they like it.

I don't want them to like it. I want them to hate it, so they stop. I want them to stop. Why don't they ever stop?

I'm as small as I can make myself and the footsteps start retreating. This is so much worse. If he leaves, the others will come in. I need to keep this one happy enough that he doesn't get the others... at least until I can remember how to reason with them.

Sometimes if I negotiate, it doesn't hurt as much, and they think I'm still in my heat. They don't hurt me as much if they think that. They like my pain, so if I act like I want what they're doing, they leave me alone quicker.

I don't hear a door open, so I glance up through my hair to look around the room. The man is seated on a sofa as far away from me as possible. That's perfectly fine for me. He can stay there...

My wolf is whining at me. He knows I can't understand him yet, so why bother getting my attention? It's not like we can shift and bust out of here. They don't let us shift unless we're in the basement. We can't get out of the basement.

Don't make them put us in the basement I tell my wolf and he whines again.

The man has his head in his hands and his shoulders are shaking. Is he laughing at me? Of course, he is. I guess I would find it hilarious too if I had total power over someone who is essentially drugged out of their mind by horny hormones.

Maybe he's going to ask for a refund. Did he get his money's worth? I don't care. He comes near me now I'll bite his dick off...

won't be the first one. But then again, that's why they got the new gags for me. I'm a biter...

Here come the panic giggles, right on time. Hopefully these will stop before reinforcements come in.

The man is moving around the room, but I force myself to ignore him. I have to stop the giggles. If I don't, Pete will fill my mouth and I don't want to die choking on my own vomit again. Four times is enough for that death.

Please? Stupid brain, stop giggling!

Something drops on my head, and I try to scramble away, getting tangled in whatever the man dropped on me. Is it a net? Is this how he's going to tie me up to finish? I don't want it anymore. I don't want to anymore! I never wanted it!

"I never wanted it!" I scream into the room.

The man staggers back as if my words physically hurt him. I don't care. I just need someone to know for once that this is not my choice. It's never my choice. The Goddess is the one who made me an omega. These monsters put the man in here, not me. It's not my choice. I don't want to be omega anymore. I don't want to be me anymore.

I don't want to be alive anymore. I send it out into the ether. Maybe the Goddess will hear me and take back her deal. I just want to be done with it all...

The man goes to the desk on the other side of the room and opens a drawer. There's a beeping noise and some clicking and whirring from somewhere else in the building. The adrenaline is leaving me since he's leaving me alone and my eyes start to droop.

I'm fighting to stay awake, but my energy is gone after the heat and the constant need to be alert. I fall over, succumbing to the need to sleep as I hear the door open to the room and the man walks out.

THIRTY-TWO

<u>Ethan</u>

I wander the house looking for someone to talk to. It's been over a week since my heat ended, and I haven't seen Ric once. He isn't answering me when I reach out to him, and he hasn't been home for longer than maybe five minutes at a time. I'm pretty sure Max and Connor are helping him avoid me because he only comes home if I'm away from the house. I don't like it.

I get the feeling something happened during my heat. Was I that bad at it? I know I'm not a virgin, or wasn't a virgin, or whatever. But I've never been *free* during a heat. I've never had any control over anything during a heat. I didn't know what I was doing. No one ever told me what I'm supposed to do.

I must be really bad considering how everyone is avoiding me now. I guess it would take a monster to want someone like me after all.

My wolf whining at me is getting annoying. He hasn't said a

word to me since before this heat and I'm tired of him being a little bitch over how terrible we obviously were.

If all you're going to do is whine, then just go the fuck away for a while. You're good at leaving me alone, I think at him.

They all leave me alone now, even Jack. The little ball of sunshine gets all cloudy when I'm around now, so I don't bother to go near him anymore.

I'm getting treated with kid gloves everywhere I turn.

The warriors who come into the house or guard the outside either look at me with pity or disgust. Connor flinches at the sight of me. Max actually leaves the room when I walk in.

I don't even know what I did in my heat, but here I am taking the blame as always.

All my life, I've been getting punished just for daring to be alive. First by "Mom" because I bothered to be born and disrupt her perfectly planned life. Then by the pack for existing, I guess.

I never did find the reason why the Alpha gave the all clear to anyone who wanted to hurt me. Goddess knows he saw it happening. Hell, he even had to give me CPR and restart my heart after the vault incident.

There has never been a punishment for hurting me. Mom never faced any. Dad didn't care. Alpha didn't care. Ric and Connor don't care. The only one who ever cared before was Max and I've obviously used up his goodwill now, too.

I should have never taken that deal. I would have died in that place and been done with all of this. Everyone would be just fine right now instead of tip toeing around the broken little psychopath that was forced into their lives.

I try shifting so that I can get the hell away from here and give them all back the good lives they had before, but nothing happens.

Oh yeah, I told him to leave me alone.

So I grab my backpack and load up some clothes and necessities and walk out the front door. At least with me gone they can go back to being happy now. I need my ball of sunshine to go back to normal. He needs to shine even if I'm not there to see it.

As I drop down on the other side of the fence, I let the tears start to fall.

I'm never going to be free.

I'll never get out of this deal, not unless I break it... But I can't be the reason Connie dies. I just have to find a way to keep going until he's old and gray. Then I'll break the deal. Give him an easy end in about sixty or seventy years. I made it through eight in there. I had another eight with Mom and the pack before that. I can do more... for Connie... for Jack...

For Daddy

I start running for the woods that will take me away from here. They're all better off without me...

Ric

My phone rings as I lock up the storage shed behind the concession stand. Tonight is the full moon and I'm using the high school football stadium to host the mandatory pack gathering. I'm going to discover just how many of my people will be exiled or executed tonight. I'm going to find out who actively hurt my mate and who was complicit. Very few will escape my wrath, if any. Jessica and her brother are going to make excellent visual aids.

I miss the call, but it rings again. I manage to make out that it's one of my warriors that I have set to watch the house. They let me know when Connor or Max takes Ethan out so that I can get home to get some fresh clothes. I've been living in the school and using the locker room showers for the past week.

"Hey Boss-man," he says when I pick up. I can't remember his name off the top of my head. Max calls him Thing 2 in conversation but I don't want to call him that directly. "Wanted to let you know your puppy has left the building."

The growl that I send over is enough to bring him to his knees. I hear his gasp as he hits the ground.

"That *puppy* is my mate you little shit," I spit out. "You WILL afford him all honor and respect."

"No offense meant, Alpha," he apologizes quickly.

My wolf cuts off the growl, accepting the warrior's supplication.

"But if I may suggest, Alpha?" he hesitates.

My grunt seems to be consent to continue, so he does, "You, your Beta and even Max don't talk to him. They barely look at him. You actively avoid him," he explains. "We're giving him the same level of respect that you all are. Perhaps, if you treated him as your mate, there wouldn't be these kinds of misunderstandings... *Sir.*"

I'm in shock as he disconnects the call. I don't know about the others, but I haven't let myself be in the same building as Ethan since the day his heat broke. Now that I can recognize it, his scent is everywhere in the house. I can't stand myself when I scent him after his screams that morning.

That was the reason I didn't want to be with him for his heat. My worst nightmare came true. I hurt him just like those monsters did and I can't forgive myself.

But my warrior is right. The pack follows the lead of the Alpha. If I ignore and avoid him, the pack has every reason to believe that I don't care about him. It's time to man up and make things right with him.

If he's left the house, I'm sure he's with Connor since Max is currently walking my way with a laughing Jack on his back.

"Sup, bro?" Jack calls out to me with a wave. Max just smiles and shakes his head, setting Jack down on his feet in front of me.

"Thing One and Thing Two reached out to me to say Ethan left the house," he tells me. "Did Connor say where they were going?"

"Where who's going?" Connor asks coming around the corner of the bleachers.

My heart stutters in my chest. If we're all here, who took Ethan out?

"Call your man," I growl to Max using my authority. There will be no more skirting orders today.

Max already has his phone to his ear and the warrior on the other end answers on the third ring.

I snatch the phone from Max and demand, "Who took him out?"

"Alpha?," the guy is obviously surprised. "He's fine. No one hurt your mate, *Sir*."

I pinched the bridge of my nose in frustration and managed to ask through clenched teeth, "Who did he leave with, you over muscled baboon?!"

Max grabs the phone back before I crush it through my frustration.

"No one, Sir," the warrior squeaks out. "He walked out, hopped the fence and took off into the woods. By the time my brother got to the tree line, his scent was gone. We weren't worried since, you know. What we talked about earlier."

My knees give out on me and I'm staring at Jackie's shoes as Max continues the conversation with his warrior. I need to work on Jackie's knot tying abilities some more.

I'm not sure how much time has passed, but Connor is shaking me out of the fugue state I fell into. My mate ran from me. I am finally able to scent him and he runs away. I'm not even sure why I can scent him now, but it hit me about halfway through his heat and it's the most delectable scent I've ever smelled.

That's why I couldn't stay at the house. After his heat, his scent just flashes me back to seeing his terror and his screams and the pain and lack of recognition on his face. But I'll take the pain if it means he's here and he's safe. I'll swallow my guilt and suffering and hide it from him so he can be safe again.

"Alpha," Connor says softly, "The pack is gathering."

I look up at the darkening sky and realize it's time to make the pack safe again for my mate. I reach up to my neck and rub the new scar that wasn't there at the last gathering. "Time to take care of some monsters," I say to my Beta as he grins and pulls me back to my feet.

This pack will forever change after this night. I guarantee it.

THIRTY-THREE

Ric

The gathering starts like any other. The older members of the pack reminisce and speak of the history of our pack, the brave warriors who banded together to fight off our enemies to make our people safe.

Really fucking ironic pops into my head.

Ethan is here?

I look around frantically trying to find him. I don't know if he's aware that tonight is about justice for him, but it makes my wolf happy that our mate is close by.

Another elder picks up the story remind us of how my grandfather's reign as Alpha met a nasty end at the hand of an evil vampire who was never seen again.

"Those evil fiends do nothing more than feast on the blood of the innocent and our pack has vowed to eliminate them all in the name of our fallen Alpha and his descendants." The old man announces to cheers from the crowd.

"I don't know old man," Ethan's voice calls from the shadows behind me. "I've known vampires and I've known wolves. I can honestly say the bloodsuckers aren't the ones hurting the innocent around here."

The angry murmurs and shouts from my pack are turning to growls as they take offense that a stranger would invade their territory and speak out against their beloved history. Goddess, I really hate my pack right now.

"You dare to intrude on our sacred gathering? Reveal yourself, interloper and face the justice of our pack!" Another elder demands to an outcry of agreement from the crowd.

My wolf is ready to interject, but I hold him back. I'm curious as to how Ethan is going to handle this.

Laughter fills the night, surrounding us all. I can't tell where it's coming from... and I realize he's projecting it. His ability to mind speak is evolving and the chilling laughter is just one sign of it.

This pack is celebrating saving the innocent? Really? That's laughable.

His voice is echoing through the night and a few of the younger adults are squirming uncomfortably. Seems like I've located some of his tormentors.

As Ethan steps from the shadows, there are quite a few gasps and exclamations of surprise in the crowd. I make note of the ones who look to be more surprised he is here rather than surprised he's alive.

"This pack thought it right and just and fair to ABUSE a six-year-old boy on the word of his so-called mother," he announces to us all.

"THIS PACK" he continues before anyone can interrupt, "allowed their pups to almost kill this boy MULTIPLE times over the next five years."

The murmurs and whispers are starting to build again but are silenced with Ethan's next revelation.

"This pack SOLD a thirteen-year-old omega to a human lab for experimentation, faked his death, and killed his parents..." he sighs as they all hold their breath. Even I don't know what is next.

"All on the orders of their Alpha." He says to the full moon as he closes his eyes in pain.

The night freezes. All sound is stopped. All our hearts have stopped. There aren't even any crickets chirping.

I know my dad had his faults, but there's no way. There's no way he sold Ethan to that lab. Carl sold him. We all know it. We have the paper trail. It was Carl, not Dad.

I stare at Ethan, willing him to look at me so I can tell him he's wrong. He has to be wrong. I start walking to him, to beg him to take it back. But he turns to me and says, loud enough for everyone to hear,

"The same Alpha that murdered his own father and blamed it on vampires that weren't even in the area." I fall to my knees in front of him, tears hitting the ground as I can't bring myself to refute what he's said here. He doesn't smell like deceit. He smells of the purest truth, mixed with pain.

As the pack erupts in a roar of denial, I kneel in front of my mate, begging with my eyes for him to tell me it isn't true.

I'm sorry he says for only me. *You all needed to hear the truth tonight, before I leave for good.*

For good? What is he talking about?

We'll talk more after the gathering is concluded. This isn't done between us. I send back to him and receive his nod in response.

As I stand and face my pack, my wolf lets out a growl to settle everyone down. It's time to end this farce of a community. I signal to the warriors to unlock the shed and bring out our first guest of the evening.

Noah's fate was easy to decide for the pack. No one objected to his execution even when his crimes weren't listed yet. He was a human on pack lands and that is apparently enough for some of them. Those people won't survive the night.

I nod to Max and he nods back to show he received the message.

Fucking savages Ethan sends out into the night in a disgusted tone.

"Before we proceed with carrying out the sentence on the human called Noah, perhaps you all should understand just why he is here?" I announce to the crowd.

"He's a human! He doesn't belong here!" shouts a female from the back corner of the bleachers.

A lot of the pack seems to agree based on that fact alone and I'm disgusted. The growls from my warriors shut them all up again.

"And what would you say if you knew Noah here was sired by one of our pack? "I ask them. "His sire was a very respected member of our community. His sister is still here in this pack. Does he still deserve death for just existing?"

"Of course he's welcome if he shares blood," says the elder who kicked off the night.

And the lemmings agree.

"So, I should set him free?" I ask the pack and I hear Ethan's growl building behind me. I hope he can understand where I'm going with this before he tries to castrate me.

"He is family and the only one who seems to have a problem with him is the interloper," says a confident voice from the front of the center section. Looking there, he seems familiar. It takes me a minute, but it comes to me. This is a cousin of theirs. His mother was their sire's sister.

"Will you vouch for your family and suffer the punishments

for any and all of his misdeeds against the pack as is your right as his full blooded kin?" I ask the ancient words that would tie Noah to our pack and our laws. I tried this with Jessica, but she refused to claim him. I need someone from the pack to claim him to be able to punish him.

Ethan's growling is getting louder... and lower. I need to keep him from exploding before I can set the pack to rights.

Calm Little Blue, he's not going to get away. I need his kin to claim him so I can punish him and any who helped him. This is the plan and I need you to hold on for me. Can you do that?

His growl cuts off and he meets my eyes. I have to blink a few times, but I could've sworn his eyes were glowing, like legit glowing.

Only if I get first crack at him before you kill him. He sends back to me. I nod in acquiescence to his request.

"I accept him as my kin and take responsibility for his actions. I can't imagine a kid of Uncle Frank doing anything worthy of punishment at the pack level," the kid states. He's around Ethan's age, but he and his mom came to us after we moved here. I know he never hurt my boy, so he's got a shot at making it out of this alive.

"As Jared has claimed Noah as kin, he is now to be judged according to pack law," I announce to the crowd.

"Noah Chastain, you are charged with trespass which your kin has absolved you of."

Oh look at that he is relieved. That is the least of his charges.

"You are charged with accepting money in exchange for illegal activity." A murmur goes up through the crowd and Jared is starting to look panicked.

"You are charged with forcing a pup from the safety of the pack." Some growls can be heard working their way through the crowd.

"You are charged with the attempted kidnapping of a pup of the Alpha's family"

An outraged roar goes through the crowd and my warriors work quickly to silence them all again.

Noah is looking a little bit more like he should now. The smug bastard is realizing he's got no friends here.

"You are accused of the kidnapping and drugging of an omega wolf." I growl out.

The crowd is thoroughly confused on that one. There are no omega wolves in our pack... or at least there wasn't under my rule until about a week ago. But Ethan was a pup under my father and by Goddess I will force them to accept him if I have to. He may be pack now that he's my mate, but being in this pack was his right the second he was brought to the Beta house after he was born.

Jared speaks into the silence, "Can I revoke my responsibility, Alpha?" he asks with hatred in his eyes directed at his cousin. "No kin of mine could possibly commit such things and if he did he deserves to suffer for it."

I look to Ethan and he gives me a nod. I knew my boy wouldn't hold an innocent man responsible for another's actions. My boy isn't a villain. He's the antihero in his story, and I'm fully on board.

"Let it be known that although Jared has claimed Noah as kin, Jared bears no responsibility for the actions of his kin and is to bear no reproach for what happens in these proceedings," I announce to the pack with my authority. This works well in my favor as it will also protect Jared when I bring out Jessica next.

"Regarding the one called Noah Chastain..." I announce to get everyone's attention again.

"I, Alpha Alaric Edward Jameson, declare him an enemy of the pack, an abuser of pups, a disgusting piece of filth, and unfit to remain among the living after the moon goes dark for the month. Any who suffered at his hand have the right to exact their punishment, not to include death, up to the night of the execution." The whispers in the crowd start growing. I let it continue for a while until someone in the back raises their hand.

I chuckle as I point to them to speak.

"Alpha, no offense meant, but why wait two weeks? Jackie is a bit young to exact any justice on him." The voice calls out to me. I can't really tell, but I think they're only a teenager. It's a good question and one that I expect from a good and righteous pack member. I nod to Max to take note of who spoke. They are to be protected tonight.

"You will get the answer to that at the end of the gathering, I hope," I tell the boy. I really hope the next part goes as well as the first part did.

The crowd's attention is pulled to the concession stand and Connor dragging Jessica to the center of the field by her hair. The noise level starts to rise with shocked gasps and whispers of outrage both rising up from the adults in the crowd.

I do notice a good number of my people who aren't reacting negatively to her treatment. I even see a few showing relief. I need to speak to them later.

I look at Max and he notices, but only gives me a puzzled look. How do I let him know to pick out those people?

Little Blue? Can you do me a favor? I turn to Ethan and he doesn't break his gaze away from his brother with Jessica.

Make it quick and it better not be to let the bitch go he growls at me with force. I have to stop myself from taking a step back from him from the severity in his tone.

Can you let Max know I want to speak to the ones in the crowd who are relieved to see Jessica here this way? Please? It doesn't hurt to ask nicely.

He still doesn't turn my way, but nods slightly in response. Turning back to Max, he nods at me showing he got the message and I can see him making a mental note of the people that Jessica apparently tormented right under my nose.

Time for the real show to go down...

"Jessica Chastain, you are charged..." I begin as I take note that this is the end of my family legacy. This is the end of my father's pack.

Ethan

I don't know why I circled back. Hanging in the treetops, it was easy to just pretend I was watching a show on the television. Maybe it was starting to drift into porn territory with those teenagers for a while, but then the damn phone stopped them before it got to the good part. I always wondered how things work with a guy and girl pairing and I haven't quite figured out how to get past the parental controls on the computers at the house to check it out there.

I overheard the person on the other end said something about a mandatory pack gathering and they took off running. I followed because I thought the gathering was going to be about sending a search party for me. OK I hoped that's what the meeting would be about. I hid in the shadows away from the people, listening to their speculations.

Some thought the meeting was about the Alpha finally choosing a good girl from a good family to mate with, like Jessica. I had to forcibly stop myself from losing my lunch at that suggestion.

Others thought the pack had some sort of altercation with vampires and we were all going to need to start training and go to war. Seems to me that there's some creative story telling going on in this pack.

Not one person thought this meeting was about finding the omega that walked out of the Alpha's house this afternoon. In fact, there's no urgency at all on anyone's face. Even Max is standing there calmly with all of the warriors I know and even others I haven't met yet. I thought Ric would at least have sent out a search party, but nope. There he is walking to the middle of the field to join a bunch of old dudes.

One of them starts talking about the formation of the pack and ok the story sounds pretty freaking cool. Battling it out against the other packs for survival. The Goddess gifting our Beta's bloodline to win the wars and establish peace. Yeah, it's a good story. I give it a nine out of ten. Needs some sex scenes to spice it up a bit more.

The next old dude starts talking about Ric's grandfather. Guy sounds like a good dude from what this guy is saying.... Hold up. Is he saying all vampires are evil and feed on the innocent? Seriously?

And apparently I am broadcasting again. I need to chill out a bit before I lose control completely.

After speaking up in defense of vampires, the crowd really doesn't seem to like what I'm saying, so I step out and let them see me.

I see a lot of people who recognize me now. I see anger in their faces. Are they seriously mad that I'm alive? Or are they mad that I'm free? I give them a little half smile and proceed to lay almost every bit of their dirty laundry out there.

Looking at Ric, I don't want to do this. I never wanted him to find out like this. But the asshole doesn't want to be around me so this is my last chance to tell him. I'm really going to miss him.

He's in pain now. I didn't want this. He's kneeling in front of me in pain and I caused it. Damn it, G Lady look at what you made me do. You could've made it so that I couldn't get pregnant until I want to. I'd carry Ric's baby and then the deal would be done and I could leave everyone for good and then no one would hurt anymore.

But you had to make it so only my true mate can knock me up. Well, Ric is the last guy to get to do that to me, so I guess you're going to be stuck with me forever.

Ric is going on about Noah and family and some formalities and it's sounding like a cousin or something is going to get Noah off with a warning or something. Neither I nor my wolf like that and our growl makes it abundantly clear.

Ric lets us know that Needle Dick isn't getting away with anything. It appeases my wolf for the time being.

I stand there, staring at Noah, wondering why I was afraid of him. He's big for a human, but I can beat him in strength and speed and a whole slew of other categories. He's dumb as a box of rocks. I can't figure out why he scares me. Even now, I know if he wasn't restrained, fear would have a grip on my heart. It doesn't make any sense.

When Ric passes his judgment, I only kind of hear what the punishment is. What makes it through is that he dies in two weeks. I'll truly be free in two weeks. No more looking over my shoulder. No more jumping every time the door opens, expecting it to be him coming to take me back to the table or the bench. No more hands in the dark stopping my breath just for the fun of watching me wake up in a panic.

The crowd brings me back when they're reacting to movement from below the stands. There's Connie. I was wondering where he was. The joy at seeing my brother falls away as I realize I was hoping he wasn't here because he was out looking for me. Well, that sucks donkey balls.

The woman he's dragging doesn't sound too happy, either. She's screeching like a dying cat and... Hey, I know that screeching. It's the she-bitch. My face hardens as I watch her get dragged towards us.

Ric breaks into my mind, but I don't look away from Jessica. This thing decided she would try to hurt Jackie, that perfect little ball of goodness. She will pay for every single second of fear she caused that angel of a pup.

Max, I send out. *Ric wants to know who Jessica hurt. Something about them looking relieved she's like this.*

I see Max nod to Ric to show he understood, but I add on,

Relief can mean more than what Ric is thinking. They all aren't victims.

I glance at him to see he got my message. He gets it. He's closer to being like me than being like Ric. We don't believe in the goodness of people without proof. Everyone's got some darkness. If you can't see it, you can't trust it. Max and me? We don't hide our darkness. We don't advertise it, but we don't hide it or lie about it if asked. That's why I'm going to miss him when I go. Out of everyone, he makes me feel close to normal. Or at least he did until this last heat. I wish I knew what happened.

Ric is going on and on about how Jessica was responsible for paying Noah and getting him into the territory and blah blah blah. Been there, done that. Drugging me? Yep but I wasn't pack. I hate to do it but I have to speak up for her on this one. Damn hero complex...

"Hold up, Alpha," I interrupt as every head snaps to me. Ric looks like I've grown a third head. Hehehe.

Dirty jokes aside, I hate that I'm doing this. But it's time to play devil's advocate. He motions me to continue, looking genuinely curious as to what I have to say.

"You know I hate the bitch," I start as I hear her growl as well as quite a few from the crowd. Interesting...I'll unpack that later, but I continue after flipping her the bird, "Yeah I fucked with her when I was a kid. She was a two faced bitch then and she's still a two faced bitch now."

That brings a few chuckles out of the crowd and I know Max can more easily identify who the victims are now.

"So yeah, she fucked up by sending her dumbass of a pedophile brother after Jackie."

There are a lot of growls and snarls coming from the peanut gallery... oh and the warriors as well...

I turn to Ric and ask, "Did you forget to mention the fact that

Noah forced himself on a pup repeatedly from the time he was thirteen all the way into adulthood? I don't really know since I zoned out through most of it. I'm not a part of this pack so it mostly doesn't concern me."

One of the old dudes shouts from the sidelines, "If you are not pack, you have no say here so leave before you are declared trespasser and meet pack justice!"

There's a smaller contingent of cheers from the bleachers than before. Seems to be mostly people who don't recognize me still.

Ric's growl silences the crowd. I gotta say it made me a bit tingly that time.

He turns to me but speaks to everyone and says, "Ethan Lewis Sinclair is, was, and always will be part of my pack. He was part of my father's pack until he was sold by his Uncle. He was never disavowed. He was never declared rogue. He never rejected us."

Huh? Those things need to happen? I thought the whole selling me with the Alpha's blessing would be enough to lose pack status. Actually, I'm pretty sure that WAS enough to lose pack status. I don't smell like pack, or do I?

Max, dude? I call out to him. At his glance, I ask him, *Do I smell like pack?*

He looks a little squeamish and tells me back, *You didn't smell like rogue when Alpha and Connor brought you home, but you didn't smell like pack until last week.* He hurriedly turns away to face the crowd. Why is he looking guilty?

"The interloper has declared he is not pack. He has no say!" shouts the elder to Ric. This dude is determined for me to not speak up here.

"HE...IS... MY... MATE!" Ric roars out and silences everyone. Well damn, that's sexy. Wait...what?

Uh Alpha? I can't be your mate. You got a fated one out there and I can't give you pups. My baby bits are gone.

Ric turns to me with a sad smile and shakes his head.

"You're it for me, Blue" he whispers to me. "we claimed each other, marked and all. Deal is done."

I step back and the world starts going gray around the edges.

No. No. I have to go. He's supposed to release me and I go and take out all the bad guys so Jackie is safe and then once Connie is an old man, I kill and the G Lady takes me and him and everyone lives long lives and you get to be happy and I get to keep the bad men away....

I know I'm broadcasting to Ric as he's approaching me like he'd calm a skittish horse, but I can't stop the spiraling.

Connie's grunt has us both turning to see Jessica break free from his hold. Ric rushes for his Beta as Max runs toward us. All I see is the blood pooling out below my big brother. I don't hear Ric calling for a doctor. I don't hear Max shout as Jessica puts the bloody knife to my throat. How'd she get behind me?

All I hear is Connie's heartbeat getting slower and slower while some warriors are trying to put pressure on the wound.

Ric is standing now and saying something. I don't hear him. Is this shock? I don't think I've ever been in shock before.

Connie's heartbeats are getting even slower. Goddess, he's dying and this bitch did it. I can't stop the growl that builds inside me. I can hear the smirk in her ungodly migraine inducing voice as she says something about only she gets to be the mate of the Alpha.

Yeah, no...

Connie's heart just stopped.

Fuck the deal.

As I feel the blade press into my neck, I turn and sink fang into hers. Spitting out the flesh I ripped away from essentially half her neck, I watch as the life leaves her eyes.

Life for a life, bitch. I think as the world grays out and I feel my mate lift me into his arms. I just hope this really is the end this time. I broke the deal, but he was dying anyways. At least this way, there's one less person in the world to hurt Jackie.

Last thing I register is the mournful howling of grief rising around me. Sorry Connie. I had to let your death mean something.

I'm sorry to let you down, I send out, hoping it reaches Connie before he gets to the afterlife. I don't want him hating me for eternity.

THIRTY-FOUR

Ric

It's been almost a month since the gathering. Jessica's death was graphic and violent and well-deserved. I only wish I could have been the one to do it. How dare she stab the Beta of this pack in front of everyone! I knew she was stupid, but that's some next level shit right there.

And now I'm even thinking like Ethan.

I miss him so much. The doctors pronounced him dead on arrival at the hospital, but I refuse to accept that. He said he can't die.

But he also said he couldn't kill and kill he did, my wolf reminds me for the millionth time.

I understand why everyone is saying I need to let him go, build the pyre, bury him, anything to put him to rest, but I can't. There's still magic in him. He's going to wake up. I know it.

The knock on the door has me burying my head further into Ethan's ginger locks. He really needs a haircut. When he wakes up, I'll take him into town to the barbershop. Maybe get them to show him how to use a straight razor. We'll even watch Sweeny Todd that night to celebrate. I don't really like musicals but Johnny Depp and Jamie Campbell Bower are always worth a couple hours. I think Ethan would enjoy it.

I didn't notice the footsteps, but I feel the tiny arms wrap around me and squeeze.

"Hey Jackie," I croak out as I lift my head.

"Hey broski," He says back with a tiny smile and tears in his eyes. He wants Ethan back just as much as I do.

He thinks Ethan is sleeping. He can't hear the lack of heart-beat. He doesn't notice that there's no rise and fall to his chest. The whole pack has been ordered not to tell Jack about what happened at the gathering, on pain of death.

"When is Ethan gonna wake up?" he asks me for the umpteenth time. He asks at least twice a day, and I can't blame him. I ask the Goddess every minute of every day when she is sending him back to me. The reminder is too much for me and I put my head back down and weep.

I hear Max lead him out of the room.

"It's almost a month, you know," Max says from the doorway.

I lift my head and stare at him. A month, a year, a decade.... I'll wait forever for him.

"Just saying... if we're looking for magic mumbo jumbo to help out, there's power in the full moon," he says as he heads towards the stairs.

I hear the running feet of a clumsy seven-year-old approaching the room. Jackie pants in the doorway with his hands behind his back as he comes up on the other side of the bed.

"Brother Ethan?" he starts and I'm desperate to not start crying again. "Last time you left, you gave me my best friend, but took away my new brother. I'll give Tony back if you just come back to us now."

As I watch in amazement, Jack puts his stuffed tiger under Ethan's hand, "Now you have Tony, and we all get you. So, you better not make us wait much longer. Ric is really starting to stink, and he won't listen to us that he needs a bath."

Before I can even comment on that one, the little shit runs out of the room. The chuckle that escapes me scares me silent. I'm not supposed to feel happiness. I can't be happy until my boy is back by my side where he belongs. I need my little bluebird.

I need my little psychopath to come back and help me teach some lessons to the ones that hurt him. I'm holding them all captive until he comes back. They're all learning what it's like to be locked away with no comforts, no meals, no clothes, and nothing but fear to keep you company.

I only wish I could have held off on killing Noah for him. But the sentence in front of the whole pack meant I had to kill him almost two weeks ago. I let Max have a go at him in Ethan's place. I'm not really sure if my warrior was as thorough as Ethan would have been, but it brought at least some satisfaction to my wolf.

Right now, the only thing that will bring me satisfaction is seeing those baby blues that shine like the summer sky.

Where are you, Blue? Daddy needs you.

Ethan

I'm yet again in that weird dark floaty place I go when I die. Sometimes it takes the G Lady a while to get to me, so I lay down and get comfy. Can't really rush a Goddess. Well, I mean I'm sure you *can* rush her, but is it worth pissing her off to do it?

To fill the time and the never-ending silence of this place, I start singing all of the Disney songs I can think of. My repertoire is a bit outdated, but Jackie was helping me catch up on what I missed while I was gone. Who knew there were so many kids' movies that aren't musicals now? It's really kind of nice.

Don't get me wrong, I LOVE musicals, but sometimes I just want a good feel-good kind of movie without singing frogs or whatnot. But yeah, it's tough to get that now, too. Some of those kid movies and shows get a little dark. I like it, but yeah not sure how I would feel if I was a dad.

My child you have a choice to make.

And she makes an appearance! She starts doing that weird fade in thing she likes to do when she wants to chat it up a bit before sending me back. Reminds me again of the hologram thing in that really old space movie that Connie was obsessed with back in the day. I think he was just obsessing over the chick in the metal bikini outfit, personally.

Is this a bad time? She asks me full of humor. At least she's in a good mood today. I gotta remember to not let my mind wander here. She might forget about me and ditch me.

"Sorry G Lady," I bow my head. See? Even I can show respect... sometimes.

"What choice do I have to make? I kill, you take Connie. That's what you said before."

She looks at me like I did a cute trick. Sometimes I hate her.

I'm just a bug to her, but I gotta play her games now that I've pulled her into my life.

I said I would take one you love, yes. But you have to choose. Your brother or your baby.

Baby? What baby? Wait... does that mean?

"I'm pregnant?!" I jump to my feet and stare at her in shock. I can't be pregnant. I don't have baby bits. I grab my middle and stare down at my hands like I suddenly have a superpower to see inside my own body.

You recovered just as I promised before. No lasting physical harm. They could not alter you in any way, not permanently. I take my word very seriously, you know.

She's looking a bit peckish at the mere thought of her word being anything less than ironclad.

"Not gonna lie, I kinda forgot that part in the craziness of the times," I explain to her. "But I actually have my baby bits and got knocked up? Seriously?"

I start dancing around the empty space. I'm gonna be a daddy...

Daddy...

I stop dancing and look back at her as she smiles an indulgent smile. She knows what I'm going to ask.

"Ric is my true mate?"

Her nod is the only confirmation I get, but I fall to my knees in thanks. To know that it's him and not some stranger out there... To know that the love I feel for him isn't going to fade when I meet someone else... To know that there isn't someone else out there for me, that I'm not holding him back from finding his perfect match...

"I really am Daddy's Little Psychopath, aren't I" I ask into the void.

Apparently so. The G Lady says with a chuckle.

Your choice, my child. You must make one. You must make the choice. One will live. One will die. Your brother or your child?

I can't make that choice! How does a man choose between the most honorable and loving and deserving person on the planet and an innocent baby? I mean yeah, it's an easy choice if I didn't know it was Connie. Almost every time I faced death it was the thought that Connie is alive that kept me sane. Connie being in the world is essential. I can't be in a world without Connie...

But my baby... they're innocent. They're a blank slate. Ric and I can raise them to be just like Connie. And their Uncle Jack will be the brightest star in the sky for them, just like Connie is for me. And Connie can teach him all about...

Connie won't be there if I choose the baby.

"Is this my only chance to have a baby?" I can't look at her right now. I won't be able to contain my rage if she's happy about any of this.

My child, you will be a father to others if you choose this path. If you wish to keep this child, your child of fateful joining, they shall be your only offspring. I need your choice. It is taking an extraordinary amount of my powers to keep your body whole while you keep me waiting. If you don't choose soon, you will have neither.

My heart is breaking. I didn't even know they were there and I've already lost them. I can't be in a world without Connie.

No. I can. I've lived it before. It's hard and cruel, but I can do it.

What I can't do is I can't imagine a kid of mine not having their Uncle Connie.

"Can I trade myself and save them both?" I ask desperately.

She gives me a look like I've just said the earth is flat and the oceans are made of Jello.

"Had to try," I say with a shrug, choking back tears. "There's no choice. Save my brother."

She smiles at me and nods her head.

A life lost for a life taken. Our bargain still holds. No more killing, my child...

She's starting to leave and the grief of losing what I never knew I had is weighing heavy on my heart.

No more killing unless you want to keep giving me more children...

THIRTY-FIVE

<u>Ethan</u>

"THAT BITCH!" I shout out as I sit up in the bed.

And the room is spinning. Footsteps pound towards the open doorway and I see Connie, whole and healthy, with a smile stretching ear to ear. He glances to my left and I lay eyes on Ric, my Daddy. He's beautiful as always, but really really scruffy.

I sniff the air and my nose wrinkles. "What the hell is that smell?" I ask.

I hear laughter from the hallway. Ric stands up looking sheepish and heads for the bathroom.

"What did I miss?" I asked Connie and everyone dissolves into laughter again. I can even hear Ric's delicious chuckle coming from the bathroom before it's drowned out by the water turning on.

After Ric gets out of the shower, I realize I can scent him now.

It's even better than I remembered.... Dark chocolate with a hint of ginger and lavender. Decadent and calming with a little bit of spice...

His scent reminds me of the time he gave me a chocolate bar on my eighth birthday. He was convinced he couldn't have chocolate anymore since he got his wolf and dogs can't have chocolate, so he gave me the candy.

Mom didn't let me have sweets, but he wanted to do something nice for me. I couldn't ride my bike because of a busted rim, and he came across me pouting about it. He just wanted to give a sad and lonely kid some chocolate to cheer him up. I think that's the moment I fell in love with Ric. He was a bit dumb, still is sometimes, but he's always had a heart of a hero.

He never knew the busted rim was because of some other pups knocking me and my bike off the trail towards a cliff. No one knew that busted rim is actually what saved my life that day. If it hadn't bent and thrown me to the forest floor, I would've gone over the cliff and made a splat at the bottom.

After Ric heads to the closet, I decide I need a bath as well. I have no clue how long I was out, but it's been longer than I've ever dealt with before. The G Lady may have kept my body from decomposing, but it was apparently too much effort to prevent muscle atrophy as well. Apparently, it was almost a month, but come on. It only felt like ten minutes to me.

Coming out of the shower, I'm exhausted all over again. You would think that almost a month of sleep would have me energized, but nope. Not this time.

Staring at the new scar on my neck, I'm confused. I've never scarred before. Even as a kid, before my wolf came, I didn't scar no matter what Mom did to me. What was so different this time?

Then it hits me... the baby. That was the only thing that was different.

Sitting down on the closed toilet, I let the wave of grief hit me.

Ric doesn't even know. How do I tell him that I chose to let go of our baby?

Between my grief and my inadequate strength, I can't seem to stand back up, so I reach out,

Daddy? Can you help me?

Ric practically falls into the bathroom in his rush to open the door. It makes me giggle a bit before the wave hits me again. I can't stop the tears from falling as I see the joy in his eyes.

"Ric, I'm so sorry," I choke out through my sobs. "It was my choice, but I couldn't do it. I couldn't lose him."

Before I can continue, I'm being crushed to his chest. I really missed this feeling. It's even better now that I can scent him.

"Let's not worry about apologies," he whispers into my hair. "I owe you a few, as well."

Ric

He's awake! I knew he wasn't gone from me. I just knew he would come back to me… well, I hoped he wouldn't leave me.

Changing the sheets while he's in the shower is keeping me occupied enough so that I don't rush in there and watch him. I'm trying not to fall into pure creeper territory, but I hate the thought of him being out of my sight. We almost lost him for real.

He has a scar now. I've seen every inch of his body and there are no other scars, but this time there is. I've had time to read the reports and journals while he slept… Yes, slept. He wasn't dead, just sleeping. I just need to keep telling myself that or I'm going to barge into the bathroom.

The sheets are changed and I'm setting out some of the new clothes I bought for Ethan when the water turns off. I decide it's probably better to just sit out here and wait for him. I don't want to be too eager and scare him off again. I can't handle him running away again. He'll be lucky if we ever leave him alone from now on. If it's not me, Connor or Max will likely accompany him anywhere he goes.

Before I can really plan out anything like a guard rotation, not that the thought hasn't occurred to me, I hear him call out to me. I don't know if it's in my head or out loud, but I crash through the door only to see him sitting on the toilet in tears.

He's apologizing for something, I think. I can't focus on anything but stopping his tears, so I pull him into a hug and shush him. I owe him so many apologies for so many things.

He pushes back against me to be able to look at me. He obviously doesn't know what I do or he wouldn't be so confused about why I'm sorry. How am I supposed to tell him that he was pregnant, but lost the baby due to the blood loss? How do I tell him that I've known we were mates since his heat? Does he even know now that we're mates?

"Daddy?" he whispers, "I know we are fated now."

This isn't a conversation we're going to have in the bathroom. Picking him up, I carry him to the bed to lay him back down. He shakes his head at me and points to the loveseat in the corner. I always forget that its there, but as I set him down, I notice Ethan is immediately more relaxed.

At my look, he explains, "This is where I slept before, when you weren't home and everyone was avoiding me."

My heart is splintering into a million pieces hearing this, hearing the pain in his voice.

"You weren't here," he repeats, pointing towards the clothes I had laid out on the bed. He's right, though. And this conversation needs him not to be naked, so I take the time to help him into the shirt and pajama bottoms I picked out for him. He smiles at the cartoon characters, but otherwise gives no reaction to my help.

"That week was probably the worst week I can remember going through," he continues as he sits back down on the loveseat.

One week here was worse than the years of abuse and torture? How is that even possible? I don't understand.

"How is that even possible?" I ask before he can say anything more. "You've been literally tortured and almost died... Hell, you HAVE died!

"How was that week worse than everything else you've had to suffer?" I repeat, trying to hold back my temper.

Ethan is staring at his hands in his lap. His tears are flowing freely, but if I couldn't see them, I'd never know he was crying. I don't like this version of him. He's not supposed to be calm. He's supposed to be angry or excited or throwing a tantrum or clinging to me for comfort. He's not supposed to be calm and withdrawn.

"Did you know I was pregnant?" he asks me after a long pause.

I swear I stopped breathing for a second. He knew. And he knows he's not now.

"When did you find out?" he continues after seeing my reaction. "I found out from the Goddess before she sent me back. I didn't even know..."

I pull him into my lap while he starts to weep openly. I didn't want him to find out. I didn't want him to know how badly I failed him. Because of my incompetence, I lost our child and almost lost him.

I hold him and let him cry as much as he wants. His breathing starts to even out and I'm pretty sure he's asleep. Putting him back into the bed isn't an option right now, so I just continue to hold him on my lap. I'll hold him forever; I'm never letting him go.

"She made me choose," he whispers into my chest.

The sound startles me and he meets my gaze as I look down at him.

"It was between the baby and Connie," he tells me. "I can't lose Connie. I'm so sorry. I'm sorry. I killed our baby, but I need my big brother. I can't live in a world without my big brother, not again..."

His words fall away into wracking sobs. I'm in shock. The words aren't even registering in my brain. The Goddess made him choose? Connor might have been bleeding pretty badly, but he was awake and healing before we even left for the hospital. He was healing before Ethan's heart even stopped. Why would he have to choose?

"I chose to save my brother over our baby," he manages to get out between gasps. "You hate me now, so I'll go once I'm strong enough. Please don't forbid me from seeing Jackie, though?"

He looks so broken and I can't concentrate on what he's saying. I hate him? Why would I hate him?

"I need to know he's still full of sunshine," he continues. "If I can't see him, that's fine. I don't want to taint him, anyways."

Ethan pushes away from me and goes to stand.

My brain finally catches up and I pull him back into my lap.

"You are going nowhere," I growl at him. "You are not at fault. You are not hated. And you are not allowed to leave me... not ever."

So why was I all alone? He asks in my head. I don't think he meant to send it. He's been broadcasting his thoughts most of the day since he woke up.

"You were alone in this house because I am an idiot," I tell him, rubbing circles on his back. "I thought I hurt you, scared you, during your heat. You were terrified when you came out of it."

The memory of those few minutes will haunt me forever.

"I don't remember," he whispers. In a much stronger voice, he tells me, "I don't always remember coming out of my heats. The books they teach us from lie about the process."

At my quizzical look, he explains further, seeming more confident, "The books say it's gradual and that omegas are coherent pretty much once the hormone production stops, right?"

I give him a nod because that's about the gist of what the books tell us.

"The books are full of shit," he tells me. "At least in my case, it's not gradual. It's like falling off a cliff.

"The hormones stop and my brain wakes up. Next thing to come online is emotions, human instinct. At this point, I'm apparently aware enough to think, but I don't always remember what happens here. My memory is the last thing to kick back in."

He pauses and I let that sink in. So, he didn't remember anything when he came out of it? Or is it that he did remember something, but his instinct was telling him different? Or...

"So when I saw you come out of it, you didn't remember it was me that was in the room with you?" I ask him in hope.

"When I became aware I was out of it, I was alone in your office," he tells me.

The relief upon hearing that is like a death row pardon. He didn't have that reaction to me, just the situation. I didn't hurt my boy. But the relief I'm feeling is short lived when he continues,

"I was alone after coming down from what has historically been the most terrifying event I have to experience as an omega..."

I can see the gears in his head change course.

"Did you know they used to bring in guys from the outside to fuck me during my heats?" he asks me as the emotions are draining away from his voice. I just watch as he starts playing with his cuticles. He needs to get this out. I need to hear it, but don't want to.

He looks up at me, needing to see my answer, my reaction. I shake my head while my heart is breaking for him.

"They wanted me pregnant," he says. "So they would put me in a room with paying customers during my heats and ran it like a brothel until my heat passed. Usually, I would still be restrained in some way coming out of it, so it's not like I could do anything to panic or get away..."

He takes a deep breath before continuing.

"A few times though, the guys were nice enough to untie me, thinking of my comfort after they finished. If I was good, I didn't have to worry about Pete or Noah taking a turn, so I tried to be good to the ones that were nice."

I can't hold back the growl my wolf is releasing. I want to kill anyone who ever touched him like that, but he somehow sees kindness in the actions of some of these men, these rapists...

Ethan looks at me angrily and growls back, "Not all of them knew I didn't consent. Some were there under the impression that

I was getting paid and my heat made me rather enthusiastic in the reactions I gave them."

His reaction shocks me. He was raped repeatedly during his heats, but he still defends the men who violated his body.

"The act, the violation never bothered me," he speaks, staring into the room. "It was the thought I could end up pregnant that terrified me."

"Imagine, coming out of that... not knowing who you've been with, and ending up pregnant," he continues, "Now, add in the deal with the Goddess... If I got pregnant, it would mean one of the men who paid to have sex with a stranger was my mate... and he'd have left me there."

I let that one sink in while he stares off into space, obviously reliving something and not sharing. Apparently, my boy is able to keep his memories to himself if he's awake. I'm glad because I don't think I could handle another scene of him with another man.

"The fear. The panic," he says as he turns back to face me, "those feelings were pretty much the only constant coming out of a heat. I didn't mean to show them with you."

I pull him closer and start to tell him it's ok and that it's forgotten, but he effectively shuts me up as he continues,

"Coming back to myself, seeing you all gone or ignoring me, I figured I did something wrong," he says. "I knew something bad happened, but I had no memory of it. I'm used to being the one to blame, so I assumed it was all my fault."

Before I can interrupt, he puts his hand over my mouth to shush me.

"No one would talk to me. No one would look at me. Even Jack didn't smile if I was in the vicinity," he tells me. "I was drowning in confusion and loneliness after having a taste of happiness."

The pain in his voice is cutting me deep. I didn't know how badly I was hurting him. I was trying to protect him. We all were.

"The bullshit saying that is out there about love and loss and all that?" he looks at me before he continues, "Yeah, that was said by someone who doesn't understand losing it. I survived everything up until that point because I didn't know what I was missing. I didn't know how it felt to be protected. I didn't know how it felt to be wanted. I didn't know how it felt to watch someone's eyes light up as I walk into a room..."

"To lose that broke me worse than anything I suffered in that hellscape I lived before," he whispers to me as tears fall from his eyes.

Crushing him to my chest, I vow never to let him feel that way ever again. I'm also going to have a talk with the rest of the family to make sure we are all aware to never put Ethan through that again.

Wiping his tears away with my thumb, I ask him "How about we go get some food in you and leave the rest of the heavy stuff for later?"

He sniffles and gives me a nod. Standing up seems to be a bit difficult for him still, so I lift him into my arms to carry him downstairs.

<u>*Ethan*</u>

So now I'm sitting in the kitchen, on my stool, after being carried down here like a little invalid. I'm a bit grumpy about everything after the emotional vomit upstairs, but everyone seems ok with my surly attitude. I guess being mostly dead all month grants a guy a bit of leeway...

"Did you just bastardize a quote from the Princess Bride?" Max asks me as he opens the fridge and grabs a bottle of coke out for himself.

"Ummm...how long was I broadcasting?" I ask looking around in trepidation.

"Just so you know, I didn't really believe I couldn't have chocolate. I just wanted to see you smile," Ric says with glassy eyes as he moves behind me to pull me back into his chest. "You know I still want the names of those pups, right?" he adds on before letting me go.

"I didn't see them," I tell him honestly. "The only person who may know who they are would be Shaun. He was pretty much the only one out of the pups my age who was ever nice to me, but I didn't see him at that gathering thingy where I croaked this time"

The glares I'm met with after I finish have me scooping up some more soup from the bowl in front of me.

OK so I guess it's too soon to joke about me dying in front of them…

"YES!"

Ooh stereo.

"Did you and our extremely flawed Alpha work your shit out?" Max asks to break the tension in the room.

"We talked," Ric tells him, leaving the rest hanging out there.

They don't need to know about the baby or the panic or anything like that. They don't need to know about the sick and twisted loophole the G Lady gave me for our deal. I'm not even going to let Ric in on that one. What I really need to do is get more answers.

"Has anyone seen my backpack?" I ask the room between spoonfuls of the soup.

Ric ruffles my hair before moving back to the other side of the island and saying, "It's in the safe in the bedroom."

When I look up at him, he continues, "I was reading the notes and files while you were…you know. And after reading just a few, I decided they can't be left out where anyone can find them."

I appreciate the consideration. I didn't think of it because frankly, up until about an hour ago, I didn't think I had anywhere safe to keep them.

"We should all go through them together," Connor suggests.

"No," I say at the same time as Daddy.

There are things I don't want Connor to find out about his parents and there are things Ric won't want known to anyone about his father. I haven't even finished reading everything, but I know Connor can't be involved until we can water some of it down.

My brother looks devastated, but I won't budge on this. I've dimmed his light enough. He's aware of just enough to understand that I am not his parents' child, even before we knew I wasn't biologically theirs.

"So..." Ric breaks in, "don't we have a trip to Six Flags to plan We want to get it in before school starts, right?"

I forgot about our trip plans. I feel my adult self-start to slip away as thoughts of rides and games fill my head. I have to make sure I get my strength back or else Daddy will have to carry me around the park on his back. I'll be like a koala hugging onto a tree all around the park.

I giggle and offer Mister Whiskers some of my soup. He needs to get stronger too. There are still some more nightmares to hunt down before we're done out there. The G-Lady still has us stuck in this deal though. I gotta come up with a really cool nickname, too.

Alpha's Little Psycho. That's who you are. I hear from Ric as he's giving me an indulgent smile.

That's right, Daddy. I'm your little psycho and I'm going on a monster hunt... right after a nap.

ABOUT THE AUTHOR

I am a dog mom living it up in the insanity that is Northeast Ohio. When I'm not documenting the exploits of the characters in my head, I'm either binge reading the works of other amazing authors or losing my voice at hockey games. I'm horribly addicted to coffee, anime, and Asian dramas in addition to building my ever-growing stuffie army.

To break it down to the basics, I am a neurospicy aceflux demirom hetero cis woman middle who writes about people (mostly LGBTQIA+) finding love and purpose through unexpected means. Almost all of my stories involve some facet of BDSM, but the heart of the matter is the characters and their growth.

K.A. Bauer is the paranormal alter ego of Kate Bauer. I guess you could say Kate lives in this reality while K.A. is in a reality where mythical creatures and magic exist and fate makes finding true love easier.

For links to all of my socials and to sign up for my newsletter, check out my linktree at https://linktr.ee/authorkabauer

I can be found on most social media sites under the username @authorkabauer

K.A. BAUER BOOKS

<u>Alpha's Little Psycho Series</u>
Alive
Holly Jolly Psycho (Novella)
Unburied
Afraid
Complete Series Omnibus

<u>Jameson Pack Series</u>
Fated Mistake
Doctor Mate
Half Mate
Learned Fate

All of my books that are not under an exclusivity clause are also available direct from my store
www.authorkabauer.shop

KATE BAUER BOOKS

<u>Manor Drive Series</u>
A Little Discovery
Drag Me Up
Pet Project
Teddy Tea Time
Night Shift
No Pain, No Gain

<u>Wrenshaw University Series</u>
Freshman Fifteen
Injured Reserve
Professor's Pet
Too Many Men

<u>MR DRAG Series</u>
Wish Upon DeStarr

Holly Jolly Psycho

PREVIEW

ALPHA'S LITTLE PSYCHO HOLIDAY NOVELLA

Thanksgiving used to be a favorite day of mine, back when my mother was still alive. She would cook up a turkey with all of the fixings and the house would be filled with the wonderful aromas and the sounds of her singing Christmas carols while she cooked. When I was still a pup, I would help make the sides and set the table. My father decided that it was beneath the man of the house to do the cooking, so he put a stop to that when I got my wolf. I always missed it after that and would sneak into the kitchen to snag a bite or two from Mom when he wasn't looking.

After Mom was gone, I just ordered a catered meal for four. Connor and Max would join me and Jack for the dinner and then we would just sit and watch football. None of us cared about the games, but it was something to do in order to keep our adult minds off the tragedies in our pasts. Jack would watch some cartoon Christmas movies until the turkey coma took hold. We didn't really have anything to be thankful for at the time.

This year is different. We actually *have* something to be thankful for. My Blue is back with us. Ethan is alive and here and it's the greatest gift I've ever received. This actually means we are going to celebrate and do it up right. I was planning on doing the full dinner with all of the fixings, pulling out Mom's old cookbook and recipes...

But Ethan says he is going to treat us all to the "greatest Thanksgiving dinner of all time." I'm not certain he can pull that off, but it's already the best one I've had since I was a kid. I can picture the future now, Ethan with our kids in the kitchen, making a mess while creating memories. The food might not be the best looking, but I have zero doubts that he'll figure it all out to make it at least taste good...

My memories and good mood are shattered when the smoke alarm starts going off. A second later, I can smell multiple some-things burning. I'm not surprised that Ethan burned something, but I am surprised to not be hearing him cussing out the smoke alarm. My boy seems to have a hate/hate relationship with the thing any time he tries to cook.

I'm not hearing anything from the kitchen except the shrill screeching of the alarm, and that worries me more than anything else. He might not be able to die, but it doesn't mean I ever want to see him incapacitated in any way again...

Racing into the room, I see the war zone that has taken over my kitchen. Max is two seconds behind me with a fire extin-guisher. Some of the cabinets look melted and I think what I'm seeing on the counter was at one point a stand mixer...

While Max puts out whatever is on fire in the oven, I scan the room to try and find my boy amidst the carnage.

Coming around the island, I see him curled up in the corner, head down on his knees.

He doesn't look injured, but he's done with cooking. Even if there actually ends up being anything salvageable, he's not going to worry about any of it at this point. I'm putting my foot down as his Alpha and Daddy. No more cooking for the foreseeable future... not that I think my kitchen will even be useable any time soon...

It's too late to get our typical meals delivered, but hopefully the pizza place is still open. I snag the menu out of the drawer and push it into Max's chest, breaking him out of the trance he's in, staring at my boy in the middle of his breakdown. I can't contain the growl coming from my chest and my warrior is looking a bit embarrassed to have been caught looking. I can handle embarrassed. I won't stand for anyone judging Ethan for this.

As Max leaves the room to order the pizza, I try to find a clean spot to kneel in front of my bluebird. There is not a single inch of space in the kitchen that doesn't have some sort of food residue on it. I give up on clean and just pull my boy into my arms, taking his spot leaning back against the cabinets. He's shaking and whimpering something, but I can't hear enough over the alarm to understand. I open up my mind a bit to hopefully get some insight into what went wrong today and what my boy needs from me.

Unburied

PREVIEW

ALPHA'S LITTLE PSYCHO BOOK 2

<u>Ethan</u>

Captain's log... Scratch that.

Ethan's log... today's date? Who knows... Every day is blending into the next. The wonder and joy of freedom has turned to boredom. Like, I know that shit was bad for me before and all, but being treated nice and everything is just so blah...

Here I am, sitting in a college classroom and it's just so... meh. Don't get me wrong. I'm psyched to be able to even go to school like this, but this professor is just so freaking dull. Every single class is a struggle to stay awake while he drones on and on about the fathers of modern psychology. I only took intro to psychology as a compromise with Connor.

He wants me to do therapy. I don't want any more strangers all up in my business, especially of the d-word variety. Me and docs are a big ole NOPE. Ric suggested this class so that I can "better understand what psychology is so I can make an informed decision."

If psychology is falling asleep in a classroom he's spending an arm and a leg for me to be in, then yeah I'd say my choice to not go to therapy is valid.

I'm not saying I don't want to talk about everything that happened to me. Keeping quiet isn't something I ever wanted or want to keep doing going forward. I've uncovered too many secrets already... but that trauma shit gets buried deep in you. Every time I've tried to open up to Connor or Ric, they look so broken and disappointed that I shut down again. I hate hurting them, so I stopped trying to tell them about things that bother me.

Max is really my only confidant. We don't say it out loud, but he knows some of what I feel. Not everything, thank the gods, but he knows enough to know I don't want or need to see horror or pity or anger. I just need someone to listen and acknowledge that it really happened and I'm really here now... that this isn't all just a dream even after all of these months. But even Max can't understand it all. When I forget and let him see, I feel the gap between us getting wider. I'm even too fucked in the head for him sometimes...

You know who this professor reminds me of? That teacher in the one movie from like forty years ago about the kid who skips school. Same voice. Same mannerisms. Man, now I want to pull out my phone and watch eighties movies instead of sitting through the rest of this hour. How long have I been here tonight?

Fifteen minutes...

Screw this. I'm ditching. The movie made me do it... That's my excuse and I'm sticking to it. It's not like I'll get counted as absent. This professor takes roll at the beginning of the classes, unlike my Advanced Anatomy prof who randomly selects half the names for roll call in the beginning and the other half at the end of class. Sometimes, he'll call people twice just to make sure they stayed for the whole class. Love the class, hate him.

Anyways, leaving the class, Mr. Monotone doesn't even glance my way. I don't really care if Freud slept with his mother or whatever he's talking about. I'll just read the book to catch up. Right now, my biggest hurdle is ditching the guard dog I'm saddled with. Today, I have Thing One, also known as Seb, as my not so faithful companion. Nothing wrong with the guy, but we both agree Ric needs to chill out with the guard duty. He and his brother, Bastien, are my usual watch dogs for the night class shift since the other warriors don't seem to like me too much after Christmas.

Ever since I woke up after the whole Gathering debacle, I haven't had a moment alone outside of the house. If I go to the store, I have a guard. If I go for a walk, I have a guard. If I check the freaking mail, I have a guard. Only good thing about having them around over the last few months was that I didn't have to lug everyone's Christmas presents through the mall. I had my built-in luggage trolleys. I think that was the last straw for most of them.

I honestly didn't mean to buy as much as I did. When Ric got the credit card bill last month, I thought he was going to be the first werewolf ever to die of shock. I didn't know a person could change colors like that without being strangled.

I apologized and even offered to let him return all of the things he bought for me to help pay for it, but he refused. Instead, he took away the card that doesn't have a limit and replaced it with one that limits me to only one thousand at a time. "For emergencies" is what he told me. Well, coffee is an emergency right now.

Thing One is nowhere to be found outside of the classroom. Daddy isn't going to be happy about that, but I'm super duper excited. This means I can get the coffee I like and not get a lecture about it being sugary milk with a dash of coffee. I mean, morning coffee needs to be dark like my soul. Just kidding. I need my creamer. But nighttime coffee is dessert. I'd get it iced, but early

February is just too cold for iced anything unless I'm in my jammies under a blankie.

Making my way across the quad to reach the coffee shop, I ignore the stupid beta idiots from the local pack cat-calling all the women walking by them. Who in their right mind would fall for dumbass dudebros like them? I put them out of my mind as the scent of the liquid ambrosia is wafting over to me. It's calling to me...

"Leave me alone, asswipe!" It's a woman's voice cutting through the fog created by the siren song of the coffee. Ignore it, Ethan. You want your coffee, right? Just ignore it...

"Get your fucking hands off me, you neanderthal!"

Damnit! Fucking hero complex bullshit. I blame comics.

"You pencil dicks can't get anyone with your looks, so you use force?" I shout in their direction, trying to distract them enough that the lady can get away. Most of them look my way, but one of them still has his hands on the woman.

"Because it's obvious your personalities can't carry you either," I continue as I turn towards them instead of the heavenly nectar. They are really not going to like ruining my plans if the coffee shop runs out of muffins before I can get in there. The night class students go crazy for the clearance baked goods at the end of the night and for once I have a decent shot at a double chocolate muffin.

"Beat it, twinkie," says a chubby frat bro looking douche canoe. Popped collars should have stayed out of style when the eighties ended. I recognize him. This guy is in my Econ class. He's one of those guys that his daddy (not Daddy, at least I don't think he swings that way) bought his way into a college education. Hell, I think he bought his high school diploma as well, maybe even kindergarten...

"Shit! The bitch got away!" yells another of the dudebros.

Since my job is apparently done, I turn back towards the coffee shop. I know better than to turn my back to potential enemies. I'm not stupid... but coffee... and muffins...

www.ingramcontent.com/pod-product-compliance
Lightning Source LLC
Chambersburg PA
CBHW031149160726
47991CB00004B/1593